CHRISTOPHER CARTWRIGHT

THE IRONCLAD COVENANT

A SAM REILLY NOVEL

PROLOGUE

NATCHEZ, MISSISSIPPI—MAY 18, 1863

WILLIAM CHESTNUT'S ANKLES were bound by heavy leg irons. His wrists were locked in hand irons, which were then shackled to five other prisoners. All were then restrained using the same method. The shackles were the Darby type with barrel locks made by the Hiatt Company. The handcuffs had a square bow with notches on the outside that engaged a lock mechanism shaped like a teardrop. They were the same type he'd once used on the very slaves whose trade the Union had recently announced it was trying to abolish.

He looked up. The morning's sky was already a bruised mixture of purple, red, and ochre. A violent storm was approaching. He grinned sardonically. There was a very good chance he'd be dead by the time it struck.

He turned his gaze from the horizon to the river and watched as the iron monstrosity approached the wooden jetty. Thick smoke billowed from her two large smokestacks. At 150 feet in length, 36 feet of beam, and drawing only 10 feet of water, the *CSS Mississippi* had been built to run the river system at speed. Her paddlewheel had been replaced with twin eight-foot bronze screws, powered by two large horizontal fire-tube boilers that lay below the waterline and allowed her to reach a top speed of fourteen and a half knots in calm water—a speed that allowed her to outpace any other armored ship on the river.

The ten-foot-high sloping sides of her casemate created a vaulted chamber toward the aft of the floating fortress, which angled inward at thirty degrees and extended below the waterline to form a protective bulge. She was clad in four and a quarter inch wrought iron, backed by fourteen-inch teak, which rested on a thick framework of pine and oak. The combination of iron and wood prevented spalling — the process where cannon shot would cause the brittle metal to splinter and break into lethal fragments capable of destroying the rest of the ship — and made her one of the most formidable ironclads on the river.

Built for speed, she carried just five guns.

Amidships, a single 200-pounder Blakely 11-inch rifled cannon was housed on a rotating cylindrical gun turret. The turret's rounded shape helped to deflect cannon shot. Two 120-pound Blakely 7.5-inch rifles were mounted fore and aft on pivots that allowed them to be fired in broadside, while two 68-pounder smoothbore muzzle-loading guns covered the starboard and port.

Her builders had failed to paint her and, like many of the other ironclads, she was covered in the deep rusty red of the Yazoo River, where her armor had been mounted. The outcome gave her low lying hull an almost camouflaged appearance against the ruddy color of the Mississippi's banks. At her bow, she flew the Confederate Navy's Jack.

Chestnut beamed with pleasure and disbelief as he recognized the vessel.

She was magnificent and hideous at the same time. He was forced to stand rigid with the other five prisoners as he watched the CSS Mississippi settle alongside the wooden jetty. At five feet eight inches, he was an average height. Just slightly taller than the men standing beside him with the exception of the Irish prisoner at the end, who was noticeably shorter. Chestnut had light brown, well-groomed hair, intelligent soft blue eyes, and undamaged fair skin. His hard-pressed starched military officer's uniform distinguished him from the other prisoners with jarring manifest.

His chains clanked as he stood and the iron dug into his wrists. Despite the grating pain, he smiled as he studied the ship. She was marvelous and at the same time hideous to her core. She was one of the Confederates final hopes to maintain control over the Mississippi River. She bore the same name as her twin sister who was intentionally burned before completion rather than being captured when New Orleans fell to the Union Fleet on April 25, 1862. Like her sister, she was to be an engineering marvel — the strongest, fastest and most formidable ship on the river.

William wore the wry smile of a man whose recent experiences had given him a very new outlook on the world. It was like he'd only just recognized just how wonderful his life had been now that it was about to be taken away from him. The cool air was fresh and tasted sweet on his lips, despite the thick scent of burning coal. The dawn sunlight swayed the grays of the horizon toward a deep blue of another picturesque day in hell. He breathed deeply, enjoying the cold air through each of his nostrils, with the contented resignation of a man who knew that it would very likely be his last.

His body shuddered as the whip bit painfully at his lower back. The pain shot up through his back, sending intense spasms along his spine. He clenched his teeth together and focused on the pleasure of withholding any audible response to the provost's attempt to single him out.

The provost guard cracked the bull-whip again. "Stand at attention, men — or I'll make you wish you were already hanging!"

William straightened his spine, fixed his eyes straight ahead and locked his thumbs against his thighs. Even the sting on his back felt invigorating, like a firm reminder that he was still alive. Despite the pain, he found himself smiling as amusement and disappointment shrouded the satire of his wretched life. That he would find such wonderment in the world, the very day he was to leave it. He wore the Confederate uniform, but he'd never been a soldier—not in the normal sense of the word. His expertise made him uniquely more valuable to the Confederacy than most men, who were no better than the cannon fodder that went to their slaughter day in, day out.

He watched as a number of men caught the heavy rope lines thrown from the deck of the *CSS Mississippi*. They quickly tied her heavy hemp ropes to the iron cleats and the vessel finally slowed to a stop. Confident she had been secured correctly, the commander of the vessel stepped off her low-lying bow and onto the wooden jetty. He approached the provost—a surly and bad-tempered man named Reynolds.

Commander Baker shook hands with the provost and at the same time exchanged orders. William watched as the Commander read the prisoner's consignments. His jaw was set hard, as the commander's eyes swept the six prisoners.

The Commander's eyebrows narrowed. "They're all to hang at Vicksburg as a deterrent to any other deserters?"

Reynolds nodded. "Lieutenant General Pemberton's army has taken shelter within the defensive lines surrounding the fortress city. It's believed that Major General Ulysses Grant is planning on a siege any day now. The last thing Pemberton wants now are his men thinking they're better off deserting."

Commander Baker nodded in understanding and then asked, in a steady voice, loud enough for all the prisoners to hear. "Deserters, the lot of them?"

Reynolds coughed and pointed at William. "All, except the one at the end."

The Commander's eyes lowered to meet Chestnut, with a cold and steely defiant gaze. "What did he do?"

"I'll let you read his arrest warrant." Reynolds pulled out a piece of rolled paper. "He's the only man among them who truly deserves to hang. The deserters, they have to—every man's afraid when the cannons start to fire and we can't have others thinking it easier just to slip away in the night—but the man at the end, William Chestnut, he deserves to hang for what he's done, and may God forgive his soul, because I sure as hell can't."

William noticed there was a certain coldness in the provost's voice, something about the way he said the words, which chilled the Commander to his core. William's eyes darted to the Commander, who was already reading his conviction notice.

The Commander's entire demeanor appeared somehow more serious in an instant. His stance was rigid, the muscles of his face taut, and a look of disgust embedded itself in his hard face, as he read Chestnut's crime. The man's ashen gray eyes darted toward him, and William met the Commander's vehement gaze. There was a look of hatred in those eyes. Like he was staring into the face of a monster.

Chestnut wondered if he really was a monster. There was no doubt in his mind he deserved to hang for his actions.

He expelled his deep breath slowly.

But what other choice did I have under the circumstances?

The Commander broke his eye contact, as though he'd been startled by what he saw. He turned to face Reynolds. "Get them aboard and place them down below where they can't get into any damned mischief on my ship!"

And William Chestnut grinned…

Because through a unique act of serendipity, he'd been presented with one more chance. The chariot they had chosen to transport him to his death, was about to be involved in the transfer of a dangerous Covenant of unimaginable ramifications. And like the *Deux Ex Machina* of ancient Greek Tragedies — the ironclad would release him from his enemies.

<hr>

Robert Murphy was the first prisoner in the line of shackled men to follow the provost toward the ironclad. He was short — about five feet four inches — but that had never caused him trouble. An Irish migrant, he'd come to America in 1855 to seek his fortune and was well on his way to achieving his goal when the Civil War broke out.

He'd always been quick and agile, with a right-hand hook like a sledge hammer. He had a natural cunning and mean streak that had served him well up until this point in life. The mean streak had made it so that people either respected him or feared him—either of which suited him fine and made him a dangerous and powerful man.

It wasn't fear that motivated him to desertion. Instead, greed was the driving factor. He'd discovered a means of making money helping those terrified of war to escape. It was a perfect business model, with one flaw—he got caught and charged with desertion.

He'd always been an intelligent and dangerous man, with a certain amount of moral flexibility, he was unbound by the constraints of modern society. He expelled a deep breath of air. He now had a little under twenty-four hours to use those wiles to change the course of his execution.

Murphy followed the provost onto the *CSS Mississippi* and down a series of steep wooden steps into the dark, cramped, uncomfortable bowels of the ironclad. The radiant heat from its twin boilers struck him in the face like the provost's whip. The further he descended, the more unpleasant the environment became. The air was stiflingly hot and pervasive with the odor of men working tirelessly to feed the insatiable boilers.

Through a series of narrow passages, past twin horizontal-firing tubes, where men were feeding the firebox with coal, they headed toward the aft section of the lowest deck. Only limited light reached the final compartment, where they were to be stowed like worthless pieces of equipment. The purpose-built prison cell had only three iron eyelets and would have been cramped, even if there had only been three prisoners, instead of six.

The provost pointed toward the dingy cell. "In you go, gentlemen."

Murphy stopped, his eyes greeting the two Confederate

soldiers who were aiming their Enfield rifled muskets at his head, making him rethink any earlier thoughts of trying to kill the provost with the chain between his wrists. Instead, as he moved forward, the narrow space forced him to duck into a crawl. He was immediately followed by the five other prisoners on his chain.

"You will be happy to know I've arranged for you to all sit during this trip." The provost smiled. It was oily and cruel. "In fact, I *insist* that you sit down."

The lock at the end of the linked chain that tethered the six prisoners together was undone and the chain was fed through the last of the three iron eyelets — the one closest to the door.

Murphy ran his eyes along the other five prisoners who shared his fate on the chain. Somehow, the knowledge they would all die together gave them an odd unity. Each of the prisoners had their heads tilted downward, as though they were making final prayers with their God or, like him, trying to remember those he'd loved. His mother and sister. He tried to forgive his father for his mistakes.

His eyes at last met the final prisoner. Unlike the rest of the prisoners, this one's head was tilted upward, so he could examine his surroundings with interest, like the curator of a museum of fine art. Robert met the prisoner's gaze; he had pale blue eyes and was grinning like a psychopath. The man looked like he didn't have a care in the world. He could have been at a picnic, or a carnival waiting for a photograph.

The stranger nodded to him, his dry lips tilting curiously upward in a wry smile.

It was an unexpectedly human gesture coming out of the monster's placid face, as though even the most wretched still seek human contact.

Robert recalled what the provost guard had said about the prisoner — *That one truly deserves to hang, and may God have mercy on his soul for what he's done, because I sure as hell never could* — Robert broke eye contact, driven by the tangible fear and repulsion of a child being hunted in the woods.

"Beautiful day, isn't it?" the prisoner said. "I think I'd like to hang slowly… savor the moment, you know… what do you think?"

Robert turned to avoid the man's penetrating gaze.

What the hell did you do?

The provost shut the small door, and the prisoners were now sealed in total darkness.

———◦◇◦———

Concealed by the inky darkness, Chestnut beamed with pleasure.

The oppressive stench of toiling men and the heat from the boilers did nothing to smother his senses as he settled in against the wall of the ship. The chains on his wrists bit harshly into his skin, which had started to welt against the rough iron. His feet and ankles ached in his officer's boots, and his semi-standing position kept him from sleep.

There he waited until the time was right. There was no rush. They wouldn't reach Vicksburg until tomorrow. Timing was everything. If he made his move too early, someone could notice and his execution might be brought forward. No, he would wait and when the time was right, he would do what had to be done.

But would the rest of the men still go through with it?

He soon put the question out of his mind. There was nothing he could do if his arrest had made the men cancel or change the plan. They might have felt that he would betray the secret, although he doubted it—the Covenant was too important to ever betray.

And he, of all people, had reason to see the Covenant delivered.

Chestnut turned his mind inward, finding focus on the pain as the hours dragged by. No natural light penetrated the interior of the battle steamer, so the passing of time was all but lost to him. He thought about his life and all that he'd seen. Everything had been leading to this moment. He thought about his own family, hidden in shame before their murder.

He remembered how powerless he had felt when he'd found them and then revisited his bloodlust and contempt for the entire reason they had suffered.

No, his men knew about why he was betraying the Confederacy and they would know that he would keep the Covenant's secret all the way to his vengeful grave. He had always known the price of retribution would be his life, a cost that he would gladly give.

Chestnut closed his eyes and expelled a deep breath. His men would go through with the plan, he was certain of it. He smiled in wonder at the depth of his icy rage. With nothing to lose, he felt empowered by his bitterness. He felt no fear or shame, only contempt. Nothing could hurt him now.

He welcomed the pain in his body again as his mind drifted back to the present. He looked at the other prisoners and his soul was barren of empathy or compassion — he hoped for savagery and horror. He hoped it came soon. He sucked in a deep breath of the fetid, hot air and savored it.

Somehow, with that he drifted into blissful sleep and the CSS *Mississippi* steamed North all day, and into the night.

At some stage, many hours later, he woke to the sound of cannon fire erupting. The ship rocked under the recoil as she returned a broadside. He counted off the seconds in his head and wondered idly if the gunnies would be able to meet the minimum reload times he knew so well. The ship gave several volleys of fire and then seemed to come about.

Above decks the squeal of a quartermaster's whistle was accompanied by a shift fore and starboard, which shoved the shackled prisoners into one another. The prisoner next to Chestnut cursed a mumbled apology as he tried to separate himself from William as the momentum settled. William figured they had come up alongside a jetty.

Was it possible they had already reached Vicksburg?

Chestnut's heart raced. *How long had he been asleep? Had he waited too long?* He stretched out, trying to reach the secret compartment built into the floorboards at the very back of the prisoner's alcove. He pushed on the floorboard, but it didn't move. He was in the wrong position. He was still short by a few inches. He yanked on the chain, pulling the rest of the prisoners to the side.

One of the prisoner's wrists became jammed in the iron eyelet, and he cried out in pain.

It was the Irishman who first realized who was responsible. "What the hell are you trying to do?"

Chestnut ignored the question and yanked harder. The man at the end of the chain screamed out in pain, but Chestnut continued. He felt for the loose-fitting pine board. It had three small grooves cut into the wood. He ran his fingers delicately along the marker. Now certain that he'd found the right board, he used the palm of his hand to put downward and forward pressure on it.

The board slid forward, revealing a hidden storage compartment. He reached in quickly, and gripped the handle of a fully loaded *Walch Navy 12 Shot Revolver.*

An instant later, the other prisoners pulled the chain in the opposite direction, and he returned to the original position of discomfort. He sat back and relaxed. Only now, he had 12 shots to take control of the *CSS Mississippi.*

"What the hell was that all about?" the Irishman asked.

Chestnut shrugged. "I was scratching an itch."

He thanked almighty providence and dammed good luck that he had the foresight to build a hidden compartment within the flooring where any prisoners might be held. He'd designed it with the rest of his men in mind, in case any of them were caught, but had no idea that he would ever have a need to use it.

He carefully gripped the handle of the Walch Navy 12 Shot Revolver. The unique .36 caliber revolver used superimposed chambers—meaning that each of the six chambers could hold two shots, for a total of 12 rounds before reloading. The revolver had two hammers and two side by side triggers, with the trigger for the front loading being positioned slightly ahead of the rear load's trigger, to help ensure that they are fired in the correct order.

Each cylinder chamber was loaded with two loads—a ball and powder over another ball and powder. The ignition system was farther forward in the chamber for shot number one so that would fire first. After that, the second charge was ready to shoot. Its shot was notoriously weak, but Chestnut had used the weapon since its release in 1859 and he'd developed an affinity for it. Despite its peculiarities he was confident the revolver would be lethal in his hand.

On the deck, the muffled sound of shouted orders being given was audible above the roar of the hissing boilers. The padded knock of boots and shouts of men above was accompanied by the slide and creak of the turret-house floorboards as the Covenant was carried on board.

Chestnut felt the tension disappear. *They made it!*

He listened to the voice of the ship's commander as he talked to the leader of the new arrivals.

"Here are your signed orders. You are to head North."

"North?" the commander was puzzled.

"Yes. We have men waiting with a wagon and horses at the junction along the Yazoo River, who will move that chest to safety. Its survival is the only priority."

"What about the prisoners?" the commander asked.

"What prisoners?"

"We took on board six prisoners. They were meant to hang at Vicksburg as a deterrent to would be deserters."

The newcomer's voice was undeterred. "Forget about them."

"They were meant to be executed here, today."

"Then shoot them!"

"I can't shoot them!" The commander protested.

"Why not?"

"It's not right. It has to be official."

"Oh for God's sake. Where have you got the prisoners stowed?"

"Down below, aft locker. They're handcuffed and chained to the floor."

"Good, that will make it easy. I'll shoot them myself."

Chestnut waited for the commander to protest, but instead there was only silence. About twenty seconds later, he heard heavy footsteps approaching. The door opened and a barrel-chested man with a trimmed fiery red beard stepped inside.

The stranger lowered a Colt Army Revolver and said, "I'm sorry, gentlemen. I suggest you make peace with your maker."

Chestnut grinned. "Not today. I still have a duty to my maker here on Earth."

"Good God, William Chestnut!" The new arrival audibly gasped. "What are you doing here? I thought you had been caught?"

"I was," Chestnut said. "They were taking me to Vicksburg to hang."

The stranger laughed. "What were the chances, hey?"

"Exactly, what were the chances, indeed?" Chestnut rattled his shackled wrists on the chain. "Come on, there's a key over on a hook behind the door. Get me out of here!"

The stranger grabbed the key, shaped like a small teardrop. "This it?"

"Yes! That's it, now come and unlock me."

"And the rest of us!" the other prisoners whispered.

"All right, all right!"

The stranger kneeled down to enter the prisoner's cell. It was the last thing the man would do. A stray shard of cannon shot ripped through the ventilation slit above, tearing a gaping hole through the stranger's chest, killing him instantly.

Chestnut watched in horror as the man fell backward. His dead, mangled body lying just four feet out of their reach and his hand still gripping the teardrop shaped key.

The little Irishman looked at him. "Well that's some seriously bad luck."

•◇•

The ship's boilers built up steam, and power was transferred to the screws starting a multitude of mechanized sounds and vibrations throughout the length of the metal clad hull.

Chestnut adjusted his weight and settled against the wall and briefly regarded the adjacent man he was chained to, who was whimpering and seemed to have soiled himself in fear. William turned his face away in disgust.

Is this to be my ending? Surrounded by the pathetic misery of cowards?

It was at that moment that the vessel shuddered, and a massive blast erupted above as a cannon shot struck the casement a direct hit.

136 pounds of steel in the form of a solid shot from an 11-inch smoothbore *Dahlgren* gun on a Union ship had flown 3600 yards and smashed into the weakest point of the topside, a joint between the armor plates. The effect was catastrophic on the superstructure. A shockwave slammed through the exterior plating rending it from the teak and pine subframe, smashing it wide open, and killing instantly nearly a dozen men working within. The ship's progress slowed and she faltered as the pilot crew attempted to assess the damage to the controls.

As though a red rag had been raised to an angry bull, the ship began being pummeled by shot from near and far as enemy ships positioned themselves to destroy the stricken vessel without fear of return fire.

"What the hell is that?" the man next to Chestnut choked out.

"Good news. We might still get to drown before we hang." Chestnut replied. He was unmoved by their predicament.

The provost Marshal Reynolds appeared down the gangway and moved towards William's position at the end of the chain of prisoners.

"What happened, Reynolds?" Chestnut asked.

With all the portholes covered with iron plates for battle, the darkness below decks was almost complete. It was impossible to see his face, but the breathing was unmistakable. He was breathing hard, with the resignation of a man about to die.

Chestnut persisted. "Reynolds! What happened?"

"The casement took a direct hit behind the pilot house. There's no way to steer the ship. We're sitting ducks here."

"Let us out, we'll fight!" Chestnut said, ensuring his voice was loud enough for all the prisoners to hear him clearly above the din.

"Can't do that," he replied shaking his head and holding up his hands as though powerless.

The other men on the chain started to huddle around and badgered the provost similarly, presenting their upturned chained wrists and giving assurances, pleading with the marshal.

Sensing an opportunity, Chestnut pressed the man. "What choice do you have? We're all going to die, and the ship's going to be taken over by the Union. Do you want the *Mississippi* to become a Union ship?"

That broke Reynolds out of his apathy. "Of course. We need to scuttle the ship."

"It's not possible. It will take too long. The entire hull is reinforced. You must free us to defend her. It's our only chance."

Another heavy thudding against the hull seemed to seal the bargain in the provost's mind and he started running along the chain, unlocking the soldier's hands in turn. He left them in leg irons, but freed them from one another. William Chestnut was the last prisoner.

He held out his hands to have the chain broken.

Reynolds shook his head. "Not you. I'd rather sink than

release you." He ensured the chain was fastened at the wall and made off after the other men towards the topside.

———◦◇◦———

The sounds of battle continued overhead and the ship seemed to be moving well. An hour passed and Chestnut simply endured. A few men remained below and toiled at the ever-hungry boilers. The ship occasionally fired the Blakely 200 pounder, but that was the only gun William heard firing.

The Blakely's bark continued to report through the ship until another crash ripped through the superstructure above William's head.

Commander Baker appeared below shortly afterward, searching for sailors. The remaining hands in the boiler room were ordered to the topside by Baker who was looking disheveled and frustrated.

"Commander Baker!" Chestnut called to him down the companionway. "What's going on up there?"

The commander approached him. His uniform was splotched with blood and smelled of smoke and salt-peter. His face was ashen gray, and his hands shook with a heavy tremor. Despite the 110-degree heat of the boiler room, he seemed relieved for some respite from the battle.

"They hit the bridge again, this time with a case-shot. It's like a killing floor up there. There's hardly anyone left at all. The steering controls are ruined. There's no way to maneuver the ship. I've sent the leftover fire-men from the boilers topside to try and man the last functioning rifle we have. It's over Chestnut. We'll be over-run soon I suspect."

"There's another way Commander Baker. You must free me! Between the two of us we can work the steering gear from below the bridge."

"How do you know that, Chestnut?"

"Because I engineered her that way."

"You designed the *Mississippi?*" the commander's voice was

incredulous.

Chestnut nodded. "Yes. From the ground up. She's my baby. And I swear to you that if you let me out, I will do all within my power to keep her from entering the Union's hands or sinking."

"Why did you do it, Chestnut?" The commander's voice was suddenly hardened.

Chestnut closed his eyes, swallowed, and then opened them again. "Because they killed my family."

Chestnut watched Baker as he thought it over. He knew the man was running low on options or he wouldn't be down here at all.

"I'm willing to take you at your word Chestnut. If you cross me I will not hesitate to kill you. Do you understand me?"

"I do, Sir. I do." A seedling of hope bloomed in the barren desert of Chestnut's soul as he watched Baker unlock the chains about his wrists and ankles. He guessed Baker figured he would win in a close combat match, or wouldn't be freeing him. How little he knew William thought.

The commander finished unlocking his chains.

Chestnut said, "Thank you."

"You're welcome. Now save my bloody ship."

"I will. Of that, at least I can promise you."

Chestnut picked up the Walch Navy 12 Shot Revolver from where he'd hidden it behind his boots. He cocked the twin hammers and raised the barrel, squeezing the first of the two triggers. It took a delicate hand not to fire both rounds at the same time. The right hammer struck the round, and a single .38 caliber shot raced out of the barrel. The shot hit the commander on the side of his head, killing him instantly.

Chestnut stepped back into the prisoner's alcove, opened the hidden compartment and removed a Union Flag.

Chestnut raced along the gangway, past the boilers and to the topside.

A Confederate officer stopped him. "What the hell are you doing out here?"

Chestnut didn't answer him. Instead, he leveled his revolver and squeezed the second trigger. The shot struck the officer on his right shoulder. The man wailed in pain. With his uninjured hand, the officer reached for his pistol.

Cursing loudly, Chestnut spun the cylinder chamber, cocked the twin hammers, aimed, and yanked on both triggers simultaneously.

Two shots fired.

Both striking the officer in the chest. Their combined report producing the sound of a thunderclap. Chestnut watched as the man's eyes stared vacantly at him, before falling backward. Chestnut didn't wait to see if he was still alive. Instead, he kept heading toward the pilothouse.

It was night time and the oppressive darkness was made even more prominent by the heavy storm clouds above. The air was thick with the smell of burnt powder tainted with the rich iron taste of blood.

The remaining prisoners stood on the exposed deck outside the pilot house, trying to regain control of the ironclad. Chestnut watched as the provost marshal Reynolds tried to organize the men into action, preparing to fire the Blakely 200 pounder.

Reynolds spotted him. His eyes went wide and he reached for his weapon. "What the blazes are you doing up here?"

Chestnut spoke with confident authority, "Commander Baker released me. I was the lead engineer for this ship, and I can repair the steering."

"You can?"

"Yes. There's a secondary steering lever beneath the pilot house decking."

Reynolds locked eyes. "All right. I'll take you down below in the pilot house. Then get her under control. But if you cross me I'll kill you myself."

Chestnut held his revolver behind his back. "Very good, sir."

Reynolds stepped up to the pilothouse and rotated the lock on the hatch behind them. They were in front of an iron ladder, which accessed the aft side of the pilothouse. The pilothouse was a small structure on the forward section of the casement that was a squat shape resembling a pyramid. It had been designed with angled sides to deflect cannon ball impacts. William was surprised how heavily dented it was from the heavy shot strike, despite the thickness of its iron-clad walls.

William paused and took in the scene around them. It was near dark, and the air was thick with the foul-smelling smoke from the coal fired vessels in the blockade, and from the ordnance that whizzed around them. The ship lolled slightly in the water and was only just moving forward. The sounds of battle were all around and confused the senses. William had no idea whose ships were where and wondered how anyone else possibly could have either. It certainly didn't seem to be stopping them from firing their cannons.

Chestnut watched as Reynolds climbed the first few rungs of the ladder. He aimed the revolver, preparing to kill Reynolds from behind — taking note how war can make someone stupid. In Reynold's attempt to get inside the heavily protected pilothouse, he'd turned his back on the most dangerous prisoner aboard.

Chestnut never squeezed the trigger.

Instead, he heard the loud whiz of a large cannon shot on its downward trajectory. He ducked to the deck, covering his head with his arms. Afterward, his ears rung with the almost silent aftermath of the nearby collision.

He looked up.

A second impact followed immediately afterward, causing Reynold's now lifeless body to erupt in a grotesque display of battle carnage. Seemingly in slow motion, the provost's left arm and shoulder contorted and disappeared, their place being taken by his head which twisted down from above as a solid cannon shot struck him in the side of the chest from the port side.

The deafening roar of the cannon's muzzle caught up with its projectile a moment after the impact, and for a millisecond smothered all of Chestnut's senses. From his position six feet behind the ladder, he watched Reynold's torso as it exploded to the right. The top half of his body was removed, all but the right arm which hung from the rung its hand held on to, the head and right shoulder attached to it dangling hideously beneath. A bucket of blood fell from the neck and streamed down the ladder. The legs and pelvis—contained within their boots and trousers—flopped to the deck in a pool of crimson that seemed to instantly form, and slid kicking and jerking down the starboard side of the casement into the darkness and water below.

Out of instinct, William dropped to the floor and covered his head. He closed his eyes and waited for what seemed like an eternity. When he looked up, he watched as Reynold's right hand lost its grip, and then caught sight of the provost's face as his head and arm fell to the deck in front of where he was laying. He crawled towards the ladder. The stink of fresh blood filled his senses, and he shoved the provost's disconnected head and arm over the side of the casement without making eye contact. He mastered his fear and stood erect on the deck.

In open defiance, he straightened and brushed off his uniform as best he could, trod through the blood, and slowly climbed the ladder to the pilothouse—being careful not to lose his grip on the bloody rungs.

From the flagpole on top, he removed the Confederate Navy Jack.

A moment later he attached the Union Jack to the grommet and snap-hook and pulled on the halyard. The flag rose quickly until it reached the top. Chestnut secured the halyard to the cleat with two figure eight turns.

He looked up and smiled.

High above the pilothouse, the Union Jack opened in the breeze.

———————•◇•———————

Chestnut opened the hatch at the top of the ladder and climbed into the pilothouse.

Standing inside was the wiry Irishman. He was peering through the slits of the navigation portal at the scene in front of the ship. He didn't look away from the scene outside as Chestnut approached him.

Turning inward, the man grabbed an oily rag from the side of a gauge stand and passed it to Chestnut.

"For your face. It's a real mess."

"Thank you," Chestnut replied, clearing his throat and wiping his forehead, then methodically folding the cloth over and cleaning his hands. He offered his hand. "William Chestnut."

"Robert Murphy," the Irishman said, gripping his hand with a firm shake. He glanced at the Union Flag above. "And I see you now have command of this vessel."

Chestnut met Murphy's hardened stare. "Is that going to be a problem?"

"Not at all." Murphy's lips curled into an upward grin. "I was already on my way to hang for deserting. No reason I shouldn't change my allegiance anyway. Where are we headed?"

"North. I have an important Covenant to deliver. Something that might actually end this damned war."

Murphy shrugged, as though he was indifferent to the ending of the war. "You might want to know that a casing shot ripped through the pilothouse damaging more than just the casing. We've lost transmission to the steering. We're sitting ducks here. Soon enough, the Confederate cannons at Vicksburg are going to start taking their shot at us."

"So I heard. Don't worry, there's a redundancy steering tiller down below." Chestnut ran his eyes across the pilothouse. "What about the rest of the controls?"

"The throttle seems to be still connected, but there's nobody manning the boilers or the pumps at this stage."

"All may not be lost. I've built contingencies into her, we may be able to run her yet. We need to go below and assess the damage." Chestnut expelled a heavy breath. "The problem will be running the river. I'm no navigator and to be honest I have little knowledge about where the river runs from here."

Murphy said, "I used to be a pilot on a tugboat before the war."

"On the river?" Chestnut asked, feeling hopeful.

"Yeah, but farther south. I used to take larger vessels into New Orleans. But I know this river and if you can get my steering working again, I'll do my best to navigate her."

"Good. Let's get started."

"What do you think, the internal hatchway might be the best idea."

"Couldn't agree more," Chestnut answered and together they opened the floor hatch.

Chestnut moved quickly, descending to the lower deck, deep in the bowels of the ship. He explained how the tiller could still be driven from below decks, using a cranking point which he had included in the design for situations where the topside was compromised.

"We need five men. Two to feed the boilers, one to run the tiller, one to crank the bilge pumps, one to see where we are going and a runner. We can rotate roles to minimize fatigue. If we have five men, we can make a run for it."

"The other prisoners are basically all the able-bodied crew we have left. I don't personally know any of them, but they're soldiers, so hopefully they can obey orders. I'm sure they'll all be happy to escape the noose for a while, perhaps even for good if things work out. I'll go and gather them up and we can regroup in the pilothouse. We need to see who's capable of doing what."

"Good."

Murphy said, "One more thing…"

"What?"

"Where are you trying to go?"

"North."

"Where?"

"To a secret location where it's imperative we deliver our cargo as soon as possible."

Murphy sighed. "I'm going to need more information than that if you want me to navigate us there."

"And you'll get it," Chestnut said. "But first, we need to get this ship underway."

Robert Murphy stared out the narrow slits of the pilothouse. He watched as the dark outline of the shore passed by and distant hills were nothing more than a shadow that blended into the foreboding and tempestuous sky. But he knew, those hills were filled with enemy cannons, capable of sending the ironclad to the bottom of the Mississippi. Now, more than ever, they had enemies. Both the South and the North could possibly take a shot at him—despite flying a Union Jack.

He still didn't know where William Chestnut's loyalties lay or anything about the important cargo he'd informed them they were to deliver farther North along the river. But none of that mattered. For now, he was alive after he was supposed to be hung at Vicksburg. So, for the time being, he would obey Chestnut. He was a born leader, unaccustomed to following, but he could grit his teeth and obey while it served his need.

And right now, William Chestnut's orders served his needs.

It had taken the men just fifteen minutes to connect the emergency steering tiller, organize the boilermen to build up steam and get the ironclad moving once more. There were a total of eight people left alive on board. Five of the prisoners and three of the original boilermen. Two were badly injured and would most likely die within the next day or two, but the rest were still fit to run the ship. All of them had happily agreed to follow William Chestnut.

Once the ship was underway, Chestnut had disappeared, to inspect the ship.

Up ahead, the river turned to the left, forming a giant curve that snaked past Fort Hill and the city of Vicksburg, making a one-hundred-and-eighty degree turn around De Soto Point. Murphy calculated the steering angle, aiming to come as close as possible to De Soto Point in order to avoid any stray shots from Confederate cannons—especially Vicksburg's notorious Widow Blakely 7.5 inch, rifled cannon, mounted high up on Fort Hill.

Murphy spoke into the copper voice-pipe, which ran from the pilothouse down to the boiler room and the new steering room, where one of the men was guiding the emergency tiller, "Give me five degrees to port, gentlemen."

"Copy that," came the reply. "Five degrees to port."

He watched as they edged ever closer to De Soto Point. Once they had gone past the peninsula, Murphy said, "Full tiller lock to port, please."

"Copy, full tiller lock to port."

The ironclad turned one-hundred-and-eighty degrees around the point and headed due south. A single cannon from Vicksburg fired, but fell more than a hundred feet short of their bow.

"Okay, tiller straight ahead."

"Copy that. Tiller straight ahead."

Murphy breathed a sigh of relief as they rounded the point and entered Union waters and made a silent prayer that the lamp that Chestnut had set up on top of the pilothouse still lit up their Union Jack.

He ensured the ironclad was steered within the middle of the river, where the deepest water lay and farthest from the shore, where enemy guns traced their movements.

Chestnut climbed the ladder from below and entered the pilothouse. His intelligent blue eyes were wide and he beamed with pride. "Well done, Mr. Murphy. Well done, indeed."

Murphy smiled back. "Now that we're out of danger and you've somehow convinced the Confederates at Vicksburg to let us slip by, while now displaying a Union Jack to keep the Union's gunners at bay, would you like to tell me what's so important you commandeered an ironclad to deliver?"

Chestnut shook his head. "No."

"No?" Murphy wasn't accustomed to being defied, but he bit his tongue. Before his temper got the better of him, Chestnut's lips curled into a broad smile.

"I'd like to show you, instead."

One of the boilermen took over in the role of lookout in the pilothouse.

"Be sure to keep her in the middle of the river," Murphy warned.

"Will do," the boilerman replied.

Murphy followed Chestnut down below, along the main gangway, until he entered the third alcove on the starboard side.

There, Chestnut stepped up to the wall near the breech of a cannon, and pulled back a heavy canvas tarpaulin, dropping it on the floor. Murphy had assumed it had been covering shot crates, but underneath was an iron and brass safe, two feet high, two feet deep, and three feet long.

It was freshly painted in a decorative blue, and had the Confederate seal stamped into a raised badge on top. A hinged clasp hung on the front with a finely crafted thick brass padlock through its eye. Thick ornate handle rails ran along each end.

Murphy met Chestnut's penetrating gaze. "Is that what we

stopped for?"

"Yes, a secret change of plans from the very top." Chestnut kept his voice low, but the words were resolute. "Inside this chest is a Covenant that has the means to end the war."

I don't want the war to end now.

War makes men desperate. And I can make a fortune off such people.

"A lot of lives would be saved if we could end the war now," Murphy agreed. "What's inside that's so important?"

"You want to see it?" Chestnut asked.

Murphy nodded. "Of course."

Chestnut removed a key from his pocket. "I took this off my friend, who was supposed to be the keeper of this chest until it reached its destination, but..."

"Your friend met his untimely death earlier today." Murphy dipped his head in prayer. "I remember."

"Exactly."

Chestnut inserted the brass key and turned it three times until a sharp click emanated from a mechanism inside. He then lifted the sealed lid.

Murphy swore. There were more gold coins than he'd ever seen or even imagined. At the center of the treasure, a single unsealed note was fixed to a bed of blue velvet. His eyes darted toward Chestnut. "May I read it?"

"Yes, go ahead. Please do."

Murphy picked up the note and read it. When he was finished he turned to Chestnut and asked, "Is this for real?"

"Yes."

Murphy swallowed hard. "My God, it will end the war."

Chestnut nodded. "That's why it's so important that we deliver it to the North."

"Where's its final destination?"

"There's a wagon and horses waiting along the Ohio River,

where it meets the Allegheny River at Pittsburg, waiting to take it to Washington, D.C."

Murphy replaced the document and closed the lid to the chest. "Now what?"

Chestnut quickly locked the chest and held his breath. "Now, we do our best to deliver the Covenant."

"There's just one problem."

"Yeah, what's that?"

Murphy crossed his arms. "The river passes through any number of heavily populated cities on our way North. Someone there is going to take notice of a large Ironclad traveling north. Once they do, fake Union flag or not, we're in real trouble."

"And you think the city's defensive cannons will sink us?"

"Or we'll hang as spies."

Chestnut shrugged with indifference. "That's a possibility, too."

"Maybe we thank our good fortune at escaping, sink the ironclad and travel on foot."

"No." Chestnut dismissed it without further thought. "We keep the ironclad. It will take us all the way we need to go."

"You think so?" Murphy's thick eyebrows narrowed. "You have a plan on how we're going to sneak past the watch towers of the various cities?"

Chestnut took a deep breath and exhaled. "Well, as a matter of fact, I have a perfect solution that's going to allow us to take this ship as far North as we want."

CHAPTER ONE

LAKE SUPERIOR, MINNESOTA

T HE LOG HOUSE appeared to be a jarring study in contrast. Proudly standing just twenty feet from the lake's shore, the architecture was a strange mixture, consisting of the olden-day charm of original explorers and fur traders with the extravagant examples of the owner's significant wealth. The outer shell was a layer of mixed hard-wood conifers—pine, fir, and spruce, felled locally and milled on site. But that's where any resemblance to the early explorers ceased.

The grand, three-story building boasted ten bedrooms and fifteen bathrooms. On its roof, covered by glass was a full length indoor lap pool. At the very top of which, a Bell 407 helicopter, painted red and white, rested on its helipad that jutted out from the roof by a thirty-foot airbridge, where it then joined an elevator—presumably to the internal three levels. The building was surrounded by a thick forest of conifers, mountain ash, maple, aspen, oak, and paper birch.

The commercial pilot banked, taking them around the front of the house, before bringing the Jet Ranger into a hover and gently placing the skids onto the smooth rocky shore.

"This is as close as I can go," the pilot said, turning to face the two men. "Gotta keep the rotor spinning because of the unstable ground."

Two men climbed out. One, average height while the other looked like a veritable giant. Both had the solid build and decisive movements of once professional soldiers. They moved quickly, removing a large equipment container and then carrying a single large duffel bag each. Thirty feet away, the shorter one gave the thumbs up signal, and the pilot took off again, quickly disappearing behind the dense forest that lined the lake.

Sam Reilly took a deep breath in and leveled his deep blue eyes toward the lake. Despite the cerulean blue sky, and unabated sun, the air had a crisp bite to it. There were only two places on Earth where he recalled experiencing such an anomaly of summer weather — the icy environments of Antarctica and Siberia's Oymyakon.

A fifty-something-foot pleasure cruiser, with its sleek design and array of radar dishes was anchored in the shallow waters directly in front of the log house. The yacht appeared out of place, more like a Billionaire's toy out of Silicon Valley, than a fishing boat belonging to the remote and pristine wilderness of Lake Superior.

His eyes ran across the shore, where a small building used to house a floatplane had its hangar door open, revealing the aircraft to be currently out.

"Well, one thing's for certain…" Sam said to Tom Bower, as he admired the range of expensive toys. "Senator Arthur Perry's son knows how to have a good time in the great outdoors."

Tom turned to face the main entrance to the summer house. "That's if the young man's still alive."

Sam nodded, his mind instantly returning to their purpose for being there. "All right, let's go meet the good Senator Perry."

A fifty-something year old man, who introduced himself as the estate manager, greeted them and took them inside.

The man knocked at a closed door.

A voice from inside immediately answered, "Send them in,

please, Walter."

Walter nodded and turned to face Sam and Tom. "You're free to see him now."

Sam nodded and entered the large den.

His first impression of the Minnesota senator surprised him. The man was portly with a rotund belly that indicated his predilection toward food. His clothes were expensive, but he let his girth stretch them at their seams, instead of buying new ones. It wasn't quite what Sam expected for a man known for his high intelligence, wealth and generosity, who'd managed to get re-elected for three consecutive six-year terms.

The senator leaned across the huge mahogany desk and greeted them with a firm handshake, making a mock attempt to stand while gesturing for Tom and Sam to please sit in the two leather office chairs opposite.

"Gentlemen, thank you for meeting with me at my summer house. I realize my request is somewhat unusual, but I think you'll appreciate the need for discretion." The senator stopped, as though he'd just recalled their long trip to meet him. "Can I offer you anything?"

"No thanks," Sam and Tom replied.

Without further preamble, the Senator handed Sam a six by four color photograph. "This is the last photo my son, David, sent me. It's also the last communication I had with my boy before he went missing nearly three weeks ago."

Sam studied the image. It was taken using film, instead of a digital camera and depicted the iron bow of the submerged wreckage of an early nineteenth century, single boiler freighter. The ship listed heavily toward its starboard side, laying deep in azure blue water. Clearly visible in letter-plate below the gunwale was the name, *J.F. Johnson*. The lifelines and bollards were all intact with thick corrosion clinging to their lines, but the ship's detail could be clearly seen.

"The *J.F. Johnson*..." Sam mulled the name over in his mind.

"I've heard of that wreck. It's in deep, cold water. Somewhere at the bottom of a hundred and eighty feet?"

"Two hundred and five," Senator Perry corrected him. "They call it the time machine."

Tom scoffed at the name. "Why?"

"The *J.F. Johnson* is that deep and permanently so cold that it made the removal of any bodies next to impossible." Perry paused and his thick, wiry eyebrows narrowed. "Local divers who have ventured to her depth say that the bodies of the four men who lost their lives are now floating, entombed within the main bridge—a mixture of the freshwater and extreme cold, having preserved them in a permanent tribute to the day they died."

Sam's lips curled into a wry smile. "You're telling us that no one's dived on her since she sank?"

Senator Perry shook his head. "Not that I've heard of."

"Is it strictly forbidden?" Tom asked.

"No. Just highly frowned upon. Only someone as stupid as my own son would even attempt to break it."

"Why?" Sam asked.

The senator met Sam's eye. "Forgetting the obvious implication of trespassing on the tomb of those pour souls who lost their lives?"

Sam nodded. "Yeah."

"Have you ever dived in Lake Superior?" the Senator asked.

"No, never."

"Well. She's a special kind of lake. Of the five Great Lakes, she's the only one that's composed entirely of freshwater, and as such, she likes to preserve and hold onto her precious shipwrecks, in a way that no other lakes are capable of."

Sam was interested. "Go on."

"As you know, it's not just her depth that's lethal. The real problem with trying to reach the inside of the *J.F. Johnson* is the temperature. The water is too cold to use *Heliox* because the helium enriched air freezes."

Sam said, "So you're confined to an extremely deep air dive."

"Exactly. The locals call it diving to seven margaritas."

Sam smiled at the analogy. "Because they reckon the nitrogen built up in their bloodstream for every thirty-three feet of water — or single atmosphere — is the equivalent of having another cocktail?"

"Yeah, something like that." The senator continued. "Even if the nitrogen narcosis doesn't cause you to do something really stupid that gets you killed, you still have the problem of bottom time. At 205 feet you're going to have a maximum of about ten minutes to enter the *J.F Johnson,* get out and start your ascent — even then, you're going to be uncomfortable as all hell in the cold for nearly a hundred minutes while you decompress."

"At 200 feet oxygen becomes toxic." Sam met the Senator with his jaw set firm. "Only a fool would try to dive the *J.F. Johnson* on air tanks. Very few divers would survive more than a few minutes at that depth, diving on straight air tanks alone. No, they would need to be using helium enriched, *Heliox* or better yet, a combination of helium, nitrogen and oxygen, called, *Trimix.*"

"Yeah, well, according to a couple cowboys who run the local SCUBA diving tours on the lake, there's been a few who have made it on air alone..." the Senator sighed. "And a few who haven't ever returned to the surface again."

Tom thought about that statement. "I suppose if they managed the intoxicating effects of nitrogen narcosis at those depths, they might just get lucky and not die from oxygen toxicity. But you'd need a heck of a lot of dive tanks for the lengthy deco stops?"

Senator Perry shook his head. "It wouldn't matter. At that depth, the lake remains a constant 36 degrees Fahrenheit all year round. I don't care how thick your dry suit is, you won't last a minute longer than that in the water without freezing to death."

"What about an atmospheric dive suit?" Sam suggested.

"One of those big machines that make you look like the *Michelin-man,* used by commercial divers on oil rigs?" the senator asked.

Sam nodded and then shrugged. "Yeah, why not?"

"Too big. It would never fit inside the narrow confines of the wreck. No, to get inside the bridge, you would need to dive in nothing thicker than a dry suit."

Sam nodded. He understood the problem. If he had to dive it, he and Tom had the knowledge and means to overcome it without getting themselves killed.

If they had to dive the J.F. Johnson.

"I'm not worried about the temperature or the depth. We can overcome those the same as any other professional tech diver."

"Really?" The senator was surprised. "How?"

"We brought closed-circuit rebreathers instead of SCUBA." Sam grinned. "And electrically heated undergarments, that directly heat the torso, back and abdomen. They were originally designed for use in the military, but in all things, as commercial demand increased, the technology moved toward the realms of the everyday consumer, recreational divers. Pretty much all the major players in diving equipment now offer their own version, including, *Golem, DUI Blue Heat, and Santi.*"

"Even so, the helium's going to dry and cool your lungs until your entire body freezes from the inside out, and hypothermia kills you as quickly as drowning or the bends."

Sam smiled, patiently. He'd heard this argument for decades. Fact was, helium feels colder on your skin than air, but it carries away less heat when you breathe it. "Actually, a recent study conducted by the British Navy concluded there's no difference in core temperature heat loss in divers at depth using *Heliox* versus regular *Air.*"

The Senator smiled. "Sure. Try telling that to the local tech divers who visit the icy bottom of Lake Superior."

Sam continued without taking the bait. "Besides, we'll be using fully closed-circuit rebreathers."

Senator Perry looked blank. "And that's supposed to keep the cold out?"

Sam nodded. "In rebreathers, the scrubbing of CO_2 from the breathing gas is an exothermic chemical reaction, meaning it produces heat. The reaction's by-product is water vapor, making the overall result of the rebreather's function causing the diver to breath warm, moist breathing gas. With rebreathers, the exhaled breath is re-circulated, which means that the moisture level is maintained. The loop gas is typically at 100% humidity and is much warmer than the surrounding water."

"Sounds great. I'm still glad you're diving it and not me."

Sam barely considered the implications of such a dive. Instead, he returned to the image allegedly taken of the submerged *J.F. Johnson*.

He examined the shipwreck for a few seconds and then turned the photo over. There was a single, hand-written note on the back.

Sam's eyes rolled across the words and his lips curled into a grin.

Dad, I found it! This changes everything. History will need to be rewritten!

CHAPTER TWO

S AM GLANCED OUT the window that looked upon the glistening water of Lake Superior. He put the photo back on the table, still trying to make sense of it.

His gaze turned to the senator. "Your son dived to Lake Superior's bottom and entered the wreckage?"

"Like I said, only my son would go off and do something this stupid," Senator Perry replied. "That was the last photo he sent to me."

The large Minnesotan sat across from Sam and reclined into a mahogany trimmed, green leather desk chair that was clearly custom made to suit his ample frame perfectly. Though he had not stood when Sam and Tom had entered the office, Sam guessed his height at six feet six inches. His tailored suit and vintage Bolo tie portrayed everything a Minnesotan voter expected from a Senator, and his demeanor was benevolent and engaging. His reputation as an accomplished politician appeared well-deserved.

"Do you know what he was referring to?" Sam asked.

"Not a clue." The Senator held his hands facing upward in a supplicant gesture and sighed. "What I do know is that my son was obsessed with the story of a man named Jack Holman, who had come out here in the early twenties after the war to get away from civilization. Holman owned a custom-built float plane, which he used to deliver cargo throughout the Great Lakes and into Canada in the North. One day he made reference to finding the remains of a Meskwaki Native American campsite where a natural spring flowed with gold."

"It flowed with gold?" Sam asked, raising an incredulous eyebrow.

The Senator grinned, revealing his own cynicism. "Hey, I'm just telling you about the legend."

Tom asked, "Did Holman ever return with the gold?"

"No, but he tended to always have money, so the legend continued to grow."

"But no one ever found the Meskwaki Gold Spring?"

"No."

Sam nodded. "And you think this is what your son is after?"

"It's the only guess I have so far," the Senator replied.

"What about this Holman character?" Sam asked. "Whatever happened to him?"

The Senator stared at the lake, his eyes fixed on the horizon, but his mind appeared much further away. "Jack Holman was a local hero and a legend who was larger than life. Some have even argued that he never existed at all. That he was just the manifestation of every token adventurer and traveler, but the British War Records would argue differently."

"British War Records?" Sam asked.

"Yes. Holman received a number of medals flying a Sopwith Tabloid as a scout during the First World War. At the time, it was one of the fastest floatplanes in the world. When he came back, he built his own modified version, and flew it all across the U.S. — Canadian border for nearly a decade."

Sam persisted. "What happened to him?"

"Rumor has it he crashed in the late twenties into a lake. No one ever found the wreck of his plane, or his body."

"What was your son's interest in him?" Sam asked. "Was it just idle interest in another man who wanted to get away from the world, delving into the pristine landscapes of the secluded Canadian mountains?"

"No. There was more to it, too."

"Go on?"

"Holman was a flying ace. In 1925 he won the Schneider Cup. Do you know what that is?"

Sam nodded. "Set up by Jacques Schneider, the son of a well-known French steel and arms manufacturer who believed that floatplanes were the most practical military and civilian design, since they could fly to any country with a coast, a river, or a lake without the construction of expensive airfields. On December 5, 1912, he declared a competition in which he appealed to manufacturers of marine aircraft to develop the world's fastest airplane."

The Senator nodded. "Like I said, Holman was really something of a legend. During prohibition, it was said that he flew cases of alcohol for a local bootlegging mob. The police wanted him, but he was never caught."

"There's more to it?" Sam asked.

"In 1931 Holman reportedly found the Meskwaki Gold Spring. He even brought back some small pieces of gold to prove it. Apparently, before he could bring a team in to recoup the gold, he had an accident and crashed. But others have suggested that maybe he was killed, his floatplane intentionally shot down."

"Because of the gold?"

Senator Perry nodded. "Some think it could have been because of the gold, but others think it might have been a rival bootlegging mob. They killed him in a violent organized crime driven turf-war."

"And your son thinks something from the wreck of the *J. F. Johnson* revealed the truth?"

"It appears so."

Tom said, "And it will change history…"

"What happened to Holman?"

"He found it, but apparently there was too much for him to carry out on his little plane, so he sent a team back to Oshkosh, Wisconsin to bring in an expedition to retrieve the gold."

Sam smiled. "Let me guess. They came in on board the *J.F Johnson?*"

The Senator nodded. "Yes, sir."

"So, you think your son might have found this gold?"

"I don't know, but that's why you two fine gentlemen are here."

A silence hung in the air as Sam and Tom mulled over what the Senator had said. Tom gave Sam a look which intoned he was interested and Sam should start asking some questions.

Sam finally broke the silence. "Sir, do you want to start from the beginning here?"

Senator Perry sighed. He rose from his chair and moved to a sideboard where a pair of crystal decanters stood on a silver platter with matching heavy based whisky glasses. He poured himself 3 fingers and raised the decanter to the two men in offer. Again, both waved a polite no thank you.

Sam was struck by the size of the man, he was overweight, and on his frame, Sam guessed his weight at around 400 pounds. A big man. Probably once a powerful man, but now political luncheons as a way of life had taken their toll. His skin was red compared to the light tan of his suit, and his fingers thick and bloated.

Replacing the crystal stopper, the Senator spoke "I blame myself. If my wife, God rest her soul, was still alive today, none of this ever would have happened."

Sam made a thin-lipped smile. "Go on."

"We're a wealthy family. Always have been. My grandfather worked hard, so did my father. I went to Stanford Law for the betterment of my fellow Americans."

"But your son wasn't interested in the family tradition?"

The Senator sighed, heavily. "No. Fact is, my son's an incredibly intelligent man and a lousy student."

Sam and Tom remained silent.

The Senator finally continued. "He completed school as a solid C average student. I'd be lying if I told you I wasn't disappointed, but after my wife passed away, I viewed things very differently."

"You wanted him to go to university?"

"Of course I wanted him to go to university. We're Perrys, we all have law degrees. But my son was never going to get through law. He might have achieved a C average in high school simply by showing up, but not law. No, I could have paid to get him in of course, but he never would have completed it."

"So, what happened?"

The Senator expelled a deep breath of air. "Well, I gave him something none of the Perry fathers gave their sons."

"What was that?"

"I let him choose what he wanted to do." The Senator studied their impassive faces, searching for signs of a rebuke. When none were forthcoming, he continued. "We come from old money. That was never my concern for my son. Fact was, he never had to work a day in his life. I told him as much. I didn't even care. Hell, my wife was a good woman, a hard-working person, and look what happened to her — she died before she got to have any time for herself. So I let my son choose."

"What did he choose?"

"Well, like his hero Mr. Jack Holman he bought himself a floatplane." The Senator paused again, his eyes squeezed tight as though the memories alone were painful. "He started spending a lot of time flying and diving the Great Lakes."

"What was he looking for?" Sam asked.

"Nothing really. A good time. He saw himself as an adventurer. A wild treasure hunter. It was all fun and games. I figured I'd let him go and enjoy himself. At least he was doing something. He got his pilot's license with a floatplane endorsement. Then his diving ticket. He told me he got into something called tech-diving, which went well and beyond the depth of recreational divers."

"And that's what brought him out here?" Sam asked.

The Senator nodded. "Yes. I believe he came up here to search for something related to that damned ship. But what he found on board led him to something completely different, where no one has seen him for nearly three weeks."

"Why us?" Sam asked.

"Mr. Reilly your reputation precedes you as one of the most inventive and indeed successful treasure hunters on the globe. You may name your price, Sir, and I will meet it if you are successful. My interest is with the welfare and whereabouts of my son, but I also believe there's a decent chance you may find a prize to equal any of your previous conquests during the course of the investigation." The Senator turned to face him. "I need your help."

"But you're already rich," Sam said. "You're not interested in the gold."

"No. I've lost my son. All I'm interested in is my son."

"What about the Police? Have you filed a missing-persons?"

"They're not interested. There's no sign he's dead. He just hasn't made contact with anyone for three weeks."

"Is that unusual for him?"

"It is. He usually asks me to send money to his bank account when it runs out, which it does often."

"He spends big?" Sam asked.

The Senator sighed, sheepishly. "I send him what he needs and not a penny more. He has a shared bank account. I deposit money when he runs out."

"You keep him on a short financial leash?"

The Senator nodded. "It's the only way I can be certain he'll be in contact with me."

Sam nodded, it was a noncommitted gesture. He wasn't there to judge, just to find the kid. "What about the bank account?"

"What about it?"

"You said it was a joint account?"

"Yeah, why?"

"So, you can see if he's been spending anything lately?"

"Yeah. There's nothing."

"When was the last withdrawal?"

"Three weeks ago. It was a mighty big one, too. Nearly two hundred thousand dollars in cash, leaving the account nearly empty." The Senator shook his head. "I expected my son to ask for more money — I'd even prepared my response that he was being frivolous and I was tempted to cut him off — but instead, he never called."

"What would your son have wanted with two hundred grand?"

"I have no idea."

Sam looked at the photograph of the old shipwreck. "Look. From what you've told me, your son was involved in a lot of high risk-taking activities. Flying floatplanes through the alpine lakes, and tech-diving wrecks are both pretty dangerous activities."

"I know what you think," Senator Perry sighed, heavily. "My son's most likely dead."

Sam nodded. "It's a possibility."

"I can't explain it. But I don't think my son's dead." The Senator put his palms outward in a placating gesture. "I know, you're going to assume I'm a father who lost his son, and is hoping for the best. But I just know, the way only a father could, that my son is still alive."

"What do you think happened?"

"My guess. He found a new lead on board the *J.F. Johnson*

shipwreck, and that led him off on a completely different tangent."

Sam said, "Find that lead, and we might find your son."

CHAPTER THREE

T HE *ANABELLE MAY* was a custom-built pleasure cruiser that took the name of Senator Perry's late wife. As he motored slowly toward the main channel into the lake's deeper water, Sam noticed that he handled her with the surprisingly adept love of a seasoned sailor. She was a custom designed motor yacht by the German shipbuilding company, *Blohn and Voss*. She had a length of sixty-five feet and a beam of twenty-eight. Her hull was made of high tensile steel, while her three decks were made of aluminum alloy, with a teak outer deck and helipad. Above its bridge, were an array of high tech radar and satellite communications and plotting equipment. Powered by twin MTU diesel-electric marine engines — a marine division of *Rolls Royce Propulsion* — and with sleek, angular sides, it could achieve a top speed of forty knots.

Once outside the channel and into deep waters, Senator Perry opened up the throttles and the *Blohn and Voss* shot forward, its bow quickly riding on the plane.

"How long until we reach the dive site?" Sam asked.

Senator Perry answered without hesitation. "It's thirty minutes from here."

"Great. Do you need us or can Tom and I start preparing our dive plan and equipment?"

"Go. I'm fine. I've been navigating these waters since my dad first took me out here as a kid. It's like my second backyard."

Sam nodded. "All right. We'll be on the back deck if you need anything."

On board the aft deck Tom had opened their large storage crate and laid out the two *Dräger Closed-Circuit Oxygen Rebreathers* on the teak deck. They were originally designed for military use, police diving, and search and rescue, but to Sam their rectangular, rigid aluminum backpack, gave them the awkward appearance of an astronaut's personal life-support system. Mounted on either side of this backpack were two gas cylinders. One of these was filled with *Oxygen* and the other with a diluent called *Trimix*. Basically, even oxygen becomes lethal at varying depths beyond thirty feet and so the gas needs to be diluted with something. For extreme depths approaching two hundred feet, a combination of oxygen, nitrogen, and helium was the most practical gas diluent.

On the port side of the aft deck, at a small entrance to the *Anabelle May,* was a fully equipped dive locker that housed top of the line recreational and tech diving equipment, including rows upon rows of dry suits, dive masks, gas cylinders and a commercial grade air compressor and a mixture of large, H-sized gas cylinders for filling tanks, including, *Air, Oxygen, Nitrox, Heliox, Trimix.*

Sam ran his eyes along the cylinders.

They would need *Oxygen* and *Trimix* for the dive.

Sam and Tom agreed to do an initial bounce dive, take some photos, and if the answers to where the Senator's son had gone still eluded them, they could set up for a more prolonged dive and come back tomorrow.

The concept with a bounce dive was to descend rapidly, spend less than ten minutes bottom time and then ascend before the compressed nitrogen had a chance to significantly build up in their bloodstream. This would result in a shorter decompression time and less risk of hypothermia. Heated underlay or not, prolonged diving in near freezing water was far from a lot of fun and increased their risks.

Sam and Tom methodically and efficiently worked their way through their dive equipment, slowly going through the laborious process of preparing each part for the dive.

Sam opened the aluminum backpack. Inside was an axial type scrubber unit filled with the granular absorbent used to remove CO_2 from the closed-circuit during the dive. He removed the half-used cartridge and replaced it with a brand-new unit, filled with five pounds of sodalime and then reinserted it, locking the lid with a heavy-duty thread.

He then began to test the unit for leaks. Two leak tests were conducted. These were generally known as the positive and negative pressure tests, and are designed to check that the breathing loop is airtight for internal pressure lower and higher than the outside. The positive pressure test ensures that the unit will not lose gas while in use, and the negative pressure test ensures that water will not leak into the breathing loop where it can degrade the scrubber medium or the oxygen sensors.

The *Anabelle May's* engines reduced to an idle and the pleasure cruiser drifted into a round arc, coming to a complete stop with the port bow just next to the historic mooring buoy, which displayed the details of the *J.F. Johnson's* wreck.

Sam looked at the buoy and then stepped inside the main pilothouse. "Do you want me to pick up the mooring line, Senator Perry?"

The Senator stepped by, carrying a retractable hook, and shook his head. "No, I'm fine."

Sam smiled as he watched the heavy senator move with surprising agility toward the bow, where he leaned over the gunwale and hooked the mooring line. It took him little more than a moment to kneel down, feed the line through the cleat and secure the *Anabelle May.*

"All right, gentlemen," Senator Perry said. "I'll be here until you return. I'll have some warm soup to heat you up again when you get here. Thanks again and good luck."

Sam nodded. "We won't be too long. An hour at most. We're

going to do a bounce dive. Straight down, take some photos and back up again."

"Seems like a good plan," the Senator replied.

Sam stepped back to the aft deck. South-east of their position, he spotted the tall boreal forest of Balsam fir and White Spruce along *Isle Royale's* rugged shoreline. From what he guessed, *the J.F. Johnson's* wreck lied somewhere smack bang in the middle of the imaginary line that ran along the surface of Lake Superior and delineated the U.S. and Canada's border.

Confident that his equipment was set up correctly and ready for the dive, Sam undressed and then donned his thermal vest and switched it on. The undergarment used state of the art fiber heating technology that generates *Far Infrared Rays,* which heats and warms up the blood in two locations along the divers back, enabling heat to penetrate deep into the body core. Over which, he wore a *Thinsulate* underlay. He then slipped into a thick dry suit, putting on a thick woolen beany before pulling the dive hood over.

Tom was already kitted up and testing his rebreather. "You're slowing down, Sam."

"Give me a break," Sam said, "This is exactly why I don't like diving in the cold. It takes too long to get everything ready. Give me a shallow tropical dive in a pair of board shorts and a BCD any day."

"All right, we'll get in and get back out before the cold has the chance to hit you."

"Thanks," Sam said and then donned his full-face dive mask.

The full-face mask had several benefits in deep cold-water dives, such as the wreckage of the *J.F. Johnson.* It functions to provide a wide lens through which the diver can see clearly underwater, it provides the diver's face with some protection from cold water, while at the same time increasing breathing security because if any level of altered conscious state occurs, the diver doesn't need to keep a regulator in his mouth. Within Sam's mask, there was another benefit, it provided space to house his diving radio to communicate freely with Tom throughout the dive.

He took a deep breath and started pre-breathing the unit — a process of breathing normally for about three minutes before entering the water to ensure the scrubber material gets a chance to warm up to operating temperature, and works correctly, and that the partial pressure of oxygen within the closed-circuit rebreather is controlled within the predefined parameters.

Sam inhaled effortlessly.

The gas he breathed was humid and warm, rather than the dry, cold air divers are used to with compressed air and a SCUBA cylinder and regulator set up. In most dives, this would make for a more comfortable experience, but in the cold, deep confines of Lake Superior, it would save his life — keeping him warmer and less dehydrated — both of which, would reduce his likelihood of decompression sickness.

He checked his gauge for two things.

One, that CO_2 levels weren't rising, meaning the new sodalime scrubber was doing its job correctly and two, that the partial pressure of oxygen within the closed-circuit remained within the initial setpoint of 1.3 bar.

Sam ran his eyes across the top reading, where a nondispersive infrared sensor showed that the CO_2 levels weren't elevating.

Below that, his glance stopped to examine the reading from the oxygen analyzer. It showed the partial pressure of oxygen as 1.3 bar.

Three minutes later, he said to Tom, "I'm all good to go."

"All right. Let's stick together. I don't know what to make of the Senator, but he wasn't lying when he said Lake Superior is a uniquely deadly place to dive."

And stepped off into the frigid waters of Lake Superior.

CHAPTER FOUR

F EW THINGS ARE more shocking to the human body than plunging into ice cold water. As the near freezing water enveloped Sam, his body reacted the way millennia of evolution had intended—his arteries tightened, blood pressure and heart rate increased, and his lungs gasped for the cold, dry, *Trimix.* The heated undergarment warmed the large blood vessels to his kidneys in his lower back, where it was soon shunted to his vital organs.

Within minutes, his body had overcome the original shock of the initial dramatic temperature change and it started to regulate the warmth. He checked his gauges, confirming on his heads-up display that his CO_2 levels weren't climbing and that the partial pressure of oxygen within the fully closed-circuit remained within the predefined parameter of 1.3 bar.

Sam glanced at his buddy. "How you doing Tom?"

"Good," came Tom's cheerful reply. "I don't know what the Senator was talking about. The lake's a balmy 4 degrees above freezing."

"That's good, Tom. You and I must be diving different lakes." Sam grinned. "How are your numbers?"

"They're all good."

"All right, let's start our descent."

Sam deflated his buoyancy wing until he was negatively buoyant and started his descent. They descended quickly, more like sky divers, watching the icy-clear waters flow past them as they raced to the lake's bed. As he descended, Sam swallowed, equalizing the pressure in his ears and sinuses and occasionally inserted a small amount of gas into his dry suit to prevent its compressed air from squeezing him tight.

At a hundred feet, he switched on his dive flashlight and watched Tom do the same.

"You still good, Tom?"

"Great. You know Sam, I remember when you used to take me diving in the Bahamas. Now all we seem to do is find more and more inhospitable places to explore."

Sam smiled, unsure whether Tom was making reference to the fact that he was normally the one to complain about the cold. "Sorry. We go where the work is."

"I know, I'm just regretting not using my opportunity to take a vacation with the rest of the crew, while the *Maria Helena* was having its engines overhauled."

"Vacation?" Sam asked. "I thought this was your vacation. When was the last time I let you come along on a treasure hunt?"

"You mean, without people trying to kill us?" Tom replied. "I don't know, it's been a while."

"See, aren't you glad you came?" Sam said. "Besides, what else were you going to do while Genevieve's away?"

"I can't think of anywhere else I'd rather be."

"Where is Genevieve anyway?"

"She stayed in Russia to visit a friend of hers. She'll be back in a week."

Sam slowed his descent. They were approaching 170 feet. "The wreckage of the *J. F. Johnson* should be visible somewhere around here."

Tom turned and shined his flashlight to their east, revealing a large wreckage. "You mean that one?"

"Yeah, that'd be it."

Sam stared at the shipwreck.

Beneath the powerful beam of his Day-maker flashlight the *J. F. Johnson* looked as though it had sunk a year ago, not almost ninety. The paint on the hull, the fittings, everything was perfectly preserved. There was some buildup on the steel rope structures aboard, but otherwise only silt disguised the intact ship. The bow pointed up the slope of the ravine and the water passed the ship from bow to stern in an ever-present current, keeping her relatively clean in her frozen tomb. The surroundings were freezing, brutally inhospitable. No seaweed clung to the barren underwater seascape, and the whole area seemed completely devoid of life-forms of any kind.

Sam could already feel hypothermia teasing at his extremities, despite all their preparations. He motioned to Tom and tapped his watch, then made ten fingers to symbolize the agreed ten minutes on the wreck, and the okay signal. Tom checked his own watch and confirmed the timing.

The current was taking him along at a walking pace toward the wreck, so he had to time his approach carefully, as he aimed for the main entrance to the raised pilothouse. According to Senator Perry, only one hatch remained accessible, while the rest of the ship was now sealed permanently with rust.

Sam kicked his fins in the lead and Tom followed as they crested the starboard lifelines, which sat atop the listing ship. They headed for the back of the main dining room amidships. An eddy held them in place against the aft wall and then shoved them into the back of the base of a bridge that raised upward from the deck at a sharp angle. It was a strange feeling being hustled inside the dead ship by the invisible hand of the sea.

He gripped the edge of the door to the wheelhouse. He pulled on the door, using his legs to push off the side of the structure, but nothing shifted. The hatch was locked from within or had been permanently fixed with rust and decomposition.

"I thought the Senator said only the door to the bridge was still accessible?" Sam asked.

"Maybe there's a second hatch, portside?" Tom suggested.

"That's probably right."

The hatch was fixed in a semi-open position, leaving a gap of about three inches, leading downward into the main fishbowl-shaped wheelhouse.

Sam cracked a weighted luminescent glowstick and waited until its chemicals mixed and glowed green. He then dropped it through the gap, leading to a broad windshield that formed the semi-circle of a large goldfish bowl. The wheelhouse glowed with the eerie green luminescence, revealing four ghostly sailors who'd kept watch on the stricken bridge for nearly nine decades. The four dead men wore thick woolen coats and typical sailing attire from the 1920s.

Sam slowly exhaled as he ran his flashlight across their faces. They looked waxy, definitely recognizable as once young men, but at the same no longer quite human. More of a morphed shape that had bulged over time into a frozen vision that haunted the deep.

Tom was first to break the tension. "It's strange to think that if any of these men had survived the original sinking they'd be older than my grandfather and would have already died of natural causes."

Sam's tension eased. "Yeah. It's hard to imagine they've been down here all this time. They still look…"

"Almost human?"

"Exactly."

"It's the unique combination of fresh water and extreme cold that would have preserved them. Lake Superior is meant to be quite remarkable for it."

Sam glanced at the gauges on his heads-up display. C02 and P02 were where they belonged. His fingertips were already losing sensation due to the cold. The Senator was right, their bottom time wasn't restrained by breathable gas volume, but by their ability to withstand the freezing conditions and stave off hypothermia.

Tom shined his flashlight at his face. "You okay?"

"Yeah. Just noticed my hands were getting pretty cold."

"Come on, let's check that other hatchway, find what we're looking for, and get back to the surface."

"Agreed."

Sam swam downward, across the heavily angled goldfish-bowl shaped windshield, to the portside of the heavily listing vessel.

He found the second hatchway. It was permanently fixed at a right angle to the portside of the pilothouse hull. Sam glanced inside. The green haze of the glowstick still radiated from inside, but not immediately inside. Instead, it appeared as though the hatchway led to the bottom level of the wheelhouse and that they'd need to swim through it and then upward to reach the old bridge.

Sam shined his flashlight inside. It revealed the remnants of an old set of steep metal stairs, that most likely led to the wheelhouse. He clipped the end of his red guideline to the steel hook on the hatchway with a carabiner. He had no intention of penetrating the wreck of the *J.F. Johnson* more than he had to, but even in the relatively small and well contained area of the wheelhouse, a sudden shift of silt could cause a complete visibility block out.

He took a deep breath, slowly exhaled and then gently kicked his fins to enter the wreck. The red guideline unraveled from its spool as he swam farther inside. About ten feet inside, he shined his flashlight on the ascending metal steps that once led to the highest point of the wheelhouse. He flicked the beam in a wide clock-wise arc. He stopped, with the light fixed on a second hatchway — this one was open, and led downward, further into the ship.

He put his hand on the heavy iron hatchway. The door moved. It seemed impossible after nine decades that the metal hinges hadn't seized completely.

"What do you think of that?" Sam asked.

"I have no idea." Tom's voice was calm and collected. "One thing's for sure, someone's been down here recently."

"You think?"

"I'm certain. For a steel door to still be moving after nine decades beneath the water isn't just unlikely, it's impossible." Tom shined his Day-maker beam on the hinge. "Looks like these have been replaced sometime over the past few years."

Hidden beneath his full-faced dive mask, Sam grinned. "You want to see what's so important down there that someone went to the trouble of repairing the hatchway?"

"Yes, but not right now. We're not set up or prepared to penetrate the deeper levels of the ship. Let's see what's inside the wheelhouse, return to the surface and then set up for a more prolonged dive tomorrow."

"All right. Good idea."

Sam was intrigued by the possibilities, but glad Tom focused him to their initial dive-plan. A prolonged expedition inside the bowels of the *J.F. Johnson* could prove fatal without better preparation.

The ship was a 251-foot steel *Tramp-Steamer,* a cargo vessel built in Lorain, Ohio by the American Ship Building Company and launched in 1924. She was powered by a triple-expansion steam engine producing 2500 hp. Sam knew the rough layout of the ship from the plans they had studied prior to the dive, but because they'd been told only the wheelhouse was accessible he hadn't bothered to really study and memorize the internal layout below decks.

They were careful not to disturb the ultrafine silt layer that lay on the walls-turned-floor that they now navigated forward toward the wheelhouse. If the dust became a cloud, their visibility would become zero and they could become disoriented or even separated. Aside from the flashlight, it was pitch darkness, so the men's progress was slow and cautious. For added insurance, Sam trailed a small red guideline from a spring-loaded spool on his hip.

Sam turned left, swimming along the once steep metal steps which were now nearly horizontal due to the listing of the vessel, and into the large wheelhouse. The entire room still glowed with the eerie green glow of the luminescent stick he'd dropped minutes earlier. He made a mental note to stop using green and pick a less creepy color.

He carefully made his way past the four ghostly sailors. There could be any number of places to search. He shined his flashlight across the large, pine wheel, that looked perfectly intact. He slowly moved toward it, trying to see what the Senator's son might have spotted.

Ignoring the bodies, he moved toward the navigation station — next to the captain's quarters. He swam slowly, careful not to stir up nine decades worth of silt.

Reaching the navigation station, he shined his flashlight inside and then swore — because, written in large red letters, were the words–

STANFORD STOLE THE MESKWAKI GOLD SPRING.

I CAN, TOO.

CHAPTER FIVE

S AM TOOK ANOTHER sip of the beef stew. It was thick and hot, but not too hot that it couldn't be quickly consumed. He felt the contents warm him from the inside. When he'd finished, his hand continued to cup the mug in an attempt to extract its heat. It was doing the job, too. He noticed his hands no longer shook uncontrollably, and sensation resembling normality, had finally returned to his extremities.

Noticing that he and Tom had finally warmed enough to concentrate, the Senator asked, "Well, did you find anything?"

Sam nodded. "Yes, but I have no idea what it meant."

The Senator's jaw was set firm and his body tense. His voice was eager as he asked, "What was it?"

Sam heaped another ladle of stew into his mug. "Someone else — maybe your son — has been down there recently. Whoever it was, they left a clue at the navigation station within the wheelhouse. It was written in big, red, capital letters so that no diver who entered the room could possibly miss it."

"What did it say?"

"Stanford stole the Meskwaki Gold Spring. I can, too."

The Senator's eyes widened and his face was suddenly drawn and pale. He tried to speak. Choked. Like his tongue was too try to talk. Swallowed. And then shook his head, collecting his composure, he said, "Any idea what the hell that could mean?"

"Not a clue. We were kind of hoping the words would mean something to you."

Perry took a deep breath. "No. I've never heard any of it before."

Tom said, "What about the Meskwaki Gold Spring? Weren't you worried that David had run off in search of the ancient treasure — a local myth in these parts of the world dating back to early European explorers?"

Catching his lie with the speed of an adept politician, he said, "Yes, well, of course I've heard of that. But like you said, it's merely a myth about an ancient treasure."

"But your son *was* interested in it," Tom persisted.

"Yes, but my son's a fool. There's nothing here that gives us any indication where this would have led David to search for the fabled treasure."

"What about Stanford?" Sam asked.

"I don't know any Stanford." The Senator closed his eyes, as though searching old memories. He opened them again and sighed. "Besides, if Stanford did in fact steal the treasure years ago, it would indicate my son has no need to go searching for it."

Sam smiled. "Unless he wants to steal it?"

"No. My son's many things, but he's not a thief. Besides, there's nothing about this statement that indicates where the Meskwaki treasure — if it even exists at all — was taken."

"You're right," Sam agreed. "So, we'll analyze the photos we took inside the wheelhouse and then, if nothing comes up, we'll plan a second dive. This one, a much more protracted one with significant decompression stops."

"Why?" The Senator asked, his voice somehow tense and full of concern. "There's nowhere else to explore except for the wheelhouse. I told you before, it's the only hatchway locked permanently in the open position. The rest of the ship's hatches have rusted in the closed position."

"Yeah, about that…" Sam paused.

The Senator's thick curly eyebrows narrowed. "What?"

Sam watched as the *Annabelle May* swung round on her mooring buoy, with the evening change in the wind. When it had finished, he fixed his penetrating blue eyes square on the Senator's face, studying for a reaction as he spoke.

"We found an open hatchway leading to a set of stairs that descended into the main hull of the *J.F. Johnson*. What's more, it looks like someone's gone to the trouble of recently replacing the hinges so the door can be opened and closed at will."

CHAPTER SIX

"I T CAN'T BE!" Senator Perry didn't even attempt to hide the fear in his voice. "The ship was supposed to be permanently sealed. Any hatches leading inside the main hull were welded shut more than ten years ago."

"Why?" Sam asked.

"I can't tell you. Not yet. It might cost my son his life—if it hasn't already." Perry stood up, took two paces and then stopped. "Oh David… what have you gotten yourself into!"

Sam stood up to support the Senator. "What is it?"

"I'm sorry gentlemen. I need to leave straight away."

"Leave?" Sam asked. "Where?"

"New York."

"Why? What do you have to do in New York?"

Senator Perry swallowed hard. "Plead for my son's life."

"Is there anything we can do to help?"

"No. I'm afraid there's nothing you can do. I'm sorry to have wasted your valuable time. I'll contact my pilot, who can come and airlift me to Duluth, where I can catch a flight to New York immediately. If you two would be so kind as to return the *Annabelle May* to her mooring, my house manager will arrange for someone to pick you up. Better yet, stay on board for a few days. I'll let my house manager know you've got the *Annabelle May*. Have a short vacation at my expense. It will look better that way. What do you say?"

"Senator Perry," Sam said. "Please, there must be something we can do to help?"

"No. Really, the best thing you could do for me now is forget the entire thing has ever happened. Forget about my request for you to search for my son, forget about Stanford, and for God's sake forget about what you found on board the *J.F. Johnson!*"

Sam thought about it for a moment, watching sweat drip off the Senator's neck in the icy cold wind. The man's face had turned ashen, and for a moment Sam thought the man was about to have a heart attack.

"All right. We'll forget about it. Look, you have my number. If there's anything we can do to help, just give me a call." Sam offered his hand. "I realize that you have powerful friends and ample resources at your disposal, but if you need help, I have a lot of connections who can help in… how do I put it… difficult times."

The Senator took his hand and gripped it with a firm shake. "I appreciate that. Really, I do. Look, send me a bill for your time up until now and I'll send you the money."

Sam shook his head. "It's not about the money. I don't need your money. I was here because I was genuinely intrigued by your prospect of finding your son who'd considered himself a bit of a treasure hunter and disappeared on the trail—but now I'm genuinely worried about you and your son. So, I don't offer my services lightly. I have people who can help. No matter what your son's stumbled into."

"Thanks. I appreciate that. But I'm hoping I can go fix this myself."

"All right."

Thirty minutes later, Sam watched as the Senator's private helicopter whisked him away, leaving Sam and Tom in possession of the *Annabelle May.*

Tom expelled a deep breath of air. "Well, that was a surprise, wasn't it?"

Sam nodded. "Yeah, who would have thought that we'd see something stranger than the bottom of Lake Superior today!"

"Did you see the Senator's response when you told him about the second opened hatchway?"

"Yeah, he practically screamed, let me out of here."

"I'd love to know what he's really doing in New York."

Sam untied and then dropped the mooring line. "Yeah, whatever it is, I don't think the Senator's off to have a good time."

They made their way up to the bridge. Sam pressed the start button and the twin MTU diesel-electric marine engines roared into life. He set a course for Duluth, pushed the twin throttles all the way forward, and the *Annabelle May* quickly started to aquaplane until she was cruising just shy of forty knots.

"You still want to work for him?" Tom asked, his voice serious.

"Who said anything about working for the Senator?" Sam grinned. "I'm interested in what happened to his son and this ancient Meskwaki Gold Spring."

"So, we're not leaving Lake Superior yet?"

"No way in hell. There's answers hidden deep inside the wreckage of the *J.F. Johnson* that someone's gone to great lengths to keep hidden — Senator Perry included — and I want to find out what those are."

CHAPTER SEVEN

S AM AND TOM spent the better part of the next day in Duluth.

They spoke to a local pilot named Jeff Gads, who chartered his floatplane for scenic tours over Lake Superior. The man had said that he'd met David Perry a few months ago after the two of them got to talking about nearby lakes on the Canada side where a pilot could put down easily if he had to. Jeff had said that the kid seemed like a genuinely nice guy — particularly for a rich kid.

Sam had steered the conversation toward the Meskwaki Gold Spring. The pilot told him he'd heard of the legend, but as far as he knew, no one had ever found it, although some had claimed to find large amounts of gold in the rivers leading into Lake Superior.

Next, they headed over to the local dive shop that offered guided dives to tourists on any of the estimated six thousand shipwrecks lying in pristine waters at the bottom of Lake Superior. Out in front of the dive shop, someone was getting into a Lamborghini Urus. Sam recognized it only because of its hubris combination of Lamborghini's traditional supercar being jammed into an attempt at an everyday SUV for millionaires. He waved at the driver — a young guy who couldn't have been any older than twenty-five — who politely waved back. Beneath the brake lights was a bumper sticker that read, *I dive Lake Superior looking for treasure.*

Tom laughed at the arrogance. "Looks like he must have found some."

Sam looked at the remaining car parked in the front of the dive shop—a Porsche Cayenne Turbo, with the same stupid bumper sticker. "Looks like the treasure hunting business is booming."

They walked into the building. Inside, it was no different than any other dive-shop they'd been in around the world, with the exception that there was more emphasis on heated dry suits due to the freezing climate.

A young man with a convivial smile greeted them. "Can I help you gentlemen with anything?"

"I hope so. My name's Sam Reilly and this is Tom Bower. We're looking for a friend who came up here to do some diving recently. We're kind of hoping you might have seen him around here and better yet, have some idea where he's headed."

"Sure. Who's your friend?"

"David Perry."

The dive operator's lips curled into a broad grin. "Senator Perry's kid?"

Sam matched his smile. "That'd be the one. Have you seen him?"

"Sure have. He was in here... gosh... let me think, a little over three weeks ago. He filled up some tanks with *Trimix* and straight *Oxygen*. He likes to use a rebreather. Increases his bottom time, although how long he could possibly want to stay down in Lake Superior, beats me."

Sam took the hook. "Did he say where he was headed?"

"No."

"Did he come in here often?"

"Sure did. He dived pretty much every day for about a month through Summer."

Sam's eyes narrowed. "Did he mention what he was looking

for?"

"No. But it was pretty obvious. He was after treasure—even offered to hire someone to help him go searching for a wrecked seaplane."

"Did you?"

"Did we, what?"

"Help find the wrecked seaplane?"

"No. In the end, he didn't have the faintest idea where to look." The diver made a wry smile, like the kid was an idiot. "Fact was, he was a rich kid out on a treasure hunt with no knowledge and no experience for how to find what he was after."

"Right…" Sam was starting to get the picture. "Did he mention where he was headed three weeks ago?"

"No." The diver paled. "Do you think he's all right? He was just some dumb rich kid, but he was a good man."

"I don't know. That's what we're here to find out." Sam wrote his cell phone number on a dive pad and left it with the man. "If David happens to stop in or anyone you know sees him, can you please give me a call?"

"Yes, of course."

"What was your name?" Sam asked.

The diver offered his hand, "Mark Smith."

Sam took it, glancing at the Rolex on the man's wrist. "Thank you for your time, Mark Smith."

They were about to leave, when Tom asked, "Have you ever dived the *J.F. Johnson?*"

"No. Never. It's not really the sort of dive tourists like to be taken."

"Why's that?" Tom asked.

"For starters it's a very deep, cold, technical dive. But more importantly, it's considered bad taste to visit. Four men lost their lives when she went down back in 1931. Those who have dived her, report seeing the four men still at their positions keeping spectral watch from the wheelhouse. No, my recommendation to anyone interested in diving her, is to leave those men to rest in peace."

Tom lowered his head, respectfully. "Of course, that sounds reasonable. I only ask because I'd heard David mention it a few times over the years, so I wondered if he may have dived it."

"He could have." Mark sighed. "And if he did, it's very likely it might have cost him his life. It's a difficult dive and extremely dangerous. I wouldn't recommend diving it."

Sam ended the conversation, before Tom could continue it any further. "We'll take that into consideration. Thanks again for your help."

Thirty seconds later, Sam and Tom stepped out of the dive shop and started walking back to the *Annabelle May*.

Sam said, "Anything seem odd about that?"

"Anything not seem strange?" Tom blinked. "Yeah, what's a local dive operator charging less than a hundred dollars a dive running a multi-million-dollar Beneteau as a dive yacht?"

"Exactly."

Sam walked a few more paces and then grinned. "I don't believe it."

"What?"

"It's been staring at us in the face all this time."

"What?"

"Don't you see. The expensive boat, European cars, the Rolex watch... the tourist dive boat is shipping contraband."

"On board the *J.F. Johnson*?"

"No. But something inside it betrays their secret involvement." Sam paused for a moment and then grinned. "And Senator Perry knows about it."

A wry smile formed on Tom's lips as he thought about that. "Sure, that fits. But how are you going to prove a thing like that?"

"I don't have to. Just watch this."

Tom had a bemused smile on his face. "Okay, I'll bite."

Sam turned around and walked back into the dive shop.

Mark, the dive operator greeted him. "What did you forget?"

"One more thing I just remembered I meant to ask you about." Sam's voice was intentionally soft, timid, almost meek. "Do you have time?"

The dive operator nodded. "Shoot."

Sam's lips formed a coy smile of indifference, but his eyes focused on the dive operator's face, waiting for a reaction. "When David Perry—Senator Perry's son—dived the wheelhouse of the *J.F. Johnson* a little over three weeks ago, he wrote his father, telling him he'd found some sort of irrefutable evidence regarding the location of the Meskwaki Gold Spring."

"Okay…" the dive operator said, noncommittally.

"Any idea what that could have been referring to?"

"No, not a clue."

Sam took a deep breath, holding it for just a moment and then made a theatrical sigh. "We're thinking about diving the *J.F. Johnson* tomorrow morning, see what we can find. Do you want to join us?"

Mark's eyes widened and he visibly took a deep breath. "I'm afraid we already have clients booked to dive the Lafayette tomorrow. But please, let us know how you do."

"Okay, great, we will—and if you think of anything, let us know."

"Of course." If there was still any doubt about his involvement, the dive operator squashed it when he then lied. "By the way, I've never even heard of the Meskwaki Gold Spring."

CHAPTER EIGHT

I T WAS A little after nine p.m. and a thick fog seemed to penetrate and obscure everything. Tom kept his eyes fixed on the radar, without which, he doubted anyone could have navigated the frigid waters of Lake Superior — a testament to the six thousand or more shipwrecks that rested on the lake's seabed.

After laying the trap, he knew it was only a matter of time before Mark — the dive operator — or someone else from the dive company would head out to the wreck site of the *J.F. Johnson*. If they were involved in illegal shipping of contraband and they thought Sam and Tom's dive tomorrow might reveal irrefutable evidence to such effect, they would dive the wheelhouse tonight to remove it.

At ten minutes past nine p.m. the outline of the *Superior Deep*, the luxurious motor yacht built by Beneteau and used as a diving charter boat, came into view. On the radar, Tom watched as the vessel, with its sleek lines, crept out along the channel and into the deep and open waters of Lake Superior.

Sam glanced at Tom, who was at the wheel of the *Annabelle May*. "You see it?"

Tom relaxed into the Napa leather seat, with his legs casually up against the instrument panel, he nodded. "I see it. I'm going to let them have some space before I follow."

"Don't lose them."

Tom lowered his feet, eased the twin throttles gently forward. "Why the rush? We know where they're headed."

It was nearly two hours before they rounded the southern end of Isle Royale, headed north and reached the wreck site of the *J.F. Johnson.*

Tom eased off the throttles and let the *Annabelle May* settle in her wake, nearly half a mile behind the dive-boat.

He faced Sam and smiled. "Nice night for a dive, wouldn't you say?"

Sam visibly shuddered at the thought. "Sure. I just wished they'd picked a warmer place to shift contraband."

They stared at the radar. The Senator hadn't skimped on the hardware for his motor yacht and the radar was no different. It gave a detailed outline of the water ahead, leading to a detailed outline of the dive-boat. Tom watched as three men worked to maneuver something around the aft deck.

His eyelids squinted, as he studied the image. "What is that?"

"Not what," Sam said. "But, who?"

A moment later, the diver stepped off the aft deck of the *Superior Deep* and into the water. Tom could just make out the diver's covered head as he surfaced after splashing into the icy waters. The dive boat loitered for a couple minutes and then turned in a large arc, motoring straight toward them.

Tom watched as the *Superior Deep* motored past them. At the helm, he spotted Mark, the dive-operator they'd met earlier that day. The man waved at him, his face was fixed in a pretense of relaxed tranquility and not a care in the world, and then he opened up the throttles and raced south, toward Duluth.

Tom increased the twin throttles, heading toward the marker buoy that represented the wreck site of the *J.F. Johnson.* "So much for coming back to pick up his diver."

"Do you think he's going to return?" Sam asked.

"I don't know. There's a chance he's already planning on how he's going to get out of the country after leaving his fellow diver to freeze to death or drown."

Tom slowed the *Annabelle May,* bringing her to a complete stop with her bow just above the marker buoy. Outside, Sam hooked the buoy and pulled up the mooring rope, feeding it through the bow cleat. Tom switched the engines off and stepped down to the bow.

He said, "Someone needs to go see what the diver's doing down there."

Sam nodded. "And someone needs to stay on board, in case our friend from the dive shop returns."

Tom sighed. "Rock, scissors, paper to see who's going to go down after him?"

CHAPTER NINE

T OM LOST THE game.

With the other diver already having gained nearly ten minutes head start, he quickly donned his dive gear, which had already been set up earlier in the day in preparation for the potential need to make this dive. This time he wore an additional two electrical heating garments, aiming to keep his core body temperature toward the high end of the norm, rather than risking hypothermia during what he predicted might be a more prolonged dive. In addition to the rest of the diving paraphernalia, Tom wore a sharkstick on his right thigh — a high powered weapon with a long barrel and a waterproof shotgun cartridge capable of deterring a shark.

He placed the full faced dive mask over his head and took a few deep breaths. His eyes studied the gauges displayed on the heads-up-display, confirming that his CO_2 and PO_2 remained within their desired parameters. He signaled to Sam that he was good to go and then stepped off the back of the Annabelle May, into the frigid waters.

Tom sunk quickly, free-falling into absolute darkness for nearly six minutes. He kept his Day-maker flashlight switched off, and his eyes focused on the small red line at the top-right hand corner of his face mask that displayed depth. When it reached 160 feet, he inflated his buoyancy wing and leveled out to a state of neutral buoyancy.

His eyes turned downward, where the fishbowl-shaped windshield of the *J.F. Johnson's* wheelhouse glowed yellow, with the light of a diver. With his own flashlight turned off, Tom descended until he was level with the other diver. One of the reasons rebreather systems are popular in the Special Forces of the military is that because they're a closed system there are no bubbles escaping to the surface, making them silent.

In the darkness, Tom was able to get close enough to clearly make out the shape of the other diver. He watched, from about thirty feet away, as the diver used an underwater paint to cover the walls and insides of the wheelhouse with a new canvas of black.

It was the final proof he needed to see that someone from the dive shop's position was made vulnerable by the note they'd discovered that read: STANFORD STOLE THE MESKWAKI GOLD SPRING. I CAN, TOO.

As Tom watched, while the diver toiled at a depth approaching 200 feet to remove history, he wondered how this could possibly implicate a current illegal contraband smuggling operation. So, the Senator's grandfather was a crook — that doesn't make the Senator guilty. Did Stanford steal a bootlegging operation when the ship sunk, killing his boss? More importantly, could it still be in operation. What about the Meskwaki Gold Spring? There's nothing illegal about finding gold. How could Stanford have stolen it? Again, how did any of this implicate the local dive operator?

The yellow glow of the diver's light began to dwindle. Tom shifted his position another ten feet backward and descended until he was nearly flat along the seabed, reducing his profile in case the diver came out and directly shined his flashlight on him.

He waited as the light inside the *J.F. Johnson* shifted lower into the hull. It was no longer an easily identifiable glow, but rather a blurry haze. Tom expected the diver to exit the ship through the open hatch on the portside of the listing shipwreck at any moment. Instead, he watched as the light continued to radiate from the portholes along the hull, constantly heading farther into the lower decks and heading toward the stern of the old Tramp Steamer.

The diver didn't notice Tom in the total darkness of Lake Superior's seabed. Tom watched him for another minute and then saw that the guy was swimming into the main engine-house. Tom watched as the clear glow of the guy's flashlight moved through the old steamer's engine room.

Where the hell's he going?

There was nothing logical about what the guy was doing. No reason anything of value could be stored deep inside the engine-house. Unless…

Tom felt his heart race with excitement. The diver had entered the second hatchway and descended into the main hull.

Suddenly it was clear to Tom what sort of operation they were running. Drugs, weapons, or whatever type of contraband was being shipped was stored inside the hull of the shipwreck and then retrieved at a later date by divers to move it between the US-Canadian border. For years, the operation had gone undetected because whoever was responsible for it, had gone to great lengths to build up a dangerous mystique about the wreck of the *J.F. Johnson* — even going so far as to weld the rest of the hatchways shut and keeping the four ghostly sailors to keep watch and protect their hoard.

Tom felt for his sharkstick. It was still attached to his thigh, not that he expected to need it. Close quarters fighting was almost impossible at this depth and even harder inside the narrow confines of a shipwreck. Besides, he was a big guy — nearly 250 pounds of muscle — if it came to a fight, he had no doubt he could win it. Worst case scenario, he had his sharkstick. He weighed up his options and decided this might be his best chance to ever catch the criminal operation in the act. If he could get closer, his facemask mounted camera could capture a digital recording of the event.

But it wasn't his job. Catching criminals shipping contraband across the border was strictly Border Patrol, Homeland Security, and the FBI's responsibility. He wasn't being paid for it. No reason he should risk his life to stop it. Take down one operation and another one will just pop up in its place. Tom swallowed hard. Then again, this might be the only chance he and Sam might have to save the Senator's son's life.

The light continued, deep into the stern of the ship's 251-foot hull, all the way to the very end, where the engine room had once been. Once there, the light stopped. It remained perfectly still. It didn't make sense. Every minute they spent at this depth was adding up to hours of decompression time. No one simply waits inside a shipwreck, even if they're trying to shift contraband.

Had the diver become trapped in the wreck?

It was enough to convince Tom to follow the diver inside. He carefully swam toward the hatchway, keeping his own flashlight switched off. Inside the lower level of the pilothouse, he spotted the open hatchway to the right, and swam through.

Mentally, he pictured the long passageway leading to the back of the ship, where the engine room had been. A faint glow of light radiated from a passage beneath a set of stairs. Tom descended two back to back metal stairs, until he reached the working deck of the old Steam Tramp—where men had once toiled to feed the boilers for hours.

He kicked his fins gently, trying not to disturb the thick layer of dark silt. The water was currently crystal clear, but he had no doubt that would all change in an instant if the silt became disturbed. He glanced at the end of the tunnel. A bright light was fixed at the end of it. The light no longer flickered. Its beams were fixed, shining away from him. Behind the light, he just made out the shadow of the diver. The man seemed completely still. There was a chance he'd made a mistake with his gas mixture and was no longer conscious, or even dead.

Tom swam faster, making a mental map of his surroundings

as he moved. It was a single straight passageway, two sets of metal stairs, an open hatch, a small rectangular entrance compartment within the base of the wheelhouse, and then an open hatchway to the outside world. He could make it in the dark, if he had to. If things went bad, he could do it without laying any guideline down. Urged onward with the hope that he might still have a chance to save the diver, he raced toward the light. Drug smuggler or not, the stranger deserved a chance—if not for himself, but because he might provide the only link to the Senator's son.

Tom was within arm's reach of the diver. He took in the diver's open eyes, which stared vacantly directly at him, his limp body, and guessed in an instant the man was already beyond hope. There was no rise and fall of the diver's chest, suggesting he'd already stopped breathing. Tom reached out to grab him.

But his hand never reached the man.

Instead, Tom watched as the stilled diver suddenly came alive. The diver's lifeless hands became animate and squeezed the twin throttle triggers of his sea scooter. The headlight brightened and shot past Tom, through the hull, like a bullet. It raced along the passageway and up through the stairwell, heading toward the open hatchway. The electric motor of the sea scooter whirred as it went past him. In seconds, the crisp, clear water was churned by the sea scooter's propeller, and ninety years of silt was spread through the water like an impenetrable mist. The now distant flashlight turned into an obtuse blur, before total darkness extinguished the light completely.

CHAPTER TEN

TOM SWITCHED HIS own flashlight on immediately.

But it made no difference. The silt permeated everything. Its fine dust particles merely reflected his own light, confining him to the same visibility of darkness. He couldn't see his own hand in front of him if he held it up in front of his dive mask.

The mental map of the *J.F. Johnson's* interior hull shattered.

Fear rose in his throat like bile and he felt the unaccustomed symptoms of claustrophobia envelop his world. In seconds his clear vision had been completely tainted and all points of reference stolen. Neutrally buoyant, his world was spinning. He tried to grasp something ahead, feeling with his hands as a person suddenly blinded might, trying to form a new mental map.

Unable to reach anything, he turned his attention to simple priorities needed to keep himself alive. He breathed in, working to consciously slow the process and avoid hyperventilation. Making a conscious decision, he savored the icy cold *Trimix,* as it entered his mouth and passed down through his windpipe into his lungs. He felt his chest rise gently, and his belly expand subtly. His diaphragm relaxed, and the gas slowly left his lungs.

His eyes couldn't see anything in front of his mask, but that didn't mean he was completely blind, either. The heads-up-display still provided a series of gauges. His eyes scanned those numbers. At the current rate of consumption, his gas volume meant he was capable of spending another three hours and five minutes at this depth. It wasn't gas volume that concerned him. At 36 degrees Fahrenheit, he would suffer from hypothermia and freeze to death well before he ran out of breathable gas.

Tom eased his breathing. He could hear the sound of his heart thumping in the back of his head. At this rate, his metabolic rate would skyrocket and he would burn through his gas supply. He needed to stop himself from sliding down the slippery slope of panic.

Locked in the interminable space and unsure if he was facing upward or downward, Tom quickly released all air from his buoyancy wing. Air bubbles ran downward past his eyes and a moment later he felt them run past his feet. He then started to fall toward the ceiling.

He grinned.

It was the first major development he'd made toward extracting himself from the deadly labyrinth in which he'd been confined. Tom adjusted his position until he felt level, and eased the last of the air out until he sunk to his knees. He extended his hands outward, until they reached the steel wall of the hull.

He stopped and treasured the achievement for a moment, took a couple of slow, deep breaths in and then reached up to his facemask. His gloved hands ran across the sealed top until it reached a single pliable switch. He depressed the rubber. It acted like the mode button in a car and changed the instrument panel exhibited on the heads-up-display. It showed an array of dive-tables, depicting his maximum bottom time and decompression obligations. He pressed it again and the mode now displayed the outside water temperature and temperature inside the dry suit. Just looking at it made him feel chilled to the core. He depressed it again and his heads-up-display now showed a digital compass.

The arrow pointed North.

He cast his mind back to the bathymetric maps he'd studied earlier that day of the *J.F. Johnson* shipwreck. It was positioned almost precisely in a North-South direction, with the stern pointed North and the bow planted due South. He took the new information and added it to the mental image of the interior of the shipwreck he was drawing.

He turned to orient himself, level with the ground in a southerly direction. Tom felt a new surge of hope. More than hope. He was enjoying the challenge, reveling in the discipline that cave diving and wreck diving demanded. The very reason he'd gotten into the sport years ago.

Running his gloved hand along the side of the hull and his trailing fins just above the ground — occasionally allowing them to make contact and confirm that he was still moving parallel to it — Tom began swimming along the passageway.

It took less than five minutes before his hand caught the edge of the steel railings that formed the base of the internal stairs. He added gas to his buoyancy wing until he started to ascend, using buoyancy to guide him and ensure that he was moving in the right direction. Keeping hold of the railing, he was able to follow it up two separate flights of stairs.

At the top, the thick layer of silt was slightly thinner. He was starting to make out things. Part of the railing, a single step, his hand in front of his face. It wasn't much, but it was a start. He followed his mental picture of the hatchway and fixed his flashlight at the wall. Moving right up to it, he spotted that it was nothing more than hull. He turned to the right and stopped. There in front of him, his eyes caught the L-shaped lever used to lock and open the now closed hatch.

His right hand gripped the handle, trying to pull it downward. Nothing happened. He fought with the door latch. Ninety years of rust had welded it shut and no amount of pulling on Tom's part could possibly encourage it to turn.

A new wave of fear churned in his stomach. Had his map of the ship, carefully reconstructed in his mind, been wrong? Had he made a major mistake in his assumptions. Could he have headed South when he was supposed to head North? Worse yet, what if he was exactly where he was meant to be? What if his attacker had locked the hatchway shut, permanently entombing him 205 feet below the surface of Lake Superior?

The thought chilled him.

How long would Sam Reilly wait for him to resurface? Even if he did come after him, there was no certainty that he'd be able to open the door. The latch, after all, was rusted shut.

That thought made Tom stop.

Then, beneath his facemask, he smiled—because if he couldn't open the latch, his attacker couldn't close it.

Tom shook his head, and pressed on the door.

It swung open.

CHAPTER ELEVEN

S am listened to Tom as he recalled the events down below.

They waited at the site for another good two hours — much longer than any diver could possibly have stayed down below without being overcome by hypothermia. The dive boat never returned. According to the *Annabelle May's* sweeping radar, there were no other boats anywhere within five miles of the dive site.

After an hour of silence, Sam said, "There's a chance the other diver surfaced somewhere already and is now surface swimming toward Isle Royale."

Tom crossed his arms beneath a thick woolen jacket. "Unlikely. I reached the surface a long time before him and my core body temperature was already low enough that I struggled to concentrate and my fine motor-skills were shot to pieces. I couldn't even hold a compass, let alone have the attention span to maintain a heading for three miles to Isle Royale."

"So he's dead, then?"

"Drowned or froze. Either way, his friends left him to die."

Sam sighed. "And now we're still no closer to finding out what's so important about the wreck of the *J.F. Johnson* that makes her so important."

"What do you want to do?" Tom asked.

"Let's find somewhere nice to anchor for the night, then we'll go visit our friend Mark at the dive shop again."

"Really?" A wry smile formed on Tom's gregarious face. "You want to kick over that hornet nest again?"

"Sure. Why not? It's the only lead we have."

"For starters. It might just get us killed and we still don't know who we're trying to help here. There's no doubt in my mind the good Senator was involved in something he shouldn't have been or at least he knew about something and kept his mouth shut. Heck, if I had to guess, I'd say he was on the take for looking the other way. Either way, I don't see a lot of innocent parties here."

Sam said, "Except the son."

"Yeah. Except the son." Tom shook his head. "All right. Let's go find a calm bay to anchor in and tomorrow we'll go upset some nice folks down at the dive shop."

Sam waited for Tom to start the twin diesel engines. A moment later, he stepped outside the upper deckhouse and told him to drop the mooring lines. Sam slipped the rope out of the cleat on the bow and dropped the lines overboard.

"She's free," he shouted.

"Good-oh," Tom replied, as he stepped back into the wheelhouse.

Sam followed him and the *Annabelle May* quickly picked up speed, cruising toward the more protected side of Isle Royale.

Ten minutes into the trip, Sam's satellite phone — sitting in the charging cradle next to the navigation table — started to ring.

He stepped over, picked it up and answered the call. "Hello."

Elise spoke without preamble. "found something from the statement you discovered written in red inside the wheelhouse of the *J.F. Johnson* wreckage."

"You found what happened to the Meskwaki Gold Spring?"

"No. As far as I can tell, it's nothing more than a legend used to drive hoards of gold prospectors into the region during the late nineteenth century. But I know who Stanford was."

"Really?" Sam felt a surge of hope. "Who?"

"His full name was Stanford Perry."

"Go on!"

"In the 1920s he was a laborer on a number of local barges and paddle-steamers. There's no record of where he was born or when he came to Minnesota. You want to know what ship he was working aboard in 1931?"

"He was on board the *J.F. Johnson?*"

"That's right. It gets better."

"Go on."

"After the events of the *J.F. Johnson's* sinking, Stanford's life appeared to make a dramatic turn for the better. Some say that he might have used the loss of the vessel to seize control of a local organized crime syndicate he was working for at the time. Maybe the previous boss died in the accident, I don't know. But what I do know, is two years later, he was an important man about town in Duluth."

Sam said, "Tell me you know who his descendants are!"

"His grandson was none other than Arthur Perry."

"Senator Arthur Perry's family made its fortune in the bootlegging industry of the 1920s!"

Elise said, "Exactly."

Sam ended the satellite phone call and hung it back on its charging cradle.

He looked at Tom. "Change of plans. I'm going to Duluth to catch a flight."

"At this time of night?" Tom asked. "Where?"

"New York. The Senator lied to us and I want to know why."

CHAPTER TWELVE

MANHATTAN, NEW YORK CITY

VIRGINIA BEAUMONT GLANCED at the dead body on the pavement.

The decision of whether to resuscitate someone or not never bothered her. Some paramedics saw it akin to playing God. But she didn't see it that way. If there was ever any chance that her attempt might save a person's life, she would try. If a person was dead, no amount of advanced life-saving medical intervention could change that.

Her practiced blue eyes rolled across the body, searching for any sign of life worth chasing. Any agonal breaths or color left in the skin. There weren't any. Her entire experience as a paramedic told her this one was hopeless. It was only as a human courtesy that she reached down for the central pulse on the neck of the bloated body, sprawled spread-eagled on the greasy pavement. There wasn't any.

The man was dead.

The body lay on a cement plinth under the awning of a Chinese restaurant, next to a pile of oozing black trash bags. The dulled eyes of the man were open, having taken on the same featureless gray as the sky they stared at. Cold, soft stillness greeted Virginia's blue nitrile gloved fingertips, as she knew it would. The morning air was just crisp enough to confine the stench emanating from the bags threatening to split and ooze onto the Baxter Street sidewalk, and from her position at a high kneeling crouch it occurred to Virginia that the air was mercifully bearable. It was definitely crisp enough to chill the dead and dying with a savage quickness, so time of death was anyone's guess.

Without removing his hands from his pockets, Virginia's partner, Anton Mercia motioned with his elbow toward the cardiac monitor on the sidewalk adjacent to their kits. "You want me to take a rhythm strip, Ginny? "

"Nah, don't bother. He's been dead for a couple hours," she said, pointing toward the lividity at the bottom of his back. "And I've been telling you for three years now, don't call me Ginny!"

"Eh come on, one Ginny a month that's all I ask," he said, grinning white teeth through his chewing gum. Anton heaved two of the resus kits off the ground, and made for the back of the ambulance idling behind them, its exhaust bright white, tailing in the circling breeze. "I'll let 'em know to start the cops," he said.

They had been on scene for about forty-five seconds.

Virginia absent-mindedly studied the body.

The body was lying on its back, right cheek and shoulders resting on the filthy cement. The puffy right hand still clutched at the chest and the outstretched left gripped a paper bag with a tell-tale translucent spot where the fast food wrappers still permeated. A lemon-yellow shirt bulged at the buttons and peeped out between a well cut pinstriped tan and gray jacket. She heard the heavy side door of the truck slam shut, and Anton reappeared around the hood, smiling and waving at a horn blast from a brown UPS van that seemed taken by surprise by the ambulance facing the wrong way, half parked on the curb thirty feet from the corner.

"This guy's wearing probably eight thousand dollars' worth of suit, shoes and haircut," Virginia said.

"Yeah I noticed that. Check it out, Hermes shoes."

"Every day, I swear it just gets more and more weird."

"Oh you mean like as opposed to a normal person's day at work?" Anton replied.

"Hey I'm a normal person! I just do a weird job."

"Yeah well, I'm sure this guy's normal too, just dead. And rich."

Virginia's lips curled in a wry smile. "So, what's he doing dying here on a freezing corner in the trash with a bag of cheeseburgers?"

"Getting dinner, I guess."

She smiled. "Last supper more like."

"Ha. Ha. It's too early. And too freaking cold. You want to wait here while I step up to the corner for two large cups? It's my turn, and we're stuck here for a while no doubt."

They both knew that at police morning shift change, the chances of a prompt response for a not so recently deceased medical case found in the street was fairly low on the list of priorities, but a vigil had to be maintained.

"Only if it's accompanied with a cream cheese bagel in honor of our friend here's dietary choices. I think he'd appreciate that."

"It's the least we can do," Anton said. "If you need me I'm on the radio and I have my cell."

"Okay, make sure you switch them on!"

"Hmm. See you in a minute Ginny, with coffee to brighten you up a little"

Discarding her gloves into a medical waste bin inside the ambulance, Virginia balled her fists in her armpits against the cold and stood over the body. Something about the whole picture was incongruous in her mind. The premise seemed perfectly plausible, guy lives too much of the good life, clogs his arteries and drops dead of the massive coronary he didn't know he was harboring. She'd seen it a thousand times, but this one just seemed a little odd. She was trying to pin down the unformed thought when the cell phone in the guy's pocket started to ring. It was the *quack, quack, quack* of the Duck ringtone on an I-phone and Virginia winced at the inappropriateness as she bent down and fished the phone from the slick silk lining of the guy's breast pocket, and touched the green phone symbol above the words, *Private Number*.

The woman's voice was concerned, but not frantic. "Where are you?"

In three words Virginia picked the caller's accent as uptown, her age around forty, and her build probably slight.

"Ah ma'am, my name's Virginia Beaumont. I'm a paramedic with the New York Fire Department."

"Where's Rick?"

Virginia grimaced. "Who?"

"Arthur Perry. The man who's cell I just rang."

"Oh." Virginia sighed, heavily. "Do me a favor and stand by one moment ma'am."

Virginia nestled the phone into her ear and shoulder, as she crouched beside the body and patted the man's other breast pocket and then withdrew the light brown billfold. Inside were three credit cards, two black and one silver, a thick wad of crisp bills and a Minnesota driver's license, with an address in an exclusive suburb of Minnetrista. The name read, Arthur Perry. The picture seemed to match the lifeless face Virginia peered at over the top of the card she'd thumbed half out of the open wallet.

"Are you there?" Virginia asked, wondering why she'd felt the need to answer the man's cell phone in the first place.

"Yes, what is it?"

"I'm sorry to tell you this ma'am, but Arthur's dead."

Silence on the phone.

Virginia strained to hear over the din of the city. Even at 6:30 a.m. the blasting of horns was already at a feverish pitch, while the residents hit the streets fighting for a position in the morning crosstown jam.

"Dear God!" The woman's voice muttered.

"Ma'am?"

In a whisper, the woman asked, "You're sure he's dead?"

"Quite sure, ma'am. It looks like it may have been some sort of medical problem but we can't say for sure." Virginia paused a beat. "We're in Brooklyn. Are you far from here? Is there someone we can call for you?"

The stranger sighed, deeply. "Thank God, it's finally over."

CHAPTER THIRTEEN

VIRGINIA HAD AN attractive face, with a high jaw-line and full lips, which were set in an easy to get along with and engaging smile. Her short, curly blonde hair was tied back in neat double French braids that ended just above her shoulders. She had deep-set, intelligent light blue eyes and a well-defined nose with a small piercing through her left nostril, giving her a decidedly defiant appearance.

She was above average in height, maybe five-ten or eleven. Her crisp dark navy paramedic uniform emphasized her slender figure as she walked with the determined stride of an athlete. Nearly fifteen years as a paramedic — five of those on the helicopter doing primary retrievals — had left her a lithe physique, toned, and with plenty of strength in her wiry muscles.

The job just keeps getting stranger…

She returned the last of the medical equipment to the Ambulance — a *Lifepac 12 Monitor and Defibrillator* — and returned to the deceased man.

Virginia glanced at the man's wallet. She took a photo of his Minnesotan driver's license, in case she didn't get the time to write his medical records until later in the shift. She searched the rest of the wallet, looking for any clue about the man's life — where he'd been recently or any contact details of family. Finding nothing, she closed the wallet, leaving every one of the hundred-dollar bills in their place.

She was staring at the screen of the phone in her right hand, holding the dead guy's wallet in her left hand still flipped open when Anton popped around the corner, paper bag in his teeth, a large yellow cup of lidded hot java in each hand. Virginia didn't move. Anton placed the coffees on the hood of the truck and deftly dropped the bag from his teeth into his waiting hand at waist height. At six feet eight inches tall, it was a pretty smooth move. To his dismay there was no reaction from his partner.

"Did you break my personal golden rule and answer the dead guy's phone?"

"Yep."

"The wife?"

"Yep."

"How'd it go?"

"It was… well, a little weird."

A white Ford Interceptor nosed around the corner and mounted the curb with two wheels and stopped toe to toe with the Ambulance. The paramedics went quiet, waiting to hand over the scene.

An older man in a suit approached with a younger female partner. "Good morning. Who's the treating paramedic today?"

"I am," she said. "Virginia Beaumont's my name."

Without preamble, the detective asked, "What have you got?"

"Fifty-five-year-old, Mr. Arthur Perry. Looks pretty clear he had a massive coronary while eating breakfast… or dinner, perhaps? But the medical examiner will work that one out for you. His wallet and phone are here. There's a heap of cash still in his wallet and no sign of a struggle or physical trauma. The man was found clutching his chest."

The detective looked at her. Undistracted by her good-looks, he said, "That's something, at least. Should be a pretty much open and shut case. Just the way we like them first thing in the day."

"You want anything else from us?" she asked.

"Nah. You've probably got more important things to do to help the living than wait around here while we work out what to do with the dead. We've got your number if we need you."

"All right. Have a good shift."

"Yeah, you too."

The detective placed his cold hands in his pockets and gave the body a cursory glance. It was practiced and professional, without any real interest, as though after thirty years dealing with homicides, it was beneath him to look after someone who'd abused his body until he dropped dead of a heart attack.

A moment later, the detective swore.

Virginia turned around out of curiosity. "What is it?"

"That pin above his right breast pocket."

She glanced at it. "Yeah, I noticed that too. Any idea what it means? It looks like an Alumni pin or something to an Ivy League University to me, but I wouldn't have a clue which one. I couldn't afford any of them, so I wouldn't know."

The detective sighed. "That's a senatorial pin. Which means we no longer have a dead guy here—we have a dead senator. And senators don't get to die without a serious investigation, which means my day has just been thoroughly fucked."

She smiled, politely. "I'm sorry."

"It's all right. Not your fault. But I'm going to need to ask you some more questions, now."

"Sure. I understand."

Over the course of the next two hours, Virginia went through everything she'd done in the twenty-five minutes since arriving on the scene with the Senator. It went right down to the nitty-gritty of what she touched, where she touched it, why she determined the guy met their well-defined resuscitation protocol for reasons to withhold resuscitation attempts. Who she'd advised of that decision, and who she'd spoken to since.

When she'd finally finished, the detective asked, "Anything else?"

"Yeah, the wife called."

"Oh, yeah?" He sighed. "That's important. What's her name?"

"Oh, Christ! I didn't get it. I'm sorry."

"What about her number. Maybe we can ring her back."

"The Senator's cell showed her number as private."

"Really?" The detective raised an incredulous eyebrow. "That's interesting."

Virginia felt her heart race. It wasn't like her to neglect obvious things. A career as a paramedic had taught her to be specific — refer only to the facts — it was a unique combination of fatigue and an ongoing problem with her father's ill health that had caused her to start making mistakes. She sighed, and pressed on. "Why's that interesting?"

The detective shrugged. "Well, if she's his wife, you'd think her number would be in his cell phone, wouldn't you?'

"Good point."

"Did she say she was his wife?"

"No. It was sort of implied. At the time I didn't give it another thought. I assumed the guy had obviously had a medical event, and there wouldn't be much to this case."

The detective restrained a slight grimace, like he could already imagine where this sort of case was going to lead him. "All right. Not your fault. You told her he was dead?"

"Yeah."

"What did she say?"

Virginia tensed and then swallowed hard as she recalled the woman's words that all of a sudden now seemed so important. She checked the handwritten note she'd made for her own paperwork, just to make certain she got it right.

She then met the detective's accusatory eyes, and said, "Thank God it's finally over."

CHAPTER FOURTEEN

I T WAS WELL after dark when they cleared the hospital for the last time that day. The twelve-hour shift had turned into fourteen, when right before finish time, a severe asthma case dropped in which took them every bit of energy they could muster — and nearly two hours to complete. They saved the girl, but now Virginia and Anton were bone-tired weary.

Virginia was crumpled in the passenger seat, enjoying the chill from the glass with her head resting against the window as the skyline blurred past. Neither one of them talked for several minutes, and they were being overtaken by about half the traffic which pulsed around them with far more urgency than either could summon, both hovering in the familiar state of near total exhaustion. Images from the day drifted through Virginia's mind as she tucked her knees up against the dash and tried to melt into the unforgiving vinyl seat. Anton stared at the road ahead, but noticing his partner looking over he gave a convincing half smile.

"How's it going with your Dad?" Anton asked.

Her lips curled into a thin-lipped smile that took effort. "It's definitely spread into his spinal cord, so yeah not great."

"Man, that sucks. Did you hear back from the Swiss drug trial people?"

"Yeah, they said they have a clinic in Palm Springs, California. Better still, he's a great candidate and they've had

100% success rates so far in the trial with patients with the same kind of cancer."

"That's great news. How do you get him on the trial?"

"Four hundred grand."

"Wow. You have to pay? I thought they were still in the trial stage, shouldn't they pay *him* to be their Guinea pig?"

"Yeah, that's what I thought. Apparently, the issue is in the costing. They say the procedure's expensive and the trial simply wouldn't have the funding to go ahead without participant's fee."

"Of four hundred grand."

"Yeah."

"Right. Any ideas?" Anton asked, his tone intimating he knew the answer full well, but eager to allow Virginia the opportunity to vent her frustration. He was a good partner and knew what was required of him.

"Anton, I could sell my house, my car and cash in all of my 401 retirement plan, and I still wouldn't have that sort of money."

"Did you tell them you're a veteran and a NYFD paramedic?"

"I wrote to them."

"And?"

"They said at this time they're fiscally unable to fund unsupported positions in the trial."

"So basically, the rich get the cure for cancer and the rest of us get to die?" Anton snarled.

"That seems to be the gist of it."

"Yeah well that sucks."

"Yeah, it sure does."

Anton drove into the fire house and they cleaned up the ambulance, restocking it and preparing it for the next day. Virginia was just locking up the van when Anton pulled across the plant room in his three-year-old Mustang GT and reached out for the roller door button on the wall.

"Did you hang your keys up, Anton?"

"Yep, already done. No reason to stay a minute longer than you have to at this place."

"Yeah, you're right. I'll be out the door right behind you." Virginia smiled. She had once felt the same way. But now, with her father the way he was, she preferred being at work than seeing him the way he'd become.

"Thanks for a good day, I'll see you back here for another one in the morning."

"Yeah, you too," she replied. "Try to stay awake on the way home. I'll message you a sign-off time after I do my timesheet."

"Hey, Virginia."

"What?"

"If I had the four hundred grand…"

"I know. Thank you."

"Let me know if you need anything."

She smiled. "Thanks, Anton."

The station phone started ringing. There was only one possible caller, the dispatch center. It was a secured line.

Anton turned his head toward the phone mounted on the wall of the station. It kept ringing. "Virginia… No."

"It might be important…"

"Of course it's important! Someone rang for an ambulance!" Anton raced the rumbling V8, temporarily drowning out the ring of the phone. "See ya tomorrow!" he yelled out the window as he peeled out the roller door and into the street.

Virginia sighed. She really needed to get back to her father and see if he needed anything. That's what she was supposed to do. She'd spent her life helping others, why couldn't she just go home and be with her father? Was it because she couldn't face the fact that she couldn't do anything to save him?

She walked over to the phone. "Central, this is Beaumont."

CHAPTER FIFTEEN

"VIRGINIA, IT'S PETER," came the familiar voice of the radio despatcher. "Is Anton still there?"

"Just driving out the door as we speak."

"Can you stop him?"

"Not a chance in hell."

"Look. I've got a 28-year-old cardiac arrest I can't cover. It's about half a mile from the station, and the next closest is at 42nd street tidying up a non-transport but can't leave yet. Can you help me out? I wouldn't ask, but it's an emergency."

"Peter it's two hours and forty minutes into overtime already, I'm exhausted."

"I'll write you up for a midnight sign off. That's four hours overtime pay and you should be on your way home by eleven at the latest. I wouldn't normally ask but I've got no coverage at all right now."

Virginia made a noise as she breathed out. "All right, all right. Midnight sign off?"

"Right. Thanks Virginia. You're my new personal hero."

"Yeah right. I'll jump back in 326, okay, same portable radio numbers as today."

"Great."

Virginia looked down and realized she was still holding the keys in her right hand from when she had parked the van a minute ago. In disbelief she hung up the now empty receiver, and unlocked the van again.

She turned the key, sat down and cranked forward the driver's seat, and the job lit up on the mobile data screen. The computer's alarm chimed urging her to mark the van as responding before she could open up the details of the case. It was to an address she knew well, public housing, probably ground floor unit judging by the number. She could have almost driven there with her eyes closed.

She grabbed the radio mike, and for the benefit of the other crews more than anything else she voiced the job, "326 dayshift responding hot to 892 — 896 Franklin for the unconscious query arrest. Responding single."

"Thanks again, 326," the dispatcher replied. "I'll get you some back up as quickly as I can."

Virginia switched the lights and sirens on and joined the traffic. She weaved in and out. She was driving hard, alternating between heavy braking and hard acceleration — after all, she was on her way to a twenty-eight-year-old cardiac arrest victim and some emergencies are more critical than others.

Blue and red lights reflected off the buildings and the emergency strobe lights shot into the traffic up ahead. She reached sixty miles an hour, and something stirred in her subconscious. A sixth sense, developed over nearly sixteen years of service as a paramedic and highly attuned to pick up the little things that didn't make sense, was trying to warn her there was something wrong about the case.

What had happened to cause an otherwise healthy twenty-eight year old's heart to suddenly stop beating?

CHAPTER SIXTEEN

IT NEVER CEASED to amaze Virginia that no matter how long the shift or how bone-tired weary she was, there was always the clear-eyed, sharpness of mind that returned to her on the way to a critical patient, especially if she was on her own.

Red and blue lights flickered and glinted all around her as the engine roared beneath the steering wheel. The wail and yelp of the siren smothered everything audible and Virginia visualized and then committed to the route she would take. Familiar sensations of the body systems gearing up inside her were distracting as adrenaline coursed into her body. She calmed her mind by assessing the sensations individually, and rationalizing them away. The tingle at the kidneys that resonated right down to the deepest core of her gut. The involuntary deep breath as her cardiovascular system started to feed oxygen to the tissues of the body in primal preparation for the battle ahead. She enjoyed the fear in her. This was what had kept her in the job. This was what made Virginia Beaumont tick.

She entered the street and killed the noise of the siren, followed by the lights of the beacons. Finding the driveway, she pulled up into the cramped parking lot and squinted to study the red brick building, using the powerful sidelights fixed to the ambulance. Sometimes she could get a good sense of what was inside from what lay on the porch or in the yard, and this complex had all the hallmarks of a certain type of clientele. Children's toys and the discarded remains of whitegoods and most of a shopping cart lay undisturbed on the tufty unkempt grass.

Taking in the scene, she shouldered an oxygen kit and strong-armed the two other medical kits through a squeaking, heavily rusted gate, and crossed the no-man's-land grassed yard to the door. The glass and aluminum door stood propped open with the top half of a broken baby stroller. Even in the cold, the musty air smothered her senses momentarily. The hallway was long and dark. Taking her mini flashlight off her belt, Virginia shined around for a light, and found a timed night light button near the door. Worn, it popped straight back out when she pushed it in.

She muttered while holding it in and craned her neck to see the details of the hallway, and any unit numbers. The door at the end of the hall on the right was ajar. Palming her flashlight, she picked up the kits and headed in.

"Ambulance!" she called out as she approached the door.

"Paramedics! Anyone home?" Virginia nudged the door with her kit, but hung back before the threshold, keeping her feet in the hallway. There were no neighbor's doors opening, the only light was flashing from the buzzing florescent on the exit sign above the door where she entered, and it seemed far away at that moment. It was quiet. She didn't like it, and hated not having her partner there.

The alarm bells of her sixth sense kept ringing—*something's not right.*

Virginia placed her kits on the concrete hallway and used her flashlight to peer into the darkness inside the unit. She took the radio mike from her left epaulette in a wide pinch with her right hand and depressed the button. "Three—twenty—six to Central."

"Go ahead three—two—six."

"Thanks, Central. I'm at the given location at 9 of 118 Nostrand Avenue and the unit is in darkness but I have access. What's the ETA on the backup car?"

"Stand by twenty-six. Central calling nine seventy, nine-seventy are you on the air?"

"Nine-seventy," crackled the reply.

"What's your ETA to clear and back up the single in Bed-Stuy?"

"We still need a few minutes here Central, five to ten and we'll be on it."

"Two-six did you copy?" Scratched the dispatcher's voice through the speaker

"Understood. Stand by for a report."

"Ambulance!" Virginia called into the unit. "I'm coming inside now!"

From the doorway she could see the back of a three-seater sofa which was doing a pretty good job of obscuring the entry. Behind that was the much-too-big–for-this-room TV set sitting on a sideboard which also housed an imitation samurai sword rack amongst empty soda cans and other receptacles which now doubled as ashtrays. A bedroom door was open and visible to the right of the TV up a short hallway, and to the left was a kitchenette, utterly devoid of any clear surface space. Food containers and dishes piled from the sink and spilled to the benches and the overflowing trash nearby. The room had the familiar stink of cigarette ash and mildew.

"Hello? Ambulance! Anyone here?"

No one was in the living room and kitchen.

Virginia found the light switches behind the TV set and to her surprise lights blazed on in both rooms. She moved to the bedroom and found the man. He was little more than a boy really. Certainly not twenty-eight, twenty years old seemed a stretch. He was dead as dead can be. Laying in sneakers, dirty jeans and a black t-shirt on his bed, mouth open with dark doll's eyes staring up at the roof.

The bedside was a coffee table cluttered with empty pharmaceutical packet strips, cigarette butts stuck into beer can lids, empty drink bottles and candy wrappers. There was a lady's belt tied loosely around the boy's left arm, and on the quilt near his right hand a spoon and disposable hypodermic needle with its plunger right to the bottom. For the second time today, Virginia felt the cold skin of death at the young man's neck through her gloves.

Virginia turned to keep one eye on the door and pinched the radio mike "Three-twenty-six to Central."

"Central, go ahead twenty-six"

"You can cancel the backup car and start the Police instead. Patient's deceased"

"Copy that, I'll get them going for you."

Virginia stared at the dead man in front of her. He was barely more than a kid. On his left wrist was a gold Rolex. It might have been fake, but then again, if he was dealing the drugs, it might have been real. She shook her head. It was another needless death by someone who should have had an entire life ahead of him. Instead, the fool couldn't keep his hands off his own merchandise.

Taking in the room around her Virginia saw the duffle bag poking out from under the bed. It seemed out of place. New. Expensive heavy duty brushed steel zippers on thick navy-blue canvas. She turned her head and listened. Only the hum of the distant street. She withdrew the bag. It was heavy. Unzipping it she already knew what she was going to find. Cash. Bundles of hundreds in ten-thousand-dollar blocks. The bag was full of them. Probably fifty of them. Probably enough to pay for her father's treatment. The gods were tormenting her. How could she live with herself if she took this money? How could she live with her father's death if she didn't?

She depressed her transmit button on her radio. "Three-two-six to Central."

"Go ahead Twenty-Six."

She felt her heart pumping in her throat and her ears. "Can I please get an ETA on the police?"

About a minute went by. "I'm sorry three-two-six. The Dees have been diverted to a shooting. You might be stuck there a while."

"Understood."

Virginia weighed it all up in a less than a minute, like it was the most important decision of her life. If she left the money now, it would be left to dwindle away in the police evidence storage in the off chance they would one day get to prosecute someone. Given that someone was now dead, it was unlikely anything good would come of it. It might be a decade before anyone ruled as much, and by then the money would have been forgotten about. If she stole the money, she was committing a serious crime and if caught, it would destroy the career she loved, and most likely see her behind bars for a long time.

But if she got away with it, she might just get to pay for her father's treatment.

Virginia stared at the duffel bag. Her mouth set hard with the fatalistic decision and dogged determination, she started down a dangerous path. She needed to steal the money. Could she keep a secret for the rest of her life? A life of honesty and duty turned in seconds? Could she look at herself in the mirror and hold her head up high knowing what she'd done?

Hell yeah!

She made her decision with conviction, without even once stopping to answer the question, *if the kid had been dead for hours, then who called the ambulance?*

CHAPTER SEVENTEEN

VIRGINIA MOVED QUICKLY.

If the adrenaline was pumping before, now it was a torrent. Her hands were shaking as she emptied the two medical kits onto the floor next to the dead man, as though she'd attempted to commence resuscitation. She then started to frantically shove bricks of cash into the empty resus bags.

The seconds raced by.

She filled both medical kits, but it seemed to barely make a dent in the pile of cash. *How much money could there possibly be?* She was hoping to shift the cash in one go, but now it was obvious that would be impossible. The thing with $10,000 bundles of cash was that they didn't compress at all. They had been sealed tight, and like small bricks, they couldn't be manipulated to squeeze into the bag once it was full.

Virginia quickly zipped up the duffel bag. If the detectives arrived while she was still outside it would at least stop them from drawing their immediate attention to the money, where they might guess that she'd stolen the rest of it.

She picked up the two medical kits. They felt noticeably heavier, but still easy enough to move. She glanced at the scene. There was a lot of medical equipment strewn across the bed. If another paramedic turned up, it would be obvious that something was wrong. There was no reason for her to have taken out all of the equipment and even less of a reason for her to put away her medical kits without packing some of it back in. If the detectives arrived, she would have to simply pretend that it was all disposable equipment—once only use—that she would pack up with her yellow medical waste bags.

Virginia took a deep breath. There was no turning back now. She would either succeed or get caught and go to prison. All or nothing.

She stepped out into the hallway, feeling thankful for its busted light, which shrouded her in darkness. Virginia turned her head to the right, scanning for a neighbor or friend to step out of one of the adjoining apartments. There weren't any. She didn't have much to worry about, people in this part of the neighborhood know to stay indoors when they see flashing blue and red lights of an emergency vehicle.

Virginia opened the door and stepped out.

In the open, she felt vulnerable. Like a bank robber out of the vault, but not yet in the get-away car, or an escaped prisoner who'd burrowed under the main gate only to find themselves in an open field filled with spotlights. She walked with a brisk, purposeful pace. She felt like a fraud. As though someone would spot the oddity any minute and question her. But there was nothing abnormal about a paramedic moving quickly while carrying two kits full of emergency medical equipment. Even if she was walking back toward the ambulance.

It didn't matter what she looked like. She had to keep moving. The general duties police officers might be delayed at another scene, but the detectives could show up unannounced whenever they felt like it.

She crossed the front lawn, stepping over the clutter of broken toys, and a moment later unlocked the ambulance. She slid open the sliding door, climbed into the back and closed the door behind her. She depressed the lock and let out a deep breath.

So far so good…

She didn't wait to revel in her success. Instead, she

transferred the cash into the yellow medical waste bags, hoping that the biohazard symbol, warning of highly infectious diseases, might just be enough to keep anyone from examining it if someone wanted to search the ambulance. It was farfetched and unlikely, but then again, an hour ago she never would have believed she'd have stolen from a dead patient.

Now with two empty medical kits, she raced back into the apartment. Her eyes darted from street to the various closed windows, where someone might be watching. She felt exposed and helpless, trying and discovering it was impossible to come up with any excuse for why she should be carrying heavy drug kits out to the ambulance and then back again.

Virginia reached the open room and immediately started the process again. There was no time for planning, only time to move. She quickly shifted the next set of bundled cash into the two empty medical kits.

She finished transferring the cash.

The enormity of what she was doing weighed heavily on her as she wrestled with the last of the resus gear, randomly shoving it into the top of the kit bag and trying to drag the overloaded zipper forward. It was stuck, and for a moment it wouldn't move. She tried to force it, but the zipper only broke free of the toothed running line. She wanted to just force it harder, but experience had taught her that the only solution was to return the zipper to the beginning and start again so the toothed grooves could be fed correctly.

She sped the zipper all the way back to the beginning, squeezed the equipment down as hard as she could, and then tried again.

This time, when the zipper reached a small amount of resistance, she stopped. Took a deep breath in and held it. Jiggling the zipper, she eased it forward. It slid past the obstruction, running all the way along its rail and sealing the medical kit.

She expelled the breath with an audible sigh.

Virginia stood up, gripping both medical kits. She glanced at the scene once and then felt her stomach churn with fear. A single $10,000 bundle of cash was lying next to the dead drug dealer's chest. It must have fallen while she was transferring the money from the duffel bag. If it was left there, the detectives would instantly question where it had come from and where the rest of the cash might have gone.

There was nothing she could do about it. She needed to get rid of the bundle. She dropped the medical kits and raced over to pick up the money.

Virginia gripped the bundle in her hand, trying to think where she could possibly put it. There wasn't even anywhere to hide it on the floor. The bed was just a mattress on the floor. Without a base, there was nowhere to hide it. She frantically searched for another place to put it, stepping toward the bathroom.

The beam of a powerful flashlight lit up the hallway.

There was a firm knock at the door. "Police."

CHAPTER EIGHTEEN

VIRGINIA HELD HER breath, counted to three, and then said, "I'm down here at the end."

She stood up, and watched two uniforms and two suits enter. One of the uniforms shined his flashlight around the room, and said, "Hello? Police."

"In the bedroom" Virginia said, walking toward the door.

The detective glanced at her, with an incredulous smile. "They sent you to this place on your own?"

"They didn't have any other crews to cover the job."

"And you entered here on your own?"

She nodded. "Yeah, worse than that I'm on dayshift."

He smiled. "You're a brave woman. I wouldn't want to do that and I carry a gun. Place like this is dangerous for anyone. I'm surprised your union lets them get away with it."

She shrugged. It was an ongoing debate. "Ideally paramedics should never be sent anywhere alone, but when you don't have the resources to cover emergencies, what are you going to do about it?"

He made a modest smile, like they'd both had to deal with the same sort of bureaucratic budget restraints. "My name's Eric Greentree. This is Paul and Doug from the 79th, and this is my partner, Kay Armstrong."

"Virginia Beaumont."

Greentree ran his eyes across the body. "This one been here long?"

"A few hours I'd say," Virginia said, taking off her gloves and hoping the Police wouldn't notice the rivers of sweat that now dripped off her saturated, wrinkled hands "I got all set up to give it a go, but once I got a better look at him, well, that's when I realized it had already become more of a job for your agency."

"Drug overdose?"

"There's injecting stuff on the bedside and he's got a belt on his arm there, but I'll leave it up to the coroner to decide. I've been wrong before and all that," Virginia added, as she tried to sound casual and risked eye contact with the lead Detective, a small waxy man who seemed all elbows and hips in a badly fitting suit.

"Do you think you're wrong here?" Greentree asked.

"No. But…"

"Go on."

Virginia smiled. "There were no track marks on the guy's arm. He did a good job finding the vein with a single needle. If I had to guess, I'd say it was the first time he ever used the stuff… but, as I said before, I'll leave that up to the coroner — I've been wrong before."

Greentree nodded and glanced at the bags of meth amphetamines and heroine. "Sure. It's unlikely the coroner's going to be interested in the case. Looks to me like you're right."

She started to pack up the remaining medical waste into a yellow biohazard bag. She could feel her heart pumping in her throat. She was close, she just had to get past the natural line of questioning, and she'd be free. "Yeah, that's what I figured. Drug dealer tries his own merchandize for the first time, and it all goes wrong."

Greentree studied her. His brown eyes intense and penetrating, like he was ready for an interrogation. "You don't look so great."

"I know, I'm sweating up a storm here. I think I'm coming down with something."

"Are you from the fifty-seventh?"

"Yeah."

"I can catch up with you later in the week for your statement if you like. You must by dying to get home if you're dayshift." The Detective reached for his notebook. Before the policeman could ask, Virginia volunteered her details.

"I'd appreciate that." Virginia sidestepped closer to the man and the odor of stale black coffee and cigarettes crept over her. "My name's Beaumont, I'm in car three-twenty-six. I'm back on dayshift tomorrow and nights after that for two."

"Okay, thank you ma'am," Greentree replied, without writing down any of the details. "Talk to you later, we've got it from here."

Virginia tucked the first medical kits over her shoulder and then picked up the second kit, followed by the biohazard waste bag.

Detective Greentree stared at her. "Here, let me carry one of those for you. You look totally wrecked. Maybe you should call in sick tomorrow."

She headed toward the door. "It's all right, I'm fine. I'm used to it."

The detective ignored her and removed the larger of the two kits from her shoulder. "It's all right. I want to head out to the car and make some calls, anyway."

"Thanks."

Greentree gripped the medical kit. "Wow. It feels like it weighs a ton. I can't believe they make you carry this stuff into each case. What have you got in this thing?"

She made a thin-lipped smile as he held the front door open for her. "Yeah. You get used to it. It's meant to all be for emergencies, but half the stuff we almost never use."

Virginia walked down the stairs, across the grass-covered

lawn, and out to the ambulance. She felt a slight, uncontrollable tremor in her hand as she felt for the keys and unlocked the ambulance. It beeped twice and she slid the side door open.

She slipped the medical kit into the side compartment and dropped the biohazard waste bag next to the other two.

Greentree handed her the last medical kit. His eyes peered into the ambulance. She held her breath. It was an involuntary response, and she hoped he wouldn't spot it.

"Thanks," she said.

Greentree leaned into the ambulance, his eyes raking the pile of biohazard bags. "You've had a big day by the looks of things."

She smiled. "You have no idea."

CHAPTER NINETEEN

D ETECTIVE ERIC GREENTREE looked around the room of the dead boy and then to his partner, Kay Armstrong. It occurred to him that what she lacked in frame, she made up in attitude. Her mousey hair severely gelled back into a tight bun made the thin-lipped, pencil brow features of her face seem marooned in the center. She impatiently rolled her palm up and eyed the patrolmen for him to see.

Reading her look loud and clear Eric spoke casually to the uniforms, "Ok thanks gentlemen, we're pretty good here, we'll catch up with you later if we need anything. "

The uniformed officer closest to him raised an eyebrow. "Are you sure?"

"Oh yeah, no problem, you guys have a great night, we'll see you at the next one. We're gonna be here a while anyway, waiting for the body snatchers. Not much to this one. You guys go, while we finish our paperwork."

"All right. Thanks. See you around, Kay."

"Bye guys. Thanks," she replied.

Detective Greentree waited until the general duties police officers' car disappeared down the street. He then finished searching the apartment.

When he was certain they were now alone, he turned to Armstrong. "So, where the hell's our damned money?"

CHAPTER TWENTY

E RIC GREENTREE WANTED to hit someone. He was normally a well composed man, who bottled up his rage and only used it out of necessity. It was a part of his job. The men who hired him to fix things expected him to be violent, but it was rare for him to lose control. Right now was one of those times. He let himself go, swearing and wrecking what little furniture was still intact.

He finished swearing.

Armstrong stared at him. Her hardened face was set with curiosity. It was one of the things he liked about her. She was tough and didn't give an inch. He'd known men six feet tall and built like Sherman tanks who'd be frightened of him in his current state. Yet, she simply stared at him, her lips slowly curling upward into a wry smile.

He shook his head, expelling what was left of his rage. "What?"

She smiled. She'd worked with him long enough to know his whims. "I bet you the paramedic knows something."

"Who?"

"The paramedic. Maybe she spoke to someone or saw something. Did you see her face and her hands?"

Greentree stopped. "What about them?"

Sensing an opportunity to impress her boss, Armstrong eased

quickly into her theory. "She looked rattled, like something was threatening her. Her face was dripping with sweat, her eyes were darting everywhere, like a frightened child. You could see she was consciously trying to control her breathing and her hands had a fine tremor."

"Maybe something about the job got to her?"

"No. If she's responding by herself, she's not new to the job. And any paramedic in New York will tell you they've been to a thousand overdoses. Run of the mill jobs. No way a seasoned paramedic would get rattled by it."

Detective Greentree thought about that. "She said that she'd started working on the kid. They normally work in teams. Maybe it was more than she was prepared for. Besides, she said she was coming down with something."

"That's the other thing. Why did she start in the first place?"

"Why did she attempt to resuscitate the kid?" Greentree smiled. "It's kind of in their job description."

"When it's possible. But you and I both know this kid was murdered hours ago. The paramedic would have taken one glance at him and realized there was no point starting the resuscitation attempt."

That hit an important point inside Greentree's brain. In an instant, he knew Armstrong was right. "Ah, Christ! I didn't even get her name. She started telling me, but already I was planning how to cover the whole thing up, so I sent her home. She looked wrecked like she'd just worked sixteen hours straight."

Armstrong shrugged. "Don't worry about it. Give the Central Fire Station a call. See if they can tell you who was on duty. The paramedic said she was due back on duty tomorrow morning. We'll have a chat with her then."

"You're right."

Greentree stepped outside, lit a cigarette and made the first of the two calls. A few minutes later he flicked his cigarette on the ground and walked back inside.

He looked at Armstrong. "I phoned the fire station. The night shift duty manager looked up the roster. He said he wasn't a hundred percent certain who got called back in, but thinks the surname is Mercia."

"That's something, at least." Armstrong looked up, having finished taking some photos of the scene. It was an easy case, and there was no reason to involve anyone else.

Her eyebrow cocked with concern. "Did you make the other call?"

Greentree lit another cigarette and inhaled deeply. He'd been trying to quit, but needed something to calm his nerves and at this rate, lung cancer was the least of his worries. "Of course, I did. I didn't want to. But you don't put something like this off, do you?"

Armstrong's eyes narrowed. "What did he say?"

"What do you think he said?"

Armstrong smiled as she removed her blue nitrile gloves and placed them in a plastic waste bag. "So, he said, take care of it?"

Greentree stubbed his cigarette out. "That's right. Close all the loose ends and get him his damned money back."

CHAPTER TWENTY-ONE

S AM ATE DINNER alone at an exclusive restaurant overlooking
the Hudson River. He was at a table for two, but the second
chair was conspicuously empty. It was now late and the
restaurant was empty. He was the last patron remaining, and
the staff had left him alone.

His cell phone rang, and he raced for it. Tom's name appeared
on the caller ID. He answered it before it had the chance to ring
a second time.

Sam asked, "Did you and Elise find anything about the
Meskwaki Gold Spring or Stanford?"

"No to the first one, and yes to the second," came Tom's
immediate reply.

"Tell me."

"As far as Elise can find, the Meskwaki Gold Spring is
nothing more than a legend."

"What about Stanford?"

"That's a different story. It turns out Stanford was a nobody
in Minnesota until the sinking of the *J.F. Johnson*. After which,
his entire fortune turned around. He became rich overnight,
although there was no record of where his good fortune had
come from. Most of his money was being funneled through local
businesses, but there was no doubt on the local law enforcement
agency's minds that the money was dirty."

"From bootlegging?"

"The police never found the connection. They once tried to make a circumstantial conviction, but the evidence just wasn't there. In the end, Stanford had counter-sued the city of Duluth for harassment and won."

Sam asked, "What does Elise think happened?"

"Her guess is that the Meskwaki Gold Spring never referred to Native American gold. Instead, it was a secret code for where, or how, they were transporting illegal contraband into the country. She asked the question, what if Stanford didn't just get lucky with the sinking of the *J.F. Johnson,* but instead he caused it."

Sam smiled. "You mean Stanford stole the Meskwaki Gold Spring?"

"Exactly."

"That's great. But how is that going to get us any closer to finding the Meskwaki Gold Spring?"

"I have no idea, but we're certain the wreckage of the *J.F. Johnson's* going to hold the clue."

"Why?"

"Elise has checked satellite surveillance of the region over the past two months."

"And?"

"Guess what ship can be seen slowing to an idle directly above the wreckage once a week, before returning the exact same time the next night?"

"Let me guess, a luxurious motor yacht built by Beneteau called none other than, *Superior Deep?*"

"Bingo."

"So they're storing contraband inside the wreckage. The question is, why? I mean, it's not like its crossing the border. I know the *Superior Deep* never crosses the international border, because I already checked. So, what are they doing, going to the trouble of making a difficult dive, just to store something illegally?"

"I don't know, Sam. But when you get back here, we're going to find out." Tom sighed. "On that subject. Did you find the Senator?"

"No."

"I thought Elise tracked him down?"

"She tracked down the hotel where he was staying, but that's where everything ran dry. She hacked into their security system and discovered that the Senator left his cell phone in his room."

"Should we be worried?" Tom asked.

"Probably. His name hasn't made the news yet, which means he probably isn't dead—or at least, his body hasn't yet been found."

"How long are you going to stay there?"

"Not long. If Elise can't track him down there's little I can do to find him in a city of eight and half million people and rising."

"You'll be back tomorrow?" Tom asked.

"No. The day after. I want to visit an old friend of mine. A girl I met working as a medic in Afghanistan all those years ago."

"An old girlfriend?"

"No. Just a good friend of mine. We like to catch up every couple of years. It's been too long and she's had trouble with her father's failing health, so I wanted to go visit her. I was meant to have dinner with her tonight, but she got stuck at work. She's promised to try and finish on time tomorrow."

"All right, I'll see you then."

"Yeah, then we go and find this stolen Meskwaki Gold Spring."

CHAPTER TWENTY-TWO

V IRGINIA KNEW SOMETHING was wrong the moment she stepped into the plant room the next morning. The supervisor's office overlooking the garage was standing room only with two senior ranking managers awkwardly stuffed into the tiny office, standing around the Station officer's desk, hands resting at their waists in the universal non-confrontational stance. One of them motioned toward her presence with a look, and their conversation instantly faltered.

She accidentally glanced back in the direction of the door through which she'd entered, and fought the overwhelming urge to run for her life back through it. As though sensing her apprehension, the Station officer stepped across the threshold of his office door and beckoned to Virginia. "How are you Virginia?"

"Not bad I guess." Getting closer she added conspiratorially. "There's a lot of brass in your office this morning Andrew," trying to project her usual cavalier attitude.

Andrew spoke without preamble. "Come on in and take a seat, Virginia."

Virginia reeled with impending doom. There was a cheap Walmart chair way beyond it's intended lifespan waiting for her. As she sat heavily she regarded the three, gray headed, gold-emblazoned uniforms that stood across from her, each wearing the same somber, downcast expression. Time passed indeterminately slowly as Virginia waited for her inevitable demise to be spelled out.

The introductions were skipped. Everyone knew who each other was. The most heavily-adorned Senior Inspector spoke first. His jaw was set hard and his eyes fixed with determination. "Virginia, there's really no easy way to say this."

Virginia looked to the floor between his black tactical boots. She wondered how she was going to explain the theft of one million dollars, and racked her brain to think of a way to salvage her job, dignity, credibility, everything she had worked for over her entire lifetime. She cursed herself silently. One moment's stupidity she thought.

She tried to speak. Her voice was a dry croak. Anxiety and trepidation, jamming her tongue against the roof of her mouth. "I'm sorry, sir."

Her tongue felt glued to the inside of her mouth. Sweat trickled down her back and her face flushed. With her heart slamming in her chest she raised her face as though to the executioner for his final absolution.

"Virginia... Anton's been killed." The old man said.

She felt her heart stop. Somehow her worst imagined fear had been surpassed by an unimaginably more horrible reality. Anton Mercia was dead. His young, mischievous and vivacious life cut short unexpectedly.

"What happened?" she asked.

Andrew was the first to meet her eye. "We're all very sorry. We know you were close to him."

"But, what? How?" Virginia was now completely adrift. Confusion, guilt, shame and pure anguish washed over her like a million gallons of ocean. She pushed out short, heavy breaths for a while and stared into the middle distance as they gave their answer.

"He was driving into work early this morning and had an accident with a stolen garbage truck. He was killed instantly.

Nobody's really sure how it happened but the truck crossed over the divider and got him head on. They think maybe the other guy was drunk or something, but he left the scene before the police arrived. His body's been identified and he's up at County waiting for the formal from his wife."

"Dear God!" Virginia said to herself, running her open palms across her face.

The office walls pressed in on her as anxiety took hold and threatened to strangle her. "I need some air," Virginia said, rising unsteadily and making for the door. She made it to the exterior door of the building and leaned against the rail of the massive shutter door. She watched the traffic buzz past and idly wondered if anyone would stop her from wandering out into it. She heard the familiar shuffle of her station officer's approach from behind. She turned to meet him. "You got any cigarettes, Andrew?" Virginia knew her supervisor had long since given up trying to quit smoking, and would certainly be holding a packet."

"I thought you quit?"

"I did," Virginia said, gratefully inhaling the smoke as her boss lit it up for her.

They said nothing for a time, just stood there and smoked in the door of the Fire Station. Clearly contrary to all possible regulations, both knew the gravity of the moment outweighed any possible admonishments from their superiors standing only a few feet away. "I know you two were close Virginia, real close. You want to take some days?"

Virginia paused for a moment, sucking back another deep lungful. Her disdainful words came with thick smoke streaming from her nose and mouth "No. I want to work, and then I want to drink until I forget."

"Fair enough. Almost figured you would. There's a single over at the 288th at Maspeth, nice guy too. You should have a pretty decent day over there. Take three-twenty-six when you're ready, it's right where you left it last night."

Virginia drew down hard on the end of her smoke, and with a practiced finger flicked the butt far into the street. She still had the muscle memory even though she hadn't smoked a cigarette for probably fifteen years. She made a beeline for the bathroom, her head spinning wildly with both nicotine and emotion. A sudden cold sweat and she just made it to the toilet to violently empty her gut. Staring down at the bowl through the blur of tears with acid dripping from her mouth and nose, Virginia elected to switch over to her default emotional setting. Absolute numbness. A necessary, and well-honed skill in her line of work. She counted to ten, took a deep breath and washed her face and hands.

She didn't wait around to talk to any of the senior brass who'd come to comfort her. Instead, she knew the best thing for her was to get back into her ambulance, and work another day. Few things were a better distraction than the problems of people whose medical conditions or injuries were in the process of very nearly killing them.

Virginia climbed into three-two-six, started the engine and drove out the large roller door. She knew the way to Maspeth in Queens well. She took Flushing Ave, skirted the top of Bushwik and around the back of the Newtown creek area. She was in a detached daze as she drove the familiar roads. It was as if she was now watching the events in front of her eyes from afar, completely separated from reality as her mind struggled to compartmentalize the events of the last 24 hours.

It was because of this that her reaction time was so poor when she spotted the oncoming garbage truck. She wasn't moving fast. It was a quiet road and she was set in a sort of mental autopilot, lazily making her way to the fire station on the other side of town. The garbage truck wasn't moving fast either, but it was moving fast enough.

Three seconds before the collision, she spotted the driver take the corner wide. She jammed on the brakes, but it didn't matter.

The garbage truck collided with the passenger's side of the

ambulance. The truck was probably going less than fifteen miles an hour, but it had momentum.

Her world spun wildly, as the ambulance was thrown in a two-hundred-and-seventy-degree arc. She felt the rear tires of the ambulance edge off the gutter, across the pedestrian strip, and nearly head into the Newtown Creek.

She had enough aptitude remaining to jam on the brakes and then pull up the handbrake. The ambulance's tires gripped the blacktop, coming to a complete stop.

Virginia expelled a deep breath. Her heart hammered in her chest and adrenaline surged through her body. Her eyes were wide with fear, but she was alive.

What the hell just happened?

To the side of her she heard the 600-horsepower turbo diesel powerplant of the garbage truck grunt, as it edged closer to her.

Her head turned around with a snap.

It all happened so slowly, her mind, unable to make sense of the strange events, struggled to accept the inevitable.

Her eyes locked with the driver of the garbage truck, whose face was set with unnerving resolve. She heard the engine whine as the driver shoved the gear into low and slowly drove toward her.

Virginia reached for her door handle. It moved, but the door wouldn't open because the first hit had damaged the locking mechanism. Her eyes darted to the passenger seat.

It was too late.

Her passenger's wing mirror was suddenly filled with headlights, bullbar and Mack grille, and all she could hear was the wind up from a 600-horsepower turbo diesel powerplant. She saw the front heave up under the torque of the motor, and then the bulk of the machine as it swayed out and away as the wheels steered harshly in toward her ambulance.

In the time before the impact Virginia's mind ran through the list of possible options and outcomes. There was no mistaking the intent behind what was about to happen. No accidental take-off or underestimation of braking distance was at play here, someone was about to plow in to her as hard as possible.

A garbage truck weighs between thirty and fifty thousand pounds depending on how full it is, add to that the torque from the Mack engine within and you've got a crushing tidal wave of kinetic energy. She figured that the brake force created by her Dodge P4500 quad cab chassis was no match, at best she might slow his progress a little. From her experience on the road, Virginia also knew any diagonal impacts in a motor vehicle crash were by far the most lethal. Vehicles are engineered to withstand frontal and rearward assault, and to some extent are reinforced against a direct side impact, but the shearing forces of the diagonal hit threatened to tear her very heart from her aorta.

She pulled her body to the right and braced on the steering wheel in an attempt to prevent being knocked unconscious. The truck rammed into the side of the Ambulance, unleashing an expulsion of smashing energy through the chassis and her body. The safety glass from her window cubed and shattered into the left side of her face with the violence of the impact and the ambulance reared up underneath her, bucking wildly as the roar of the truck's diesel powerhouse again filtered into her perception.

She was now being shunted brutally across the sidewalk and into the rusted rail fence that would either crush her in the cabin, or give way—allowing her to freefall twelve feet into the freezing Newtown Creek below.

It was the latter that occurred; the posts tore easily from the clay at their long-eroded bases and the rail fence went free as her ambulance was shoved through. Virginia felt the floor rise up and around to her left as the van tipped over the edge and rolled, passenger side first down the steep embankment. A moment of weightlessness during freefall preceded the crushing impact and deafening roar as the inverted Ambulance landed flat on its roof in the water.

Virginia was jolted head first toward the ceiling. Her head clashed with the B-pillar, knocking her unconscious.

CHAPTER TWENTY-THREE

UNDERWORLD

V IRGINIA WAS SHOCKED awake by a torrent of freezing water that surged throughout the sinking ambulance. She was hanging upside down from her seatbelt which had been tightened by the safety pre-tensioners during the initial impact. The ringing in her ears was overcome by the noise of the swirling eddy that was gushing in an ever-widening stream where the dash met the windows. The smell of the burning oil and engine fluids that streamed from the vents in the console around her, and the vibration and sound of the faltering V8 from under the sinking hood all confounded her brain.

It took her a full five seconds to orient her mind to the sensations and visual images of her surroundings, and another five to formulate the linear thoughts required to react. She was trapped, in a vehicle, sinking fast. There were only a few options left to her and her failure to utilize them immediately would result in her death.

The fingers on her right hand scrambled for the release on her seat belt. It didn't matter. The damned mechanism was jammed. She frantically tried it again but didn't get anywhere. Water was already rushing up to her downward facing head and she needed to tilt her head just to keep breathing.

She'd been to thousands of motor vehicle crashes. There was nothing entirely alien about her environment. No reason she needed to panic—except this time it was *her* life at stake.

Her training kicked in.

She steadied her nerves by focusing on priorities. Right now, the first one was to free herself from the seatbelt. Without that, nothing else mattered. She would drown in the next few minutes. But the mechanism had jammed.

So, how could she free herself?

Her mind came up short. Instead, she returned to her training. More importantly, how would she free someone else trapped in the same position?

Scissors!

Her right hand moved up to the small holder on the inner thigh side of her cargo pants, removing her trauma scissors. She withdrew them and used her straight left arm to brace against the remaining dashboard to slow her fall, with her left elbow locked and wedged against the roof of the cabin she cut the seatbelt.

Virginia allowed her legs to bunch up and she came to a crouch on the roof, turning to be head upward. The ambulance suddenly dipped as the heavier engine end sucked the van downward from the hood, causing her to lose balance again.

She stepped off the slippery wet dashboard and climbed vertically into the rear of the ambulance as water completely flooded the driver's cabin. The airtight seals on the rear compartment were slowing the progress of the water, but not by much. She guessed she had around thirty or forty seconds before she was completely swamped.

She stood on the seat backs and concentrated on a solution to overcome the next two equal priorities—she needed to get out of the ambulance without getting killed by whoever attacked her in the first place.

There was no doubt in her mind that whoever was driving that garbage truck was probably watching to make sure she sank with the car, and she was determined not to disappoint them. After all, it's much harder to murder someone who's supposed to be already dead.

Virginia reached down into the side locker and grabbed the mobile oxy-viva kit they used on jobs, and a three-foot oxygen tube from the shelf next to her. She unzipped the kit and connected the hose to the spigot, starting the flow at six liters per minute. With fifty liters compressed into the bottle, she could relax a little. She had what she needed — some time, and probable survivability.

She held the backpack in front of her like a life-jacket and waited as the freezing water climbed up to her chest. She breathed air for as long as she could until the icy waters finally flooded the entire ambulance. With her face now fully submerged, she placed the oxygen tube into her mouth and started to take slow, full breaths.

Virginia closed her eyes and waited.

The ambulance remained partially afloat for nearly another two full minutes, before finally becoming negatively buoyant and sinking.

It moved quickly, and she had to swallow to try to equalize the pressure in her middle ear, but still her ears felt like they were being crushed. There was nothing she could do about it. The ambulance was going to sink at whatever rate it was going to sink at and there was nothing she could do about it. In her head, she counted the seconds, trying to guess how deep Newtown Creek was.

In the back of her mind, she recalled something she'd once read during her initial training, regarding diving physiology and hyperbaric treatments. What she remembered, now terrified her.

Symptoms of central nervous system oxygen toxicity, which include seizures, neurological deficits, and death, may occur after short exposures to partial pressures of oxygen greater than 1.3 atmospheres.

In simple terms, death may occur in divers breathing pure oxygen at just ten feet of seawater.

CHAPTER TWENTY-FOUR

BELIZE

VIRGINIA DIDN'T WAIT for the ambulance to sink any farther.

She reached up over her head and unlatched one of the rear barn doors with her right hand. The cabin was filled with floating debris consisting of packaged medical items and bandages. It was strangely quiet in there, just the sound of sucking swirling water, and the creaking of the ambulance chassis. Virginia took fast deep breaths as the truck gathered speed, starting its inevitable descent. She let the last of the air in the cabin shove the back door ajar as the ambulance slipped under the surface, and she made her way through the opening with the kit held at her chest. The ambulance slipped past her, down into the murky depths below.

Navy flight training kicked in as she steadied her nerves. She stayed below the surface and bit gently on the hose between her teeth from the oxygen bottle. She was sinking with the weight of the kit, and from the downward eddy caused by the car. She needed to lose her tactical boots to swim, so she shouldered the backpack straps of the oxy-viva and secured the waist belt.

She unzipped the sides of her boots and pulled them loose, discarding them and her socks. It was very dark now, so she figured she must be either deep, or in the progressively thickening sludge that no doubt lined the bottom of the creek.

Virginia traced the path of the bubbles, until she was confident which way was up and which way was down. She kicked her legs, and fought her way toward the surface. The visibility was less than a few feet. After about fifteen seconds, the water above turned sepia.

She stopped a few feet shy of the surface and continued to swim toward the opposite side of the creek, hoping that the murky waters might still keep her hidden from her attacker.

In her helicopter training, she had been made to swim a length of 100 feet underwater after escaping the Dilbert Dunker submersion simulator. The concept was that immediate surfacing would place you at risk of being burned by the giant puddle of fuel at a crash site. During training, early surfacing resulted in a sharp stab from the drill Sargent's stick as he prowled the side of the lane next to the escape swim path. This was the first time she'd truly appreciated the wisdom of the training.

Virginia continued to swim underwater until the C-sized oxygen cylinder finally ran out. She held her breath just that little bit longer, and then slowly surfaced with her eyes and mouth just above the waterline.

She glanced around. She was now more than a hundred yards from where her ambulance had been knocked into the Newtown Creek. There was no longer any sign of anyone watching her from the opposite end of the bank.

Virginia turned and faced the Queens side of the creek. She swam quickly until she reached the stone embankment along the wall. Detritus a foot thick, made of trash and rotting shards of timber, blanketed her as she raised up. Looking back across to the Brooklyn side there was no sign of anyone watching. Virginia could see the damage to the fence on the lead in to the hundred-year old swing bridge, but no garbage truck, no emergency responders, nothing. They thought she was gone, and that worked for her just fine.

She climbed out onto the bank of the creek.

Virginia had no shoes and her paramedic's uniform was soaking wet. None of the eight cars that passed her on 46th, 47th and 48th streets seemed to notice her trudging along the sidewalk. She pulled out her smartphone from her left cargo pocket and glanced at the screen. It still worked. *What do you know, the waterproofing on these modern smartphones must be improving?* She scrolled through until she found the name she was after, and pressed call.

The answer came halfway through the second ring as she knew it would, from the familiar voice. "Virginia Beaumont!"

Virginia smiled. "Sam Reilly, I need your help."

CHAPTER TWENTY-FIVE

BELIZE

S AM REILLY PULLED his rental into the open space beneath the Brooklyn-Queens Express overpass. It was a white Toyota sedan, the most invisible car he could find. He turned the car so that he could see the Newtown Creek and the adjoining roads. His eyes raked the surroundings for any sign of trouble. There were none that he could see. Some kids were playing street baseball in the flattish land that ran between the two, but apart from that, the place appeared completely devoid of people.

He set the handbrake, but left the engine running.

Sam reached down to his left boot holster and withdrew his concealed carry weapon, a Bersa Thunder 380 CC. With it he carried the required documents, obtained throughout his classified employment to the Secretary of Defense, that allowed him to legally carry the weapon in New York.

He removed the magazine and checked it. There wasn't anything to do to it, Sam kept the weapon clean and well oiled, ready in case he ever needed to use it. He chambered the first round, cocking the slide to double action for the first two cartridges. The pistol mimicked the concept of the Walther PPK made famous by the original James Bond movies, but this piece was eight ounces lighter and had a polymer grip making it preferable to Sam for concealment. He glanced at his watch. It was 11:05.

She was already five minutes late.

At 11:08 the kids picked up their bat and ball and left. Sam eyed the small field where they were playing, his head slightly tilted as he tried to listen for any sign of trouble. Out the passenger side window he thought he heard something move.

His head snapped around.

With his Bersa concealed under the cover of an open book — *The Devil Colony*, by James Rollins — Sam swept the safety lever into the fire position.

The clear ground outside the passenger's window was empty.

His eyes went wide.

Behind him, he heard a female voice say, "Sam Reilly, you don't know how glad I am to see you!"

He turned to the driver's side window, where Virginia was now standing.

Sam lowered the handgun and smiled. "Virginia."

He glanced at her.

She looked a disheveled mess, but otherwise no different than the last time he'd seen her more than two years ago. Her feet were bare and she wore a pair of paramedic blue cargo pants. She'd discarded her conspicuous paramedic top, keeping just her black tank top instead. It revealed her slim figure and muscular arms, the way he remembered her. Her clothes looked like they had recently been wet, but were now close to dry. Her blonde French braids were wet and windswept, giving her a decidedly sexy appearance, that Sam hadn't quite seen when they were both in the military.

Sam felt the tension leave his body in an instant. His lips curled into a grin. "Well, are you going to get in the car or are we going to have a picnic here?"

Without responding she moved to the passenger side door. She moved with the commanding gait of a professional soldier.

Her face was set hard and her eyes determined. She opened the door, climbed in and closed it.

He stared at her for a moment.

She smiled a full set of even white teeth, bare one. Sam recalled it had been knocked crooked during an attack in Afghanistan by a small fragment of shrapnel that ricocheted off a protective wall by an IED blast. She'd once meant to get it fixed when she returned stateside but decided against it, telling everyone it reminded her that she should have died that day, and now every day is a bonus — as such she didn't want to waste a day of it.

She had a small gold piercing through her left nostril. *That's new. Certainly wouldn't have met Navy regulations.* Her blonde, windswept hair had a pink tinge to it where it appeared she'd taken a blow to the side of her forehead.

Her full lips curled into a grin. "What?"

"You look like hell, Virginia."

"Thanks." Her soft blue eyes examined him, noticing differences in him, too, no doubt. "I missed you, too."

"Hey, you made the news this morning!"

"That's good. Anything interesting?"

"Not really," Sam admitted. "They found your Ambulance and they've had divers out looking for your body all morning."

"Well, the longer they think I'm dead the longer I'll get to live."

Sam carefully scanned the underpass for people. "You hungry?"

"Starving."

He released the handbrake and took off. "Good. Let's grab a bite."

CHAPTER TWENTY-SIX

D ETECTIVE ERIC GREENTREE peered upward past Armstrong through the dirty windshield of the unmarked police cruiser from the passenger seat. There were several rows of cheap houses, not unkept, just decidedly working class living.

"The red brick one here," he said, squinting through shards of afternoon sun.

Looking toward the building on their left, Armstrong braked and rolled one wheel up over the curb into a space. "1349 Greene avenue, apartment 2. Lodgings of one Charles Michael Beaumont."

"At least it's probably ground floor," Greentree said. He removed his Glock 9 from his shoulder holster, checked it, and replaced it.

"This building looks old, thirties probably, must have survived the blackout here."

"Our boy probably watched it all burn from the front window." He said, flicking his cheap suit lapels with a shrug.

"Let's go see if he's home," Armstrong said getting out and slamming the ballistic panel door.

The building appeared run down compared to its neighbors. Graffiti was scrawled on the ajar steel and glass door, and trash bags were piled on both sides of the stoop. A broken security camera hung from its wires above the entrance. "Nice place," Greentree said, running his eyes across the peeling paintwork and pushing the door with his fist. "I thought this area was trendy now?"

"I think Paramedics earn even less than us, if that's possible — he probably bought this place twenty years ago for a song."

Greentree placed his ear to the worn black door marked 2, taking care not to obstruct the looking glass, or step in front of the threshold and make a telltale shadow. After a moment he shrugged and withdrew his handgun.

"Timber door," he said to Armstrong as she pulled her own from its hip holster under her jacket. He looked at Armstrong, stance ready, fearless. He knew she would have his back and would wade straight into battle at a moment's notice if that was what happened right now, no question. He hoped he wouldn't be ordered to kill her at some point.

He took half a step back, paused, and kicked the timber door just below the striker with the full force of his body weight. The door crashed straight off the frame and fell open, hanging from the lower hinge.

"Police!" Armstrong yelled as she blazed in and left, Greentree a step behind and moving right.

The unit was dark, and silent. It was instantly obvious to both from the stale air and stillness that they were alone.

"Anyone here?" Greentree called, as he turned and hoisted the door back up into the frame with his left hand. He gently pushed the lock, keeping his handgun in his right hand. With flashlights and gun sights they swept the apartment as they had a hundred others. Both satisfied with the search they holstered their weapons.

Greentree found the lights. "Maybe she's dead?"

"I watched that water for ten minutes, and nothing came up from that wreck. I told you Virginia was dead."

"So the cash has to be here somewhere right?" he said, moving toward the kitchen.

"Right."

Greentree tore at the contents of the cupboards, anything he could grab clattered to the floor beside him. Armstrong had pulled the cushions from the sofa and was dragging a switchblade from one end of the interior fabric to the other when Greentree read aloud from the flight itinerary he had just found on the refrigerator door.

Mr. Charles Beaumont. Thank you for choosing Delta for your upcoming flight from La Guardia to Palm Springs International Airport.

Armstrong snatched the itinerary off the fridge and read a couple lines and smiled. "Well how do you like that?"

Greentree snatched the itinerary from her. And read the intended destination — a medical clinic that specialized in a new type of cancer treatment. "Virginia comes into a million dollars and the next thing you know her father is on a flight to a specialist treatment center."

"He's not going to be happy."

"No. And it gets worse."

"How?"

"He called last night. Said there was a mix up with the assassin. He said after she killed the Senator and stole the map, she placed it in the duffel bag with the kid's money. The idea was when we got the duffel bag, we would retrieve the map."

"But we checked he duffel bag?"

"Exactly."

"Oh shit. Which means, Virginia accidently stole the map when she took the money."

"Yeah, and now she's at the bottom of the river and we have no way of knowing where the damned money and map went."

Armstrong picked up the itinerary again. "No, but I know someone who's currently the prime beneficiary of her good fortune. If anyone knows where the map got to, it will be her father."

CHAPTER TWENTY-SEVEN

S AM FOLLOWED VIRGINIA through the belled door into the diner and they took a seat in a booth on the back wall. Sam scanned the street in the mirror over Virginia's shoulder while he spoke to the server and ordered coffee for both of them.

Over the course of the next half hour Virginia filled Sam in with every detail of the past twenty-four hours, since her life had been turned upside-down. She told him about the young drug dealer who appeared to have taken his own drugs only to overdose and about stealing the money so that she could fund her father's experimental treatment. She then explained how the next day she discovered her partner, Anton, had been killed by a stolen garbage truck, finally finishing with the rundown of how she'd been attacked by a different garbage truck on her way to another ambulance station, which was how she ended up in the river.

Sam waited and listened, letting her get it all out. When she was finished, he said, "All right. I have some questions, then we're going to decide exactly what we're going to do about all this."

"Shoot."

"How old was the kid?"

She raised a curious brow. "The drug dealer?"

"Yeah."

"I don't know. Mid-twenties. Possibly late twenties."

Could it be Senator Perry's kid?

"Describe him for me. What exactly did he look like?"

A wry smile formed on Virginia's lips, but she thought about it for a second before she answered. "He looked well groomed, wore an expensive gold watch... a Rolex or something grotesquely expensive. Definitely didn't look like he'd been doing it hard."

It definitely could have been the Senator's son...

Sam persisted. "Was it a gold Rolex or something similar?"

"Why?"

"I don't know. Something about a gold Rolex. I've seen it on someone recently. I can't remember where."

She paused, thought about it. "Yes. It was definitely a gold Rolex, I recall the distinctive five-pronged golden crown, the emblem associated that's often advertised when you watch tennis."

"Interesting." Sam tried to think back to where he'd seen it recently. The Senator was wearing an expensive watch, but nothing stood out in his memory as it being a Rolex. He'd seen photos of David Perry. Had the man been wearing a Rolex?

"What are you thinking?"

"Nothing. It doesn't matter. I'm just trying to work something out. Tom and I were recently asked to help track down someone who recently went missing. For a second I thought the two events might be related."

"Really. Why?"

"The kid was twenty-eight and the sort of rich kid who'd probably wear a Rolex. It doesn't matter. It wasn't him."

Sam turned his focus into a different direction. "What about the rest of your shift?"

She cocked her left eyebrow. "You want to know what I did on a fourteen-hour shift as a paramedic?"

"Sure. Maybe you were attacked because of something else

you did? You have an interesting job. You see a lot of people in vulnerable positions. We already know this has something to do with what you and your work partner did yesterday, so maybe it's something else. Did you have any unique cases?"

"No. Nothing particularly out of the ordinary. We saved a five-year-old kid's life after she had a bout of severe asthma. We returned a ninety-five-year-old woman with dementia back to a nursing home, after she was found walking along Fifth Avenue without any clothes on. We attended a guy who was found dead in the gutter."

"Anything suspicious?"

She smiled. "No. A heart attack."

"Anyone important?"

"No. Wait... we did look after someone pretty high up in the government who died, but there wasn't anything suspicious. It just looked like he'd had a heart attack. The detectives only became interested when they recognized the congressional pin."

Sam sat up and went rigid. "Who exactly was it that died?"

"His name was Arthur... something... Parry I think..."

"Senator Arthur Perry?"

"That's it."

"Senator Arthur Perry's dead?"

"Yeah. He died of a heart attack first thing yesterday morning. Why do you look so concerned? The guy was the epitome of gluttony. It was only a matter of time before he dropped dead."

"Sure. But I don't think that's what killed him yesterday."

'You don't?" Virginia asked

"No. He was murdered."

CHAPTER TWENTY-EIGHT

VIRGINIA LET THOSE words hang there silently for a moment.

The waiter arrived through the port-holed kitchen door and placed their lunch in front of them. Burgers, fries, and a soft drink. She took a bite. The burger was fantastic. One of those genuine hand made burgers with a thick patty, tomatoes, lettuce, beetroot, and cheese. It probably went a fair way toward clogging her arteries, but right now she didn't care.

She finished two more bites and then said, "So, you want to tell me why you think Senator Perry was murdered?"

"The Senator approached me four days ago to search for his son who'd gone missing nearly three weeks ago. Something we found in our investigation frightened the Senator. He said that if the message got out, he and his family would be dead. Then he told us to stay where we were and pretend nothing had ever happened, while he caught the next flight out of there to New York, to go and put things right."

"And so you thought maybe the drug dealing kid was his son and had been targeted, too?"

"The thought crossed my mind." Sam took another bite of his burger. "But then I dismissed it. The Senator said that his son was an adventurer. There was nothing about him being a drug addict, much less one from New York who made money dealing the stuff. God knows the Senator was wealthy enough that his son never would have needed to make money selling drugs."

Virginia recalled the Senator's *Hermes* shoes. Any kid of his would never have needed to sell drugs. But she also knew with experience that drug addicts didn't always come from broken families. Some of the wealthiest and most successful people she'd known had become hooked on some sort of addiction. The only difference between them and those who aren't so well off was that the rich could afford good quality drugs.

Rich kids don't generally overdose.

Her focus kept shifting fractionally in and out. The shape of her mouth changing, as if she was constantly thinking. There was something important there, she just couldn't quite reach it. Rich kids buy high quality drugs, which aren't laced with additional chemicals, and as a consequence, they don't die as frequently as the drug addicts on the street.

Virginia smiled. "He wasn't a drug addict!"

"What?"

"The kid. He wasn't a drug addict."

Sam asked, "How do you know?"

"Professional gut instinct, but I can tell you with some level of certainty, he wasn't a regular heroin user."

"Go on."

"His teeth were white and well cared for, which suggests he's never become dependent on methadone — the drug used to help wean heroin addicts of opium — and his arms didn't have track marks."

Sam finished his mouthful of soda. "What?"

"Track marks. It's the name we use to describe the multiple pin-prick type marks on the inside of a person's arm, where the easier veins to access are generally located. Basically, they're scars from regular needle use by drug addicts."

"And the kid with the pile of cash didn't have those?"

"No."

"So, he could still be the Senator's son. Seems like a hell of a coincidence that he should be murdered on the same day." Sam grimaced. "You couldn't find his name or details, could you?"

"No. He didn't have any ID on him."

"So he might be the Senator's kid and he might not."

Virginia finished the last of her fries. "Where was the kid last seen?"

"Not in New York, but that doesn't mean he didn't follow his father over here."

"But where was he?"

"He was apparently searching for treasure in Lake Superior."

Virginia's eyes went wide. "Really?"

"Yeah, why?" Sam squinted as though he was trying to see what she was getting at. "What does that have to do with your drug dealer?"

"Probably nothing... but possibly everything."

"Go on."

"When I finished my shift last night and hid the cash I found something attached to a bundle of banknotes."

"What was it?"

Virginia reached into her cargo pocket and pulled a Mylar sleeve. She rolled it backward and flattened it on the table as she slid it open. "This."

Sam's eyes twisted into a crooked grin. "You found a treasure map?"

CHAPTER TWENTY-NINE

S AM RAN HIS eyes across the document.

Within seconds, he knew the item inside was either genuine, or a very good forgery. At least a hundred years old, the coarse paper within was tattered and yellowed, but still legible. A crude hand drawn map showing a main river, smaller tributaries and a dotted pathway to a mine shaft. An X was located at the end of the tunnel with a small drawing of a shovel next to it, most likely indicating that the treasure was buried at the end of the tunnel. It was like a caricature of a classic treasure map. The left-hand edge of the map had been torn by hand as if from a ledger.

Sam studied the map, looking for any distinguishing landmarks that matched with his memory.

"Any ideas where it might be?" Virginia asked.

He held the pouch up to the light and found a watermark depicting a man in uniform saluting on horseback, the animal passant with its right foot raised while walking. Sam recognised the Great Seal—*Confederate States of America 1862, Deo Vindice.*

He made an audible gasp. "This is official Confederate States stationery Virginia. *Deo Vindice* is Latin, meaning, With God as our Protector. It was a national motto of the Confederate States."

"Wasn't there meant to be some old story that when the Confederacy fell to the Union, Jefferson Davis took the huge gold stores from the Confederate treasury and attempted to flee to Havana to raise a new army?"

"Yes. Jefferson Davis denied it and no one's ever found any evidence of the treasury, but the rumors still persist."

Virginia sighed. "And if they were true, how much gold are we talking about?"

"At the lead up to the Civil War, the southern states amounted for nearly eighty-five percent of all tax revenue coming into the country. One thing's for certain, at some point the Confederacy had an enormous treasury."

"The sort of money that could change someone's life forever."

"If this map is true, it would explain why someone's willing to murder for it. Which means, you're in real trouble, Virginia"

Virginia expelled a deep breath of air. "Tell me about it."

"With you now dead, is there anyone else they might come after for it?"

"No. I lived alone until my dad got sick."

"What about your dad?"

"He's leaving for Palm Springs, California, to start treatment now that we have money to pay for it."

"Which means…"

"Oh Christ! They're going to go after my father, aren't they?"

"For a treasure like this, they'll go after everyone until they get what they want." Sam dropped a fifty on the table and stood up. "Let's go."

CHAPTER THIRTY

DISTRICT.

T HE TOYOTA PULLED up to the front of her father's house.

Virginia's eyes reached the damaged front door. She felt her chest tighten and her heart hammer faster. Light was shining from underneath the door, and up along the hinged edge, indicating it was not properly hanging as it should.

She watched Sam move with the same military precision he was capable of when she'd first met him, back at Afghanistan. Sam withdrew his handgun from its holster, and stepped up against the door, so that he could listen for anyone still inside.

He waited a full minute. Sam glanced at her. "I don't suppose the door was like that when you left it this morning?"

"No."

"All right, you'd better unlock the door."

Virginia stepped beside him and edged her key in tooth by tooth to the hilt. Sam counted down three on his fingers and she turned the mechanism as he pushed the door and swept his handgun in an arc through the sections of fire as he entered. The door sagged loose from its broken bottom hinge for the second time that day. Sam side-stepped it as he moved toward the single bedroom and cleared it for persons. He shook his head at the violence that had been wantonly unleashed on his friend's home and belongings.

Looking back towards the door he watched Virginia take in the vision of her destroyed apartment. He guessed everything she owned was here, and was now opened, smashed, upended or displaced. Even the sofa was slashed open bulging it's stuffing to the floor. She stood firm, feet rooted to the spot. A slight quiver on her lower lip the only hint of how violated he guessed she must have been feeling. She stepped to the kitchen bench and picked up the admission confirmation for her Dad's hospital treatment and showed it to Sam.

"I have to call my Dad," she choked out.

"Yes, of course."

Sam waited, while she tried his cell number twice.

She studied the original itinerary. "He might still be on the flight."

"We should meet him there," Sam said without hesitation.

"I agree, but in case you forgot, I'm supposed to be dead. It might be a little hard to keep up the pretense if I board a commercial flight."

Sam shrugged. "I have a plane waiting for me at La Guardia."

She grinned. "You really don't have to play by the same rules at the rest of us who have to work for a living, do you?"

Sam grinned. "Not even a little."

"All right. Let me get changed and I'll be out in a minute."

CHAPTER THIRTY-ONE

PALM SPRINGS, CALIFORNIA

S AM STARED UP at the entrance to the medical clinic.

The building towered above the surrounding California low rise, housing a tan and glass behemoth, set against the deep blue sky. It was as imposing as it was impressive, with a sprawling front setback complete with palm trees and a water feature centered turning circle. Sam pulled the rental up to the curb and a vested valet promptly arrived with a friendly greeting and handed him a voucher for the car.

Sam stepped in through the automatic doors into the crisp interior of the lobby. "This place is more like a five-star hotel than a hospital."

"I should hope so for the money they're charging," Virginia said.

Sam stopped to casually study a painting in the foyer while Virginia approached the reception counter, giving her some privacy. He took in the sprawling vaulted room, complete with lounge, cafeteria and florist. He waited a few minutes before his eyes turned to Virginia.

One glance and he could see how much Virginia carried her father in her stride and countenance. Sam remembered meeting him at an award ceremony that he and Virginia had coincidentally both attended post Afghanistan, and how much pride they showed in each other. Her father was the hardened New York city Paramedic whose daughter had followed in his footsteps.

Virginia had cut her teeth in the Military first, taking training as a Navy combat medic and then helicopter Med-evac specialist, and this was where she and Sam had crossed paths. He had flown some mercy missions for crews against the odds, and found her a ready and capable crew member — and a cracking medic in the most difficult of treatment scenarios. Assessing a major trauma in the back of a moving helicopter is a skill set all of its own and Virginia was always composed, calm and effective, no matter what she was up to her elbows in.

Leaning up against the counter now it struck Sam that Virginia was toughness and femininity combined. She wore black cargo pants into combat boots, and her tightly bound French braids met the back of her plain white t-shirt tucked in up top. It seemed she was still most comfortable in fatigues. Some things just become second nature.

The clip of hard soled flat shoes on the polished faux-marble floor drew Sam's attention back as a well-rested looking blonde lady in her early thirties came down the counter towards Virginia where she leaned up. She greeted her brightly and asked how she could help today.

"We're here to see Charles Beaumont, please"

Sam noticed a shift in the body language in the reception woman instantly — something was very wrong. He tensed as he stepped closer to hear what had happened.

"Are you his family Miss…"

"Beaumont." Virginia nodded. "Yes. I'm his daughter."

The receptionist made a theatrical sigh for their benefit. "I'm afraid Mr. Beaumont signed himself out this morning against medical advice."

Virginia stepped closer, looking over the counter. "I'm sorry but you must be mistaken. Could you check for me please?"

"I'm sorry Miss Beaumont but I'm quite certain, you see I processed the paperwork myself. Your father was quite unwell so I was trying to reason with him along with one of the nurses but he insisted. He said it was a family emergency. He left with his sister and her husband."

"He doesn't have a sister. In fact, he doesn't have any family at all aside from me. Could you double check for me please? Charles Beaumont." Virginia's voice started to crack.

"I'm sorry, ma'am. I remember the man. He was adamant that he had to leave straight away. He said that it was important. There had been a problem with his family and he needed to leave. There was nothing we could do to talk him out of it."

Sam glanced at the ceiling and counted six inverted black domes placed discreetly in a network of sightlines throughout the expansive area. "Excuse me ma'am, do you have access to the security footage in this area?" Sam asked, approaching the counter alongside Virginia.

"There's a security office down the hall sir, but I'm not too sure how it all works."

"Could you show us please? We have reason to believe Charles Beaumont has been coerced to leave…"

The receptionist looked like she wanted to protest that Virginia's father didn't look like he was being coerced, but saw something in his face, that dissuaded her from the idea. "Of course. Follow me, please."

Sam turned to Virginia who looked up at him, her icy blue eyes glassed with emotion and frustration.

"Come on soldier. We'll find out what happened to him," he stated as fact.

She maintained eye contact with Sam as she hardened herself and drew in a long hard breath and pushed it out, then picked up her bag and he followed her as she hustled to catch the reception clerk clip clopping down the hall toward the security room.

Sam and Virginia stood in the doorway of the security office, which was about the size of a small store-room. It contained a desk which was joined around three walls with room for one chair. On the wall behind the chair there was another small table housing a drip filter coffee machine, and a few of the other essential dietary components required to survive a nightshift in a setting such as this. The main wall was covered in a matrix of out-of-date monitors each showing a view of the hospital sections, each rotating vision through its various assigned cameras.

It smelled of stale coffee and cheap aftershave. In the one chair sat the classic portly middle-aged security guard. He was dressed in the usual white epauleted garb that says, *I'm not police, but I may be useful in an emergency, and you should listen to me generally speaking.* The reception clerk was explaining the situation to him and he seemed eager to help. Sam guessed by his reaction that this was probably the first time someone had ever wanted to see any of the vision this system harvested day in and day out.

He typed some commands into a PC on the desk and indicated a screen on the wall. Sam watched as the scratchy playback rolled images of a withered version of the man he had met years before standing at the reception counter, half being held up and half strong-armed by a pair of what looked like police in cheap suits, then watched him get jostled out to a locally produced sedan at the curb. Neither one was talking to each other, except the occasional instruction which seemed to be given by the female of the two accomplices quietly into Charles' ear, after which he would nod and hang his head.

Virginia was peering at the screen, her face inches from the glass, a look of horror and confusion frozen across her face.

"Do you know those people?" Sam asked her.

"That's the thing. I've never seen them before in my life."

"We need to find out who they are."

Sam turned to the guard still leaning back in his office chair.

"Sir, is there any chance we can grab a copy of this part of the tape? We think this might be a kidnapping."

"I don't see why not," he answered. "Give me an email and I'll send you what you just watched. Let me know if it needs to go to law enforcement, too."

"We will sir. Thank you for your help"

Behind them came a two-tap knock on the doorframe and standing there Sam saw the reception clerk, holding a small basket of yellow flowers. "Miss Beaumont, this is going to sound really strange, but these flowers just arrived for you."

"I'll take those," Sam said.

He gently snatched the basket and made a beeline for the exit door. Stepping outside, he placed the flowers on a sandstone railing in an empty courtyard. He stepped back and examined the package carefully in the afternoon sun. He looked for any sign of powder, grease or shadowing on the accompanying envelope. Seeing none he looked closely among the stems for signs of wiring or a device that constitute ignition components. Nothing. It was just a few daffodils in a small basket with a note attached in a matching yellow envelope.

Sam gingerly opened the envelope, leaving it attached to the rest of the gift, and slipped out the note. He motioned for Virginia to join him from where she stood looking in the threshold of the exit door.

Virginia read the note. Her eyes were wide with fear, her lips parted in a panicked breath.

Sam met her worried look and asked, "What does it say?"

She handed it to him. "Here, read for yourself. I'm afraid I've dragged you into my problems, but I don't know how. For what it's worth, I'm sorry, but I couldn't think of anyone I'd rather be stuck in this sort of mess with. I hope to hell you know what this is all about, because my father's life now depends upon it."

Sam ran his eyes across the lines.

Dear Virginia Beaumont,

I see now why you decided to steal my money. You needed it to save your dying father. Just so you know, I ordinarily would have killed you for your simple mistake. Nothing personal, but you know... in my line of work, a reputation is the most valuable thing.

As it is, it turns out you may have access to something I need. It has been brought to my attention that you're currently being assisted by a Mr. Sam Reilly, who, among other attributes, is regarded highly as an excellent treasure hunter.

It just so happens I'm currently in the process of finding a particular treasure myself.

Somewhere along the Canadian alps, east of Lake Superior, legend has it there is a vast treasure named the Meskwaki Gold Spring. For more than a century, westerners have searched for it, without any luck. But in 1931 an explorer and a seaplane pilot named Jack Holman discovered the treasure. It is believed that the man made detailed notes on the treasure's location and was on his way back to Lake Superior to organize a team to perform the retrieval of the vast sums of gold, when he crashed and was never seen again.

Now, I'm not an unreasonable man, I don't expect you to find the Meskwaki Gold Spring that has evaded western explorers for more than a century. All I ask is that Sam Reilly locates the wreckage of Holman's seaplane and retrieves his journal for me.

Do this by the end of the week and I'll return your father to the clinic to receive his next treatment.

Good luck.

Sam noted that whoever they were dealing with had intentionally left out the consequences of failure.

Virginia looked up at him. There was a softness about her that he hadn't seen before, as her wide eyes stared at him imploringly. "Tell me you've heard of Jack Holman and his Meskwaki Gold Spring!"

Sam grinned. "As a matter of fact, I have."

Royal Alexandra Hospital
Corsebar Road
Paisley
PA2 9PN
28/06/2022

James Campbell
11 Wright Street
Renfrew
PA4 8BJ

Dear James Campbell

CHI Number: 2809553319

An outpatient appointment has been arranged for you as follows:

Consultant: RA Generic Orthoptist

Specialty: Orthoptic

NHS
Greater Glasgow
and Clyde

your appointment and no earlier that 5 minutes prior to your appointment time.

In the time between receiving your appointment letter and your appointment date, should you develop any symptoms of COVID 19 and therefore require to self-isolate please contact us to rearrange this appointment.

If this appointment is not suitable or if for any reason you no longer need or are unable to keep this appointment, please telephone **0800592087** or email **Appointmentsbookingcentre@ggc.scot.nhs.uk** as soon as possible so that other arrangements can be made, and you appointment can be offered to another patient. Not attending costs NHS Scotland approximately £135 per appointment.

Please note, should we require to contact you by telephone about your appointment, this will be from an 0800 number. If your contact numbers change please contact us in advance of you appointment to update these.

You can contact us between the hours of 9am - 5pm Monday to Thursday and 9am - 4pm on a Friday, excluding Public

If you are contacting us by email you should include the following information:

Your name

Your CHI number

Consultant name

Date and time of your appointment

Reason: e.g. Unable to attend and require a further appointment

For security purposes, pleased no not include any clinical information in your email.

Your sincerely

Donna Lansdowne

Date and time: Friday 19/08/2022. at 15:30

Please attend the following clinic on the date and time of your appointment:

Desk 2 Outpatients Department Royal Alexandra Hospital

Royal Alexandra Hospital

Due to the ongoing COVID 19 pandemic some changes are being made to how outpatient clinics are managed and as a result you will see some differences when you attend your appointment.

To try and keep the number of people in the department to a minimum we ask that you attend your appointment on your own wherever possible. We also ask that you arrive on time for

CHAPTER THIRTY-TWO

LAKE SUPERIOR, MINNESOTA

T HE *ANABELLE MAY* cruised toward Isle Royale at speeds just shy of forty knots. The yacht turned sharply around the southern point, sending sea-spray high into the air. Sam watched as Virginia played with the controls, getting an easy feel for the luxury *Blohn and Voss* sports cruiser.

He'd sent the image of the strange treasure map Virginia had found to Elise, in an attempt to extract a location from the topographical reference points. As it was, the person who wrote it was obviously no cartographer. The map lacked any form of legend to indicate the distances. Instead it simply used reference points such as rivers, valleys, and a shipwreck as a starting point. Elise's computer search of North American topography returned more than eighteen thousand locations that could have met the basic requirements of the map.

Unable to locate the treasure from the map, Sam decided their best efforts needed to be focused on finding *Jack Holman's* wrecked aircraft.

It was getting dark and they were nearing the end of their first day. Six more days to find the Holman's wreckage and the Meskwaki Gold Spring. Tom had shown Virginia the sports cruiser's controls and she quickly became confident enough to be left alone with it. Sam was still certain that the wreckage of the *J.F. Johnson* still held the greatest clue to the location of the Meskwaki Gold Spring.

Senator Perry died after he and Tom found the message inside the pilot house of the wreckage—STANFORD STOLE THE MESKWAKI SPRING. I CAN TOO. Something about the strange message lead to his death and the attempt on Tom's life. When Elise ran a search on the overhead Defense satellite's data, she discovered that the local dive charter boat, Superior Deep, motored above the wreckage site of the *J.F. Johnson* every night at eight ten p.m. It was one trip, every night, same time. The *Superior Deep* always slowed, but never stopped, on its routine trip across the western side of the Isle Royale.

One thing was certain, someone was diving the wreck nightly. It was most likely they were using the shipwreck to store drugs or weapons, or some other type of contraband. The question that kept plaguing Sam was, why? They weren't crossing any borders. It wasn't like they were shipping contraband into or out of Canada. The wreckage was clearly well within the U.S. side of Lake Superior, so why were they going through the trouble of diving on board every night? There was something else, too, that kept disturbing Sam.

The *Superior Deep,* nor any other vessel for that matter, ever returned for another twenty-four hours. It was far too long to be submerged in the near freezing waters. Even with a thermal suit, batteries would run out, gas supply would fail, and divers would die.

So where did the divers go after the dive?

Sam had no idea, but he was certain that finding out would lead him to the Meskwaki Gold Spring. The sound of the Rolls Royce engines eased and the bow of the Anabelle May dipped and settled back into the water. He watched Virginia shift the twin propellers out of gear, letting the sports cruiser coast.

She glanced at the GPS map. "We're here."

"All right. You know the plan?"

"I've got it," she replied. "You make the dive and I'll head off, taking anchorage on the opposite side of Isle Royale. You and

Tom are both wearing satellite tracked homing beacons, that will notify me of your precise GPS location when you're on the surface."

"Right," Sam confirmed. "Remember, we'll be using Sea Scooters, so we might surface miles from the initial dive site. Also, there's something keeping the other divers down there for twenty-four hours. If we don't find anything that indicates where the Meskwaki Gold Spring is while we're down there, we'll hide and wait for the nightly SCUBA diver."

"Are you planning on staying somewhere else for twenty-four hours?"

"No. But the other divers do, so I'm not ruling it out."

Virginia nodded. "And if I don't hear from you within twenty-four hours?"

"Contact my friend, Elise, on the number I gave you. She'll track down the rest of my crew from the *Maria Helena*. They're currently vacationing all around the world, but she'll find and recall them if I get into trouble."

"And they'll come rescue you?" Virginia asked.

"No. By then we'll most likely be dead, but they'll be sure to finish what we started."

"You think they're going to finish one of the most dangerous organized crime families in the history of the United States of America?"

"You haven't met the rest of my crew. They're a determined bunch, professional and dangerous in their own unique way." Sam smiled and turned to Tom. "When is Genevieve back?"

Tom's eyes lit up and he smiled at the name. "End of the week."

"Do you think she's going to be upset you got into all this fun without her. Not to mention risked your life in the process?"

Tom nodded. "Yeah, she's going to be pissed."

Sam grinned. "Then we'll just have to make sure we've found the Senator's kid, saved Virginia's father, and found the Confederate gold before Genevieve gets back, won't we?"

CHAPTER THIRTY-THREE

T HEY DROPPED INTO the water approximately one mile to the South of the *J.F. Johnson* wreckage. After recognizing how easily Elise was able to obtain the satellite images of the diving charter boat, *Superior Depth,* stopping at roughly the same time every night above the location, Sam decided not to risk any chance that someone was tracking their movements. Particularly after the attack on Tom. This time they would put in farther away, and use a Sea Scooter, capable of running at 4.6 miles per hour for up to 1.5 hours to reach the *J.F. Johnson.*

On the icy surface of Lake Superior, Sam slowly deflated his buoyancy wing until he was negatively buoyant and started his descent. Like their previous dive, they descended quickly, free-falling 170 feet before leveling out.

He switched on the Sea Scooter's electrics. The soft red glow of the machine's instrument panel lit up like the dashboard on a motorcycle. "How are your gauges looking, Tom?"

"Good," Tom confirmed. "Yours?"

"All good." Sam checked his digital compass, setting a bearing for the *J.F. Johnson.* "All right, let's go."

The twin Sea Scooters whirred into life, quickly reaching their maximum speed of 4.6 miles per hour through the pitch-dark waters of Lake Superior's seabed. Sam switched his headlights on for a moment to confirm there was nothing but cold water ahead of them, before switching it off again to conserve power.

Riding in the dark, Sam turned his concentration to his sonar display, which gave a visual outline of the submerged seascape ahead of them.

Within minutes the large outline of the *J.F. Johnson's* hull came into view. He altered his course another degree to the east, setting up to make a direct approach for the single opening on the portside of the listing pilothouse.

It took a total of fourteen minutes to reach the main hatchway at the base of the pilot house. Sam and Tom kept their headlights and flashlights switched off so they could see if anyone else was already on board the shipwreck. They both carried shark-sticks in case they ran into trouble, but their aim was to remain hidden if anyone came on board so they could see what they were shipping and where they were disappearing to over the twenty-four-hour period before the ship returned again.

Confident that they were alone, Sam switched on his flashlight. The entrance lit up beneath his beam, revealing the ascending stairs to the wheelhouse, the horizontal passage to the opposite end of the hull, and the open hatchway leading to the descending entrance to the lower decks. The same place where Tom had nearly drowned after his attacker merely closed the door.

Sam had no intention of repeating that incident this time round. He swept the beam of his flashlight across the hatchway, over the hinges, and all the way along the edge of the door. He was searching for any iron eyelets or latches, where the hatch could be permanently locked from the outside. It's one thing to be attacked or become temporarily lost once inside, but a totally different, and far more frightening event to be sealed within — to wait until their gas supply eventually ran out and they drowned.

No way I'm letting that happen.

Sam finished running his beam along the exterior edge of the entire hatch, confirming there was no way they could be locked inside the wreck, either by accident or by the divers from the

Superior Deep.

He swung the door open and closed. The hinges were obviously new — certainly not original anyway — and the hatchway moved freely. Sam glanced at both sides of the door. The main latch was rusted in the open position. He studied the rest of the door. There was no other possible way to become stuck.

Sam slowly pulled himself through the opening, turned and proceeded with the same process on the opposite side of the door. The hatch appeared free of anything that could be locked, but a single rusted iron eyelet was welded to the heavy bulkhead to the right of the hatch.

With his gloved hand, he took the iron eyelet in his grip and pulled. Despite nearly nine decades of rust, the ring was solid. It would take a lot more than they had to break it if they needed to. He swept the flashlight beam from the eyelet back to the hatch. There was no sign of anything that could be used to lock the door onto it. Sam guessed the device might have once been used to hold the door in the open position, when the *J.F. Johnson* still sailed.

Sam fixed his beam on the eyelet. "What do you think of this?"

Tom ran his light across it. "I wouldn't worry."

"You don't think it could be used to lock us inside?"

"No. It could be used to lock us inside, but then, whoever did so would be trapped here, too."

Sam smiled. "I hadn't thought of that. Good point."

He removed a small device from a small pouch on the side of his diving vest. It was cylindrical in shape and small enough to fit comfortably in a single one of his gloved hands.

Sam switched it on and attached it to the bulkhead to the left of the hatch, somewhere low enough that any movement would conceal its view with silt. There were no little blue or green display lights to show that the device had been switched on. He gently pushed himself backward, until he could stare at the hatchway.

A small upward crease formed on his lips. The device was almost undetectable without knowing precisely where it had been placed. There was no way any diver would stumble across it and even if they did, it was even less likely that they would have any clue what it was.

The device was an underwater location beacon known as a ULB. It was a smaller version of the one used in aviation, fitted to flight recorders such as the cockpit voice recorder and flight data recorder so that crashed aircraft flying over water could be located. It transmitted an ultrasonic 10ms pulse once per second at 37.5 kHz. The sonar used on the Sea Scooters would pick up that pulse as it bounced around the interior hull, creating a visual map, the same way bats used echolocation.

As a consequence, despite any damage to the silt within the confined space of the inside hull, both of them would have a real-time map of how to return to the hatchway. Ideally, they would have laid out guidewires, but that would have given away their position to whoever might follow them inside.

"Are you picking up the signal, Tom?"

"Got it." Tom calibrated his instrument panel toward the ULB. "Where do you want to begin?"

"You said you originally followed your attacker below decks, toward the aft storage compartment, before he turned and fled?"

"That's right."

"How about we start there, then." Sam glanced at the dark outline of Tom's face mask. "Do you think you can remember how to get there?"

"Sure. I found my way out of there in a total blackout, I'm sure that I can find my way back in now the water's clear again."

"Good man."

Sam watched as Tom recalled the image of the interior hull

that he'd mentally constructed the last time he entered the *J.F. Johnson* wreckage. Sam couldn't help but admire Tom's ability. He moved with the confidence of a dive master, leading a tour through a wreckage he'd been to a thousand times before. Despite nearly being killed there only three days earlier, the man dived without displaying any apprehension, let alone trepidation.

He switched off his own flashlight. In the darkness, Sam followed the haze of Tom's light, as he led the way down the first two sets of metal stairs into the long passageway heading aft. Tom moved quickly, and Sam found himself having to work to keep up.

Using long, powerful strokes with his fins, Sam followed Tom to the end of the passageway. There, Tom swept the area with the beam of his flashlight. A metal door blocked any further progress into the ship.

Sam switched on his flashlight and shined the beam across the door. "It looks brand new."

Tom gripped the aluminum handle. "No way this has been down here ninety years."

"I bet whatever's behind that door is worth a fortune."

"Enough worth killing for, anyway." Tom gripped the handle and sighed. "But we're not going to find out any time soon."

"Why not?"

"Because the door's locked."

Sam shined his light on the small circular hole, where a modern security key might be inserted. Inside his full-face mask, his lips curled upward in a wry grin, full of curiosity. *Whatever's behind that door, someone's gone to extreme lengths to keep it protected.* He looked at it, wondering whether the blast from one of their shark-sticks might be powerful enough to damage the lock.

The flicker of a beam of light swept across his back.

Sam switched his flashlight off and turned sharply.

A second light approached. "We've got company!"

Tom turned his light off. "Behind you, there's an open alcove."

Sam moved quickly into the alcove. His eyes focusing on the shimmer of light approaching. It was filtering down from the stairs at the end of the passageway. He held his breath, hoping that he spotted the light early enough that whoever was coming down hadn't spotted theirs.

Sam gripped the handle of his shark-stick. "Did they see us?"

"I don't think so."

Sam stared at the light as it approached. Its beam focused on the locked door. Sam listened intently for the sound of expelling bubbles. There were none. The divers were using rebreathers, too. Deadly silent.

No wonder we didn't see them coming.

The diver paused. His head turned to look straight at Sam and Tom. The man seemed to be staring vacantly through them. Sam watched the crease in the diver's forehead deepen and the diver tense. If the diver hadn't spotted them, one thing was certain, he felt uneasy about something as though he was being watched. There was always the possibility the diver routinely checked the alcove for other divers before opening the door. But if that was the case, why hadn't the diver shined his flashlight on them?

Sam placed his trigger finger on the shark-stick.

The diver turned and faced the locked door again.

Sam expelled his breath of air.

The diver casually turned and started swimming back the way he came. He wasn't racing, if anything, it was merely as though the diver had been practicing a wreck dive, reached the end and turned around.

Sam asked, "Where the hell's he going?"

"Beats me," Tom replied. "Maybe there's a different door?"

"So why did he come all the way down here?"

"I don't know. Let's follow him."

Sam waited another fifteen seconds and then moved out into the passageway. The faint glow of the diver's flashlight dimmed.

"Where the hell's he going?" Sam asked.

"He must have spotted us!" Tom said.

"Quick! After him. We can't let him escape."

Sam started to kick hard, racing toward the end of the passage. The diver swam up the twin stairs well ahead of them.

Clank!

The hatchway slammed shut and the diver's light disappeared.

Sam switched on his own flashlight. He raced to the top of the stairs and then swore — because the closed hatchway was now locked shut.

CHAPTER THIRTY-FOUR

V IRGINIA CHECKED HER timer. Sam and Tom had been down for thirty-two minutes. Sam and Tom said they could be down there for as much as four hours if need be, still she remained vigilant, watching the radar for any signs of them surfacing.

The GPS showed her position to their location as two miles, give or take. The *Annabelle May* would close that gap quickly once Sam and Tom's personal locator beacons indicated they were on the surface of Lake Superior again.

She took a sip of coffee and watched.

The radar screen blipped as another vessel came into the five-mile radius on the screen. She had a digital pin dropped on the screen at Sam and Tom's co-ordinates where the *J.F. Johnson* was located, and watched as a mid-sized vessel made a beeline for the very same spot. A trickle of adrenaline tingled at the base of her spine as she turned for their position at a slow idle. All she could do was wait. The radar showed the boat stopped directly above Tom and Sam for about five minutes, and then retraced its path back toward the protected waters of Isle Royale. Again, she waited, while all the worst-case scenarios were being borne out in her imagination.

She thought about Sam's hardened ability as a soldier and Tom's size. From what he'd explained to her, fighting underwater was extremely difficult, and few people chose to attempt it. If there was a problem, it would be when they resurfaced.

Virginia glanced at the loaded Remington double barreled shotgun next to the *Annabelle May's* helm and hoped she wouldn't need to use it.

CHAPTER THIRTY-FIVE

S AM STARED AT the door. The beam of his flashlight pointed at
the iron eyelet. A thick steel chain had been fed through the
side of the hatch and was now padlocked to the ring. He checked
the door for any movement with his hand. There wasn't any.
The door was locked shut. His heart hammered in his throat.
He'd suffered with claustrophobia since he was a child. Wreck
diving and cave diving was his ultimate achievement in
overcoming that fear. But it had never completely left him.
Instead, he'd learned how to manage it. How to keep it at bay,
hidden. But those fears were still there.

And right now, they came flooding back.

He breathed deeply, consciously making the effort to slow his
rate. "Tom, was this how you found the hatchway last time they
tried to trap you down here?"

"Afraid not. Last time there was no chain."

"You think our shark-stick might take that padlock off?"

Tom ran his gloved hand across the grooved padlock. "No
way in hell. That's a German made Granit. Almost
indestructible. It can withstand up to six tons of pressure and
hold together the same amount of tensile weight. The core is
extremely pick resistant and uses disk detainers instead of pin
tumblers."

"Meaning?" Sam asked.

"There's no way we're breaking this lock."

"Great." Sam glanced at his gas supply. "So, we have a little under four hours to work out how to get through this hatchway. You got any ideas?"

"Yeah."

"What?"

"Let's not go through it."

"That wasn't quite my plan. I mean, it's nice down here, but I'm kind of keen not to spend the rest of eternity entombed here."

"No. That's not what I mean."

"What do you mean, then?"

Tom swept the surrounding chamber with his flashlight. "I plan to go out the same way the diver does."

"Ah, Tom. I hate to mention this, but the diver's already gone out through the hatchway there."

"No, he hasn't."

Sam glanced at the locked chain. "You're right. That door's locked from the inside. That being the case, where did the diver go?"

"I don't know." Tom shined his light down the horizontal passage. The silt was still and the water clear.

"You go that way, I'll check out down here," Sam said, pointing to a second compartment next to the stairs.

"Agreed."

Sam moved, quickly recovering his confidence, having now been given a task to concentrate his attention.

Halfway down the stairs, he noticed a horizontal opening to another room. He guessed that it was a ventilation shaft from the main engine room when the ship was afloat, and ordinarily unable to be accessed. But now that the ship was flooded, it formed an open tunnel to another part of the ship. Sam flashed his light into the gap.

The silt stirred and settled near the base.

Had the diver swam through there?

With his left hand on his flashlight and his right on the shark-stick, Sam slowly entered the gap. It traveled approximately twenty feet before opening up into a large room in the deck below. Sam swept the room with his flashlight.

It looked empty. The silt was all still. He swam to the end of the room and turned around. His light fixed on a small section of silt beneath the opening he'd just come through. The ground was a brown murky sea through which his gaze barely penetrated. There were two small streams where the debris and iron particles were slowly filtering downward.

Had he caused both of them?

A small eddy started to form. Murky water swirled for an instant. *What the hell is that?* Sam gripped his shark-stick.

He watched as the swirls gradually increased in diameter.

An instant later the nose of a sea scooter pierced the debris cloud. Its electric motor whirred. The propeller blade suddenly sped up its revolutions and the rider shot out, racing through the opening into the main passage.

Sam switched his sea scooter on and squeezed the dual triggers. "Tom. He's heading back to the door!"

An inaudible crackle followed as the solid bulkhead of the *J.F. Johnson* disrupted their close proximity radio waves.

"Tom!" Sam shouted.

"What?"

Sam's scooter raced out through the opening and turned left down the main passageway. In front of him he could see the glow of the diver disappear behind the door. "He's heading for the locked door at the end of the passageway."

Tom's sea scooter whirred behind Sam. "I'm right behind you. Don't let him close that door!"

"I won't!" Sam hoped he was telling the truth.

He watched the diver open the door up ahead and race

through. The door closed. Sam gritted his teeth and mentally begged his sea scooter to go faster.

Clang!

The nose slammed into the slight crease between the door and its iron frame.

For a moment the sea scooter became stuck—wedged between the door and the iron frame—until he adjusted the angle slightly and squeezed the twin throttle triggers. The machine whined as 350 watts of power were used to make its way through the door.

Behind the door, an open hatchway indicated a set of vertical ladders leading into the lowest levels of the ship. The slightest of glows illuminated from the opening. Sam drove his sea scooter downward into a room of large mechanical pieces. Sam stopped the sea scooter. He swept his new environment with the beam of his flashlight.

The engine room of the steamship was the largest single space inside the hull. It incorporated a room from the keel amidships—right up into the chimney at the top of the forecastle. There was room to swim down both sides of the mighty steam engine. Perfectly preserved in the icy water, the brass fittings and green casing of the engine shone in the diver's flashlight beams. It was a double action inverted triple-expansion vertical steam engine made by Joshua Hendy Ironworks in Sunnyvale, California. Three giant cylinders each larger than its predecessor allowed for re-cycling of the precious steam, producing economy of fuel. State of the art for its time. Machines like this were shrinking the globe before the jet airliner. The back of the engine was connected all the way to the stern by the propeller shaft.

Tom brought his sea scooter to a standstill beside Sam. "Any idea which way he went?"

"Not a clue. I followed his light into the engine room, but I have no idea where he traveled from here. He's hiding somewhere in here. You take the left side and I'll take the right."

"Got it."

Sam and Tom swam the length of the room on either side of the engine.

On the opposite end of the room, they met across the prop shaft. Splitting the engine bay in two, Sam and Tom swept the entire place. Every access door and hatch had been professionally sealed since the *J.F. Johnson* had sunk all those years ago. They circled the room in opposite directions, carefully checking each hatch. All were permanently welded shut.

Sam shrugged at Tom with palms upward. "I don't get it. He can't have just disappeared!"

CHAPTER THIRTY-SIX

AN INCREDULOUS SMILE formed beneath Tom's full-face dive mask.

He scanned the empty room. Why would the diver draw them into the old boiler-room? More to the point, why go to the effort of strengthening the place? He glanced at the heavy-duty, commercial grade underwater welding performed deep inside the hull. It was similar in quality to what could be found on an offshore oil drilling rig, where expert commercial divers lived in a pressurized habitat for weeks. So why would someone go to the effort with such craftmanship inside a ninety-year-old shipwreck?

"I'm all out of guesses what's so important down here, let alone where he's hidden," Tom said. "You got any ideas, Sam?"

"Must be in hiding at the end of the propeller shaft?"

Tom raked the beam of his flashlight carefully down the length of the tunnel that housed the propeller-shaft. A flicker of light twinkled off the wall at the most distant point of the tunnel. As he approached it he ran his gloved hand across the bead of a fresh weld. The welding framed the outline of a hatchway which was more recently cut into the base of the hull just near the stern on the port side of the vessel, the side on which she listed.

Tom flashed his light toward the engine room to call Sam down to his position. Together, they turned the hatchway lock and opened the curved door outward. A current of warm water flooded over the two men from the bilge. It wasn't hot, but compared to the near freezing water inside the *J.F. Johnson* the water felt like it had come straight from a hot bath.

Tom swam through the small hatchway into the bilge.

He shined his flashlight around the perimeter of the rounded hull, starting along the starboard side. Littered everywhere, were the remnants of more than a few hundred damaged wooden barrels. Most were cracked and empty, but some were still intact and others still, revealed dozens of bottles packed inside. At a guess, he figured the *J.F. Johnson* went down with a small fortune worth of prohibited rum.

The bilge ran the entire length of the ship, and by the looks of things, had been filled with contraband rum during prohibition.

Tom stopped and picked up a single bottle of rum.

He fixed the beam of his flashlight on the label. He ran his eyes across the bottle's intricate craftmanship. The label was white with the words: *Philadelphia 1876* set at the top — most likely a reference to the year Bacardi rum had earned a gold medal at the Philadelphia Exposition of 1876. Below that were the words *Ron Bacardi Superior* and at the bottom of the label it read, *Graduacion 44–5*. The cork was intact, and had a foil seal with the Bacardi Bat embossed on top. Toward the lower half of the label were the words, *Santiago de Cuba* and below that, *Habana – New York.*

He handed the bottle to Sam. "I bet you this is part of what they were after."

"Broken old bottles of Bacardi rum?" Sam asked, not bothering to hide his doubt. "Couldn't they make it to their local liquor store?"

"Not the broken bottles, but I'm sure there would be some intact ones down here." Tom smiled. "They could try, but I'm doubting their local store has one of these lying around."

"It's a rare bottle of rum?"

"You could say that."

"How rare?"

"Rare," Tom said. "In 1912, while Emilio Bacardi traveled to Egypt to purchase a mummy for the future promotion in Cuba, his brother Facundo M. Bacardi continued to meticulously supervise the training of the third generation of Family Master Blenders back in Santiago. Meanwhile, Henri Schueg, their brother in law, began to expand the company. He opened new bottling plants in Barcelona, Spain and New York City."

"Get to the point. What's this got to do with organized crime and trapping us inside this ninety-year-old shipwreck?"

"The Habana-New York distillery was opened in New York to produce Bacardi Rum in 1916, but it had to shut down production by 1919 prior to prohibition coming into effect."

"Meaning?"

Tom laughed. "So, you're not much of a drinker. It doesn't matter. The fact is, a bottle of Habana-New York Bacardi Rum could fetch upward of fifty thousand dollars depending on its condition and guess what? Look around you. The ice-cold waters of Lake Superior are a natural preserver, capable of maintaining everything in pristine conditions."

"So why have they been diving here every night for nearly three weeks?"

"Maybe there's a particular bottle they're searching for. A shipment that's so rare, it's worth spending a fortune to steal."

"Of course. The J.F. Johnson would be registered as a National Historic Place and as such, would prohibit the removal of any items found within. If they got caught, it would be a criminal offence, but more importantly, they'd lose out on potentially millions of dollars' worth of rare prohibition era rum bottles."

"Exactly."

"All right. So now we know what they were doing down here, how are we going to find our way out?"

Tom scanned his gas supply numbers. They still had nearly

three hours. It would be plenty of time to wait until the diver unlocked the hatchway — that was, assuming that's how he reached the surface again.

"Come on, let's see where this thing leads."

He swam along the bilge, toward the bow. The J.F. Johnson was a 251-foot steel Tramp-Steamer. It would take some time to reach the opposite end of the hull. Tom squeezed the twin accelerator triggers on the sea scooter and started heading toward the bow.

He trained the light toward the port side up ahead.

What he saw made him take an involuntary breath. Where the bottom of the hull should have been, a giant gash now tore through at least thirty feet of the iron hull. Tom would have expected the steel hull to be bent inward, but instead the jagged edges were curved outward — meaning the J.F. Johnson hadn't run into a reef or collided with another vessel, but the damage had been caused by an explosion from the inside. Most of that gash had been buried by the seabed of Lake Superior, but two thirds of the way along, someone had gone to the effort of digging through it.

He fixed his flashlight at the opening. "There's our way out."

There was relief in Sam's voice. "Great. What are you waiting for. Let's get out of this damned shipwreck."

Tom swam through the manmade opening within the buried ruptured hull. The tunnel continued for approximately twenty feet before expanding into what he guessed would be the open seabed of Lake Superior.

Before he swam out the end of the tunnel he switched off his flashlight.

Behind him, Sam asked, "Can you see the other diver?"

Tom's eyes went wide. "Yeah, but you're not going to believe what else I can see!"

CHAPTER THIRTY-SEVEN

S AM REACHED TOM'S side an instant later, expecting to now be
in the open, 205 feet below the surface of Lake Superior. He
watched the diver's light diminish in size, over a hundred feet
away.

"Think he's far enough away not to notice us if I shed some
light on our new environment?"

"Not to notice our lights?" Tom asked. "Yeah, should be all
right."

Sam switched on his flashlight.

He shined the beam upward, expecting the light to be
absorbed and disappear in the darkness of the deep water that
reached toward the night's sky. Instead it showed the ceiling of
a large limestone cavern that extended due west in a gradually
upward slant. Strewn throughout were potentially more than a
thousand wooden barrels.

Sam turned to meet Tom's wide eyes. "I guess it might take
our friends more than a few dives to locate the contents of a
specific barrel."

"Yeah, no wonder they've been so devious about diving here.
It could take months to search their massive stockpile. The first
time they were to get caught removing anything from the J F
Johnson and their dreams of gold would be lost."

"The question still remains. Where did it all come from?"

Tom watched the last of the mysterious diver's light dissipate into the distant cavern. "I don't know, but I'm betting our diving friend over there has some idea."

Sam focused his flashlight into the cavern. "If nothing else, I'd feel better knowing we can reach the surface."

He depressed the sea scooter's accelerators and the machine whirred, as though eager to get going again. The cavern continued in a gradual upward slope for approximately two miles. Their course was perfect because it graduated their ascent in such a way that they progressively decompressed in the process, removing the need for prolonged decompression stops.

About twenty minutes into their journey, the cavern changed direction, angling in a near vertical section that appeared more like a sinkhole than a subterranean cavern. Up ahead, Sam spotted the diver's light and guessed the man was performing a dedicated decompression stop.

Sam switched his flashlight off. "Guess we're in the right place. It looks like he's preparing to surface."

"Looks like it." Tom followed suit and switched his light off, too.

Soon the diver's light diminished in size as the diver ascended far above them. Sam waited in the dark, maintaining neutral buoyancy and their closed-circuit rebreathers concealed their very breath, he ensured nothing had given away their presence to the diver they stalked.

The icy waters of the lake were crystal clear and devoid of sea-life and the detritus which would otherwise obscure them, so extra care needed to be taken. They had followed the man North along a subterranean tunnel for what seemed like miles before the roof opened up above them to where they could see sunlight beyond the surface.

Confident the diver had left the area, they increased their depth to thirty feet and stopped to make a mandatory safety decompression.

Once it was complete, Sam and Tom silently ascended to the surface.

Sam broke the surface first. He allowed no more than his facemask to show. He carefully turned 360 degrees in search of the other diver, or danger. Unable to spot either, he allowed himself to fully surface above the water.

"Clear," he confirmed.

Tom said, "Copy. Coming up."

He swept the area with his eyes. They were still underground. Blue-green bioluminescent lights of firefly larvae adorned the ceiling of the grotto eight or so feet above, reflecting like stars on the slow moving shallow stream that led toward the mouth of the cavern. A lightly worn path followed the edge of the water, leading over several boulders.

Sam listened to the silence.

On the edge of the path was a Canadian National Parks wooden placard which read: This creek is of cultural significance to the Meskwaki First People who once inhabited the region.

Sam glanced at the sign. "Check that out, Tom. The Meskwaki Gold Spring was never about gold. It was a secret spring that led between Canada and the U.S. waters on Lake Superior."

Tom grinned. "You're right. Only there was never a spring, either."

"There wasn't?"

"No. A river that flows from the surface to underground is called a siphon."

Sam's lips curled in an amused smile. "Thanks for the vocabulary lesson."

"Just saying…"

Sam smiled. "What do you think happened here, back in the twenties?"

Tom looked around the grotto from the entrance at the mouth

of the cavern, back to where the water disappeared underground. "My guess is someone must have known about this spot and realized that barrels of rum or other contraband could be dropped into this creek, where they would be pulled underground by the flow of water and the slightly warmer waters of the siphon would disperse at the bottom of Lake Superior."

"There the *J.F. Johnson* would have been waiting, ready to pick up the bobbing barrels and ship them onto receiving ports anywhere along the Great Lakes."

"So, what went wrong?" Tom asked.

Sam thought back to the message they'd found inside the wheel house of the J.F. Johnson that terrified Senator Perry — STANFORD STOLE THE MESKWAKI GOLD SPRING. I CAN TOO. "Stanford stole the Meskwaki Gold Spring!"

Tom shrugged. "Yeah, I was there. I read the note, too. But how?"

"How would you shut down an operation like this and at the same time get rid of your old boss and any competition?"

"Of course, he's filled some of the barrels with dynamite on a long timer!"

"Right! He then dumped the barrels, into the subterranean river, where they were carried into Lake Superior. There the *J.F. Johnson* loaded up her secret bilge compartments with what her captain assumed was rum. Somewhere, hidden among those were explosives."

Tom grinned. "Only Stanford made a mistake, didn't he?"

"Yes. Stanford miscalculated the fuse length. He assumed the *J.F. Johnson* would have pulled away from her anchor by the time the explosion occurred. Instead, the ship was still there, right above the mouth of the cavern. Which meant when it sank, the ship became wedged into the mouth of the cavern."

"Stanford, assuming that he now had control of the new operation, kept using the Meskwaki Gold Spring until he discovered his barrels were no longer coming through the other side."

"Decades went by until advances in SCUBA diving and closed-circuit rebreathers made it possible for the Meskwaki Gold Spring to be reopened. Only this time, Prohibition no longer existed, but drugs and weapons had become major business. A business that would make Senator Perry rich."

"There's just one thing I don't understand."

"What's that?"

"If Stanford didn't make his fortune by stealing the Meskwaki Gold Spring, how did the Perry family rise to its current position of wealth and power?"

CHAPTER THIRTY-EIGHT

I T WAS SILENT on board the Annabelle May. The water along Lake Superior deceptively gentle. From the bridge of the pleasure cruiser, Virginia studied the radar screen. The dive boat still hadn't returned, but neither had Sam or Tom. She felt tense and focused. With her senses heightened, everything from the splash of a gentle wave through to the intermittent, sibilant breeze made her rigid with fear.

The satellite phone rang.

Virginia answered it before the second ring. "Hello?"

It was Elise, Sam's computer expert and hacker. "Has Sam and Tom dived yet?"

"Yeah, they put into the water about twenty minutes ago. Why?"

"I think I have an idea what's happening. During the 1920s when prohibition was in full force, a number of organized crime families made a fortune in the bootlegging business. Some of the most successful of these operators were from Moosejaw, Saskatchewan—along the Canadian border."

"Go on."

Elise said, "There were a number of mob families, but the most notorious of these was a man named Alphonse Gabriel Capone. Nicknamed, *Scarface,* for a three-inch scar across his face, which he received after making an indecent comment about a woman at a bar, whose brother then slashed him across the face. Scarface was an American mobster, crime boss, and businessman who attained notoriety during the Prohibition era as the co-founder and boss of the Chicago Outfit."

"You think Al Capone's descendants are running another contraband business at a shipwreck in Lake Superior?" Virginia asked, her voice, incredulous.

"No. Al Capone was finally indicted for tax evasion in June 5, 1931. At the time, he supposedly brought in rum to the tune of a hundred million dollars from Moosejaw, but to this day no one knows exactly what secret method his rumrunners used in doing so."

Virginia asked, "So what does any of this have to do with the wreckage of the *J.F. Johnson?*"

"When Al Capone was indicted and his empire toppled, do you think bootlegging ended?"

"No, of course not."

"Right, neither did the supply of arms, illicit drugs, or other contraband."

Virginia smiled. "So, someone else picked up the mantle?"

"Exactly," Elise said. "I found a buried police document dating back to the thirties, which reveals a new family had taken over Al Capone's supply chain, moving into illegal arms and drug sales after December 5, 1933 when President Franklin D. Roosevelt announced that prohibition had been repealed with the 21st Amendment."

"Did they ever catch the new organized crime family?"

"That's just it. The document noted that evidence was hard to produce because the new family had such strong connections to the police and politicians. Unlike Al Capone who flaunted his new-found wealth, the new family predominantly lived normal lives. In the end, the internal police decision, signed off by FDR agreed not to pursue the new organized crime boss—quoting huge collateral damage of hunting local police and politicians."

"What happened to the family?"

"It's suspected the family eventually made their fortune and assimilated into legitimate businesses. You want to guess where Stanford Perry — Senator Arthur Perry's father — used to work as a boilerman?"

"On board the *J.F. Johnson*?"

"Exactly."

"And you don't think it was a coincidence that Al Capone was indicted two weeks before the ship met its ignoble demise?"

"What happened to Stanford after the shipwreck?"

"No one really knows for sure. He started up a number of legitimate businesses, which all were highly successful, until he became a prominent and successful man in town. His son, Arthur, studied Law at Stanford university — I'm not sure if the choice of university was Stanford's humor there, but afterward Arthur became a successful criminal lawyer who quickly earned himself a position as Minnesota's District Attorney."

"He ruthlessly went after all other crime figures within the state, making room for his father's original business to thrive!"

"Yes. In doing so, Senator Arthur Perry never got his hands dirty. His record was crystal clean. He cleaned up any organized crime in the state, and got rich doing so."

Virginia thought back to the photograph of the note found inside the wheelhouse — the same one that Senator Arthur Perry thought would get him killed the day before he died of a heart attack. It read, STANFORD STOLE THE MESKWAKI GOLD SPRING. I CAN, TOO.

She swore. "Whoever's in the process of taking over the Perry family crime business knows the wreck of the *J.F. Johnson* is the secret to the Perry's wealth."

Elise said, "I've gone over satellite images of the area for the past three months."

"And?"

"Three weeks ago. The same time David Perry, the Senator's son, went missing, a local dive operator's boat started to make nightly visits to the shipwreck."

"Sam knows about the dive boat," Virginia said. "He and Tom believed they would be back before the nightly divers arrived. If not, they hoped the divers would lead them to the *J.F. Johnson's* secrets."

"When were they due back?"

Virginia stared at the radar screen that showed nothing but empty water and swallowed. "An hour ago."

CHAPTER THIRTY-NINE

S AM CARRIED HIS dive gear across the shallow stream to where a group of five small boulders, resting against one another, formed a natural pond of water approximately three feet deep. He deflated the buoyancy wing, causing his dive gear to sink to the bottom. Tom passed him the backpack, containing the gas tanks and C02 scrubber of his closed-circuit rebreather. Sam lowered it into the pond, where it, too, made its lonely voyage to the stream floor.

Stepping back for a better view, Sam studied the creek with his flashlight—the bright light reflecting clearly off the smooth, still surface of the water. He looked across at Tom who was studying the area from the path that lined the bank of the creek.

"What do you think?"

"I think it's well hidden."

"Good." Sam removed his shark stick, which was fundamentally a Remington shotgun with a single .50 caliber shot. "Let's go see where we are and where our friend got to."

"Sounds good to me."

Sam followed the narrow track through to the end of the grotto, where it combined with the creek to form the mouth of the cavern. At the opening, the creek was less than a foot deep and the cave allowed a spacing of another two feet above it. Both Sam and Tom needed to slide through on their bellies to pass.

Sam shimmied through the opening and stared with relief

into the open night's sky.

The creek was fed by a large lake, approximately two miles in length by half a mile in width. The silhouette of long mountain ridges lay in the distance to the west. The sky was heavy with clouds, and mist swirled in the air above the water.

He stood up and stretched his legs while Tom slipped through the small opening. Sam glanced at it and smiled. Without knowing the grotto was there, it would be easy to simply assume the creek flowed into a natural siphon, disappearing beneath the rocky shore. It's amazing anyone knew about it.

Wet and muddy, Tom pushed to his feet.

"Tight fit?" Sam asked with a grin.

"You bet."

They walked across the stony shore of the lake, heading toward a clearing near its edge which provided a good cover of brush, but a clear view of the water. The late afternoon was peaceful, the only sound was birds as they migrated toward their roosting positions for the end of the day.

Sam stopped walking, struck by the beauty of the place. The opposite edge of the lake was bordered with a craggy overhanging cliff of about 300 feet which gave way to conifer forested sides on the rest of the shore. The water's glassy surface reflected all the light and clouds of the late afternoon, yet was clear enough to reveal the river-stone bottom at the same time.

"Stunning," Sam observed.

"Very," Tom agreed.

Sam and Tom freed themselves from their dry suits and flopped on to their backs in the thick, long grass. Tom's face had deep red lines from his facemask, but was otherwise pale against the chill. They had been in the water for nearly two hours.

"Any guesses where we are?" Tom asked, rubbing his eyes before looking up at the sky and foliage above their position.

Sam took off his gloves and wiped the face of his digital tablet as it picked up the overlying satellites. He clicked the locate button and a map of their surroundings opened up.

He handed Tom the tablet. "According to this, we're looking at Marie Louise Lake, Ontario, Canada."

"That's some aquifer!"

"Yeah, not a bad dive after all—even if it's going to get mighty cold soon."

Tom handed it back to him. "Looks like there's a Ranger's Station toward the northeastern edge of the lake. If we start walking, we should be there in an hour. Maybe we can get a message out to Virginia."

"Good idea."

Sam and Tom started to head into the thick pine forest, before they heard the familiar drone of a De Havilland Canada DHC-2 Beaver floatplane moments before they saw it crest the ridge of the eastern shore. Throttled back, intentionally losing altitude, the Beaver was making an approach to land on the glassy lake.

Instinctively, Sam and Tom took cover against the trunk of a large tree. The plane could have been any number of commercial aircraft, ferrying in tourists or seasonal Rangers for the national parks. But there was something fundamentally disconcerting about a light aircraft landing on a small lake at night time.

With visibility reduced, you could land on a log, a boat, or a sandbar. No commercial floatplane would risk that.

The plane continued its descent; soon the yellow seaplane's floats were carving the surface as it landed. Sam hoisted himself up into the branches of the great pine tree under which they stood, climbing up about forty feet to get a better look.

On the opposite shore he watched as a small inflatable was rowed toward the airplane. The bush pilot stood on the pontoon and gave the diver a friendly wave. Once there, the man in the inflatable passed two large bags to the plane.

The pilot was keeping the De Havilland's motor running, ready for take-off. Both men were in a hurry. There was no chitchat, the transfer took only minutes. Moments later, the floatplane was taking to the sky and banking toward the north, even before the launch made it back to the shore.

"It's a drop," Sam said to Tom, as he started to climb down the tree.

"For what?"

"I'm guessing something illegal."

"Drugs?"

"Or weapons."

"Now what?"

Sam jumped down from the lowest branch of the pine. "Now we find that Ranger station and see if we can find something to eat. Then we wait for the diver to return through the Meskwaki Gold Spring."

"We don't even know when the diver's going to return."

"Sure we do."

Tom smiled. "We do?"

"Yeah. He or she will need to wait until eight p.m. tomorrow. The same time the Superior Deep makes its nightly visit out to the wreck of the *J.F. Johnson*."

CHAPTER FORTY

S AM CLIMBED THE small ridge, heading northeast toward the Ranger's station. He and Tom moved slower than they normally would. Compressed nitrogen, built up in the bloodstream from long submersion at depth, had that effect on the human body. Even young, fit people, like Sam and Tom, couldn't forego the fatigue that followed such a prolonged, deep dive.

Tendrils of fog brushed against his skin as the temperature plummeted. Sam was thankful of the warm underlay clothing he'd worn beneath his dry suit. Generally speaking, these garments appeared quirky, but they were hardly out of place among visitors to the popular camping region.

It was nearly eleven p.m. by the time they reached the Ranger's station. The place was one of those log huts built in the 1950s, when tourism in Thunder Bay was taking off. No lights were on, and for an instant Sam worried that the place was unmanned. A tiny wisp of smoke rising from a single chimney reassured him they were in luck.

Before he or Tom reached the log cabin, the side door opened. A man in his late seventies, with thick gray hair that continued into a long beard down to his chest, stepped out with a lively gait and a gregarious smile. Sam's first impression was that the gentleman belonged in an old gold rush era western movie.

Sam hastily said, "I'm sorry to intrude this time of night."

The stranger grinned. "Doesn't bother me any. I'm always happy to see people enjoying these parts of the wood. Travelers are always welcome. Besides, I am curious to know how you ended up here at this time of night with little in the way of equipment or supplies."

"There's a long story about that," Sam said. "I'm happy to tell it to you shortly, but first, is there any chance you have a working cell phone?"

The man shook his head. "I've no need and no interest in those things."

"Do you know where I could find someone else who might have one?" Sam asked, his tone set in a mixture of sheepishness and urgency. "We weren't planning on camping here at all tonight. We took our little motor boat out onto the lake and the engine gave out all the way down the southern end. We spent the better half of the afternoon paddling to shore and have hiked here in the dark. We didn't have flashlights with us, so we ended up using our cell phones for flashlights, but now…"

"They've gone flat and you need to let your wife know about why you're not coming home for dinner?"

Sam smiled. "My girlfriend actually, but I'm sure she's worried sick."

"Look. There's a satellite phone inside — meant to be used for emergencies, but you're welcome to use it to let her know you're all right."

"That would be great. Thanks." He offered his hand. "My name's Sam Reilly by the way, and this is Tom Bower."

The Ranger took it. His handshake was firm. "Pleased to meet you Mr. Reilly and Mr. Bower. Come inside, I'll throw the pot of stew back on the fire and warm it up for you. That and fresh coffee — black is all I have."

"Thank you, that's very kind," Sam said.

"My name's Yago. I've been coming out to these woods a few weeks each summer since I was a boy and my father used to drag me out here for weeks on end."

Sam wondered if Yago was their new friend's first or last name, but as the man intentionally omitted it, he decided to let the question slide. He met the Ranger's eyes. "I bet you could tell some interesting stories about the area."

"That I can. That I can." The Ranger reached into his backpack, which rested on the floor next to the entrance of the cabin, and retrieved the satellite phone. He handed it to Sam. "You know how to use it?"

"Yes, sir I do."

"Good." Yago turned to put more wood in the Franklin Stove. To Tom, he said, "Come warm yourself by the fire."

Sam set up the external antenna, stepped outside and waited for the phone to locate its satellites. He dialed Elise's number by memory.

Elise picked up on the first ring. "I see you found your way to Lake Marie Louise in Canada without getting yourselves killed."

Sam was about to ask how she knew where they were, and then smiled. "Glad our tracking system's working."

"Did you work out who's transferring the contraband across the border?"

"Not yet, but I have some ideas. At least now we know how they're shipping it. We'll set up some surveillance and find out soon enough who's behind this operation. They'll also be responsible for murdering the Senator and his son, and kidnapping Virginia's father."

Elise asked, "Do you want me to tell Virginia to come get you?"

"No. We can make our own way back tomorrow when the diver makes his return trip. Unless we get into trouble, we should be able to come up on the shore of Isle Royale."

"All right. I'll pass the message on to Virginia. You need anything else?"

"Yeah. A warm bath and some good food."

"Afraid I can't help you there."

"Good night, Elise."

Sam ended the call, dropped the antenna, went back into the cabin, and handed the satellite phone back to Yago. The heat from the fire spread quickly, warming every muscle of his body. The Ranger handed him and Tom each a bowl of warm stew.

"Want sugar in your coffee?" Yago asked.

"Sure. Two, please, for both of us," Tom replied.

Yago brought coffee. Sam thanked him and asked, "You said before that you grew up visiting these parts of the world over the summer months and your father was a Ranger before you, is that right?"

"Yeah. But my dad was never a Ranger, just an outdoorsman who wanted to pass on some of his knowledge. I've been coming here since I was a kid. Dad spent time here during the twenties, extensively mapping out the region throughout the summer months—then, when the Great Depression hit in 1930, he returned to the land more permanently."

"Why?" Sam asked.

"He needed to eat, and he needed some place to live. At the time, he could achieve both of those necessities without too much trouble out here. The gambling side of him, the side that saw his fortune destroyed by the Great Depression, also drove him out this way."

"Why is that?"

"Back then, there was many a prospector who swore they would find their fortune in these mountains."

Sam smiled. "Any of them succeed?"

"A few. Not many." Yago smiled like it was a familiar story when it came to gold and the human race. "Truth was, it didn't matter to my father. He could feed and house himself out here, which was better than most could say during those hard days. And then there was always hope, wasn't there, that someday he'd get lucky and strike it rich with gold."

"Interesting." Sam took a mouthful of the stew. It was warm and surprisingly full of taste. "I bet you and your father could tell a few interesting tales about the place."

"You wouldn't believe some of the stories he used to tell."

Sam smiled at the loquacious old Ranger. "Like what?"

"Once, my father said he was playing poker with some other vagrants. Mostly trappers, prospectors, or fur traders. A stranger asked to join the game. My dad says sure, but we're playing for gold. The stranger smiled and put down a single gold coin. Says, what will you give me for this?"

Sam and Tom listened with wide eyes at the anecdote, their interest piqued by the allure of a gold coin, but both remained silent.

Yago stoked the fire. "So my father picks up the coin. On one side is the image of an old iron warship—you know the type that were used throughout the Mississippi River during the Civil War? And on the other side, the face of Jefferson Davis."

Sam grinned. "You're talking about Confederate gold. What did your father do?"

"He let him play of course."

"Did your father win?"

"No. Lost everything he owned trying to get that damned coin. That loss just about killed him over the course of winter." Yago shrugged. "But that's the life of a gambler, isn't it?"

Sam nodded. He liked a challenge, and he took risks if he had to, but he never understood the addictive mindset of a high-rolling risk taker. "Did your father discover where the man found that coin?"

"Yeah, but I've often wondered if the stranger's story about where he'd found the coin was even true. I mean, it was more likely that the man had bought the coin and used it to entice gamblers to risk more than they could afford to lose in an attempt to win it."

"What was the guy's story?"

Yago smiled and shook his head. "You wouldn't believe me if I told you."

"Try me."

To Tom, Yago said, "What about you? Do you want to hear another wild and unbelievable tale from long ago?"

"Sure. Why not?" Tom replied. "After all, traditionally people tell ghost stories around campfires, but Sam and I here, have nothing against trading those for stories of treasure. You'd be surprised what we've found over the years."

"All right," Yago said, stretching backward on the wooden chair, putting his feet up, and getting comfortable. "The stranger tells my father that he flies a float plane on a regular trip from Moose Jaw across to Thunder Bay. Normally, he flies a mostly direct route, only a few months earlier a severe snow storm caused him to head much farther south taking him into North Dakota to refuel."

"Right," Sam said. "Not really sure how a pilot could end up so far south from Moose Jaw, Saskatchewan."

As though he recognized Sam's incredulity, Yago said, "You have to understand this was in the late 1920s or early 1930s. Aviation wasn't the thing it is today. Pilots were true adventurers and bush pilots the greatest of them all."

Sam nodded, taking another bite of stew. "Go on."

"The pilot tells my father he took an alternative route a couple times before, having known a place where fuel could be purchased. Only this time, he takes a detour. He swears he spotted a pyramid the color of rust. He said his curiosity got the better of him, so he landed on a river nearby to investigate. It turned out, the pyramid was in fact an old warship, like on the coin, and inside there was a chest full of the gold coins. Of course, he couldn't take them all. So, he pocketed a couple, made notes in his journal of the location, and continued on to Thunder Bay."

"So what came of the gold?" Sam asked, a wry smile forming on his lips.

"Well. According to my dad, the pilot returned to the location on the map he plotted, but he never found the ship again."

"It simply disappeared?"

"Yeah. Like I said, the man's story was pretty far-fetched. Apparently, the pilot was just that kind of guy where there would be only a hint of truth to whatever he had to say, yet people always seemed to believe him."

Tom nodded, nursing his coffee. "I know a guy exactly like that."

"Talking about legends," Sam said. "Do you mind if I ask you about an old one in these parts?"

"Sure. I suppose you want to know about the Meskwaki Gold Spring?"

"No, thanks. Although I've heard it's beautiful this time of year." Sam smiled. It must have been a common question in this part of the world. "Actually, I'm looking for information about a mildly famous pilot in the area who went missing in the late 1920s."

The ranger narrowed his gray, bushy eyebrows. "Ah, so that's it. You'd be looking for Jack Holman's plane then, would you?"

"That's it. A friend mentioned Holman's floatplane was never found." Sam smiled warmly and glanced at Tom. "We were thinking of trying our luck locating the wreckage. Figured if it hasn't been spotted from the air, there's a good chance she's resting on the bottom of a lake somewhere."

"And you were hoping I could tell you which lake Holman's wreckage is lying in?"

"No. I was just trying to get an idea of what lakes have been explored and if there's anywhere you think a plane like Holman's could remain lost all this time."

"Lot of places to lose a floatplane in these parts of the world.

Forgetting the lakes, there are plenty of deep ravines, dense forests surrounded by steep unmanageable terrain, where a crashed aircraft might disappear forever."

Sam felt like he'd been kicked in the guts. "I hadn't thought of that. I just figured plane crash has to leave a scar on the earth where it strikes. Someone must have noticed that scar in the past ninety odd years since Holman went missing."

Yago's brown eyes turned sharp, and his affable manner suddenly abrupt. "What's your interest in Holman's plane, anyway?"

Sam thought about lying, but something in the man's face told him that would be a bad idea. Instead, he simply told the truth. "A friend of mine's father has been kidnapped. His captors didn't ask for money. Instead, they wanted me to locate a journal they believed Jack Holman was carrying on board his aircraft when he disappeared."

Yago met his gaze, put down his cup of coffee. "And why would they think you might locate something that's been lost all this time?"

"I work in ocean salvaging and, among other tasks, I've headed up a few successful treasure hunts over the years."

"And what do these... kidnappers want with Holman's aircraft?"

Sam shook his head. "Just the flight records or a journal. Apparently, Holman spotted something unique from the air. Whatever it was, a lot of people have died so that it could be located again."

"What are you going to do if you find the aircraft and the journal?"

"Give it to the kidnappers."

"You don't want to notify the FBI?" Yago raised an eyebrow. "Kidnapping's a federal offense."

"Sure. But these people say they have connections throughout the New York Police Department and the FBI. If we cheat them, they said they'll know and will kill my friend's father."

"What makes you think they can be trusted to return your friend's father if you do as they ask?"

"Hope."

"Seems like a lost cause."

"Many things are. But you have to try, don't you?"

Yago's face was set hard and his body tense, before finally expelling a deep breath of air. A thin-lipped smile finally rose as though the man had somehow looked into Sam's face and accepted the truth. "All right. I'll tell you where Jack Holman and his float plane now rests for eternity. Not that it will do you much good."

Sam asked, "Why's that?"

Yago sighed. "Because he's at the bottom of Dog Lake, beneath three hundred and fifty feet of icy water."

CHAPTER FORTY-ONE

S AM ASKED, "HOW can you be so certain Holman's last flight ended up in Dog Lake?"

"Look, always chasing his fortune, Jack Holman was a gambler and a risk taker. He was also involved with a lot of bad people. A jack of all trades, he was someone who could get a lot done in a time when tough guys ruled the area."

"Was he involved in bootlegging?"

"Not directly. He was employed by a local organized crime gang from Chicago. They moved alcohol amongst other contraband, from Moose Jaw in Saskatchewan into the Great Lakes, where a number of ships shifted it to the cities farther downstream."

"What did Jack Holman do?"

"He flew up ahead, above, or behind the rum-runners and had an intricate coding system to notify when and where prohibition agents were setting up a blockade."

"So how do you know he ended up crashing in Dog Lake, Ontario?"

Yago smiled. "Oh, I never said he crashed, did I?"

"Really?" Sam studied his face. "How interesting. Go on. What do you know?"

"In late 1930 Holman landed on Dog Lake. A boat came to meet him. It was owned by the people he worked for. A young man was at the tiller. A man Holman called Stanford."

Sam felt his heart start to hammer in his throat at the mention of the name. He forced himself to remain silent in case Yago would close up like a clam.

Yago closed his eyes. "Holman and Stanford spoke for a few minutes. When they were done, Stanford shot Holman from behind — right between his ears. Poor Holman never knew what hit him. He fell overboard and disappeared into the icy waters. Stanford then took an axe to one of the floatplane's pontoons. It quickly filled with water, causing the aircraft to tip over on its side. From there it took less than ten minutes to sink."

Sam asked, "How do you know all this?"

Yago opened his eyes. "Because Jack Holman was my father."

"Your father?" Sam asked, incredulous. "How old are you?"

"I'm ninety-three."

Sam nodded. It was possible, albeit unlikely. Sam decided not to challenge him. He was either telling the truth and the aircraft would be at Dog Lake, or he was lying. "How did you find out what happened?"

"I wasn't supposed to be on that flight, but I was. When my father spotted Stanford approach, he told me to get into the cargo bay in the tail and stay down. I continued to hide after he was shot, until the floatplane finally tipped over and started to sink. By then, Stanford was already motoring away on his small boat."

"How did you survive?"

"I was six years old, but that day I became a man." Yago swallowed hard at the memory. "I swam through the icy waters to the shore, where I was picked up by some local fishermen. They lit a fire and saved my life."

"Did you ever tell anyone about Stanford?"

"Who could I tell? I never saw Stanford, and to this day I don't know whether Stanford was his first or last name. But I'll tell you what, it brings a smile to my old eyes to know that people are still trying to locate what's on that aircraft."

"Why?"

"Because that means Stanford never lived to see it." Yago grinned, wildly. "And I'll make you a deal."

Sam sighed. "Go on."

"I'll tell you exactly where Jack Holman's wreck is, but I want you to promise me something."

"I'm listening."

"My story about the stranger who turned up with the Confederate gold coin wasn't entirely true. He wasn't a stranger. He was Jack Holman, my father, and a terrible gambler."

"Your father found Jefferson Davis's hidden Confederate Treasury?"

"My father thought so. He was in the process of organizing an expedition to retrieve the entire fortune when he was murdered."

"This is why everyone's dying all of a sudden. It's not about the Meskwaki Gold Spring. Someone knows about the Confederate gold." Sam stopped, his eyes fixed on Yago. "You must know that Stanford's dead. He must've been dead for years."

"Of course, I do. I'm an old man now, so unless he's a couple decades over a hundred, he's long gone."

"So then, what do you want us to do?"

"If you find my father's journal, I understand you have four days to return it to the kidnappers in exchange for your friend's father."

"That's right."

"Good. Then that means you have three days to locate the Confederate gold and remove it before you hand over the journal. I just hope you're as good a treasure hunter as you say you are."

Sam grinned. "So do I."

CHAPTER FORTY-TWO

T HE NEXT DAY Sam and Tom hiked down to the river, retrieved their dive gear, and followed the diver back through the Meskwaki Gold Spring without any problem. Virginia met them near the shore of Isle Royale. Sam removed his fins and handed them to her, before climbing the boarding ladder onto the aft deck of the *Annabelle May.*

Virginia waited until he removed the heavy closed-circuit rebreather system from his back before she asked, "Did you find it?"

"The Meskwaki Gold Spring?" Sam said.

"Yeah. Did it lead you to Holman's wreck?"

"As a matter of fact, it did."

Her eyes widened. "That's great! Where?"

"I'll explain on the way, but right now, we need to get moving."

"Where are we going?"

"Duluth. There's a floatplane waiting for us to rent."

CHAPTER FORTY-THREE

DULUTH—SKY HARBOR

S AM WAITED IN the Aviation Flight School office for a rental manager to meet him. Next to him, Virginia waited impatiently. Tom had already stepped outside to enjoy the picturesque landscape of the unique amphibious air base, which accommodated both land and sea plane traffic. From where Sam was sitting, he could see the backdrop of Duluth city and the splendor of Lake Superior.

Something on the TV caught his attention.

A woman who appeared too young to be a candidate, and much too attractive, was giving a speech about her vision of Minnesota under her Senatorial leadership. She had an easy-to-watch kind of face, with an amiable smile and confident voice. She spoke intelligently and eloquently, while trying to hide the remnants of an Irish accent.

Sam listened to her speak for a while, before turning to Virginia, who was seated in the chair beside him. "Hey, for a politician, she seems all right. Much too young a candidate to be accepted by the more conservative members of the electorate — even in Minnesota that's voted Democrat every election since 1976 — but hey, she might get in one day. I hope she wins."

Virginia also watching the TV, turned to face him. "She already has."

"Has what?"

Virginia smiled. "Won the position of Senator for Minnesota."

"Senator Perry's been dead less than three days," Sam said. "How did she get the job so quickly?"

"Gubernatorial Appointment."

"Of course," Sam said, his eyes filled with a vacant expression.

Virginia sighed. "Didn't you learn anything at that expensive private school of yours?"

"I learned how to dive on the weekends, sail in the afternoons, and fly floatplanes in the summer. What more could I have wanted to learn?"

"How about how your country's electoral system works?"

Sam shrugged. "I think you've got me pegged for someone else. While I take my voting responsibilities seriously, I have zero interest in running for government."

"Obviously not and it's a good thing, too."

"What's that supposed to mean?"

"It means if you'd paid more attention during social studies at school, you would have learned that for thirty-six states, vacancies to the U.S. Senate during a sitting member's term, through resignation, expulsion, or death, are replaced by Gubernatorial Appointment. The remaining fourteen states require a special election to be called."

"Sure," Sam said, his face still not showing any sort of recognition.

"Minnesota is one of the thirty-six states that utilize Gubernatorial Appointment in this circumstance. Basically, it means the governor is allowed to appoint the interim Senator for the remainder of the term or until the following November when a formal election must be held."

"Okay. How does the Governor choose?"

"He or she doesn't choose so much, as refines the list of current pre-selected candidates."

"Meaning?"

"The candidates must be of the same political party as the Senator who vacated the seat. If the vacancy occurs before a specific number of days prior to the regular primary—in Minnesota this is six weeks—the election is held the following November. If it occurs within that period of days before the regular primary, the election is held on the second November election after the vacancy occurs. And lastly, but possibly most importantly, the governor makes the appointment by selecting from a list of three provided by the party."

A worried frown formed between his brow. "Who were the other two candidates?"

"What?" Virginia asked.

"You said the party needs to provide a list of three candidates." Sam shifted on his seat to take another look at the new Senator. "Obviously she was one of those people. Who were the other two?"

"I've no idea."

"Can you find out for me?"

"Should be able to. It should be public domain." Virginia opened her smartphone and Googled the list of possible candidates. Three names immediately came up. She ran her eyes across the list. "It says here that the three candidates included Rachel Murphy, who's the cute, vivacious redhead and Senator Appointee, and two others. It says here, the first of the other two candidates had voluntarily excused himself from the list, citing recent diagnosis of a significant medical illness."

"And the second pre-selected candidate?"

"A man named Malcolm Bennet."

Sam glanced over Virginia's shoulder at her phone, taking in the image of an elderly man with the typical stately appearance of a lifelong politician. "Why wasn't he selected?"

"I don't know." Virginia clicked on the link next to the man's name. "There's an article here that says Mr. Malcolm Bennet stood down as a candidate after the recent loss of his son, who died of a heroin overdose in New York. Bennet is currently in the process of challenging the coroner's findings, making a statement that his son had never touched heroin in his life and that there must be a mistake. His believes his son was murdered and he intends to find out."

An image of the candidate's son was displayed on the phone. Virginia's skin paled, her lips parted in a panicked breath. Eyes wide with fear, she dropped her phone down on the table as if it had burnt her fingers.

Sam picked it up, glanced at the image. "You know this guy?"

"That's the suspected drug dealer who overdosed in New York. The same person who I stole a million dollars from."

A blank look on his face, Sam silently stared at the picture of the clean cut, young, healthy man. He appeared to be of a similar age as the Senator's son. Did they go to the same school? Run in the same circles? Were they both killed by the same paid assassin?

"Don't you see? This means I was right, the kid wasn't a drug addict. In fact, if that's the case, it means it's more than likely the candidate's boy was murdered. But why did they leave the cash? For dirty cops on a mob payroll perhaps? Remember, I also found the map in that bag. Was it also left as payment to cover up the crime?

Sam thought about that for a second, but new implications suddenly struck him like a match set to gasoline. "With the two other candidates already out of the running, that would mean Rachel Murphy already knew she was a sure thing! She must have been responsible for the murder of the Senator and second candidate's son, just to get into power."

"It doesn't necessarily mean that Senator Murphy was in on it," Virginia protested.

"You don't think she just murdered two people to place

herself in the position as next senator of Minnesota?" Sam asked.

Virginia expelled a deep breath of air. "If not Rachel Murphy, then it means someone murdered two people to place her there."

Sam swore. "Either way, we have a senator who's a murderer or one who's being significantly coerced to vote a specific way."

"That means before our seven days are up, we also need to find out which one of those statements is correct—and who's doing the coercing."

CHAPTER FORTY-FOUR

DOG LAKE, ONTARIO

S AM PULLED BACK on the stick of the rented De Haviland, a Canadian-built DHC-3 Otter, climbing above the craggy mountainous coastline laid out below. It was a single engine propeller-driven seaplane, known for its suitability to the rugged Canadian conditions. Tom and Sam had picked it up from Duluth Aviation, under the guise of a week-long fishing and sightseeing vacation.

Built to seat ten, the plane had been converted to four seats and a substantial cargo area. In the second row, Virginia was checking over the sonar buoy they had brought with them. Tom was entering the co-ordinates of the lake into the onboard navigation screen.

Sam listened to the steady growl of the 450-kW Pratt & Whitney R-1340 geared radial engine, searching the tone for irregularities or out of place sounds that might spell foreseeable trouble. Finding none, he relaxed and focused his mind on the task ahead. To the left of him, Tom methodically scrutinized the gauges, while searching the horizon.

Adjusting the plane's attitude, Sam slanted a casual glimpse at his industrious friend. Comfortable with Tom by his side, Sam thought it reassuring that they were of the same mind, as usual.

Turning his head, Sam glanced back at Virginia as she absent-mindedly examined the yellow kettle-bell shaped float in her hands. It was heavy, and it made the muscles in Virginia's biceps and forearms ripple like a set of eels. It was about the size of a basketball, with a tow hook attachment at the front. It had 2 ports for USB, and an old-fashioned video RC cable with rubber grommets on its top.

"It's a narrow-beam bathymetry and sonar buoy," he said over his shoulder, raising his voice above the cabin noise.

"That's what I thought it was," she replied, a wry smile cracking her face.

Despite her good humor, Sam saw a hardness in her eyes he'd never noticed before. The stress of her father's situation was starting to tell on her. He thought she must have squared off against thousands of horrors in her lifetime of service to others.

Up ahead, Sam spotted where the end of the Michipicoten River system flowed into Lake Superior. He banked to the left and pushed the throttle in farther to increase power to the engine. Commencing his climb, he used the river, which originated at the southern outlet of Dog Lake, as a guide.

The surface of Dog Lake was roughly 1083 feet above sea level, which fluctuated depending on the requirements of the local hydroelectric dam.

It wasn't long before they spotted the southern tip of Dog Lake. The large body of water was an irregular shape with multiple islands and basins spread throughout. To the south a series of rapids and falls between Dog Lake and Little Dog Lake could be seen to create a confluence with the Matawin River to form the Kaministiquia River.

The name Kaministiquia came from the Ojibway First Peoples' word, meaning, "Where the rivers meet." It was there, at a crest of a ridge that separated Big and Little Dog Lake, that a large effigy of a dog had been found, from which the lakes took their names. Dug out of the ground, and mounded up with debris, it had been carved out of the crest to form a crude depiction of a dog-like creature.

Sam checked the topographical map that Yago had given him. A hand-written note identified the location of Jack Holman's seaplane toward one of the northern arms of the lake, where the Lochalsh River entered from the north. The water was moderately clear to slightly turbid, taking on an overall yellow-brown color.

"There it is," Tom said, pointing over the nose of the plane and down to his left.

Sam glanced at the shallow beach at the end of the basin, where several boats and another floatplane were tied to a dock. It was summer, and despite the remoteness, the entire region welcomed throngs of adventurers and fishermen who vacationed there.

He banked to the left, setting up to do a reconnaissance fly-past to rule out any floating logs, small boats, sand bars, or surface debris. He flew over a long distance, making sure his waterway was clear and long enough. The surface of the lake wasn't rough, a condition that would make it hazardous to land. Worse, though, the water was dead calm.

A glassy, flat surface reflects like a mirror — one of the most dangerous conditions a seaplane pilot can face. This made it extremely difficult for Sam to judge actual height. When landing on water, one can't rely on an altimeter. The difference between one foot and ten was a thin line between a safe landing, or flying your plane with power straight into the water and sinking.

When he was ready, Sam opened his side window, making a sharp bank to the left. Removing his cap and dropped it out the window. His hat fell straight downward, confirming there was no wind within the basin. It landed with a splash, sending a series of circular, undulating ripples flowing outward.

"Why did you drop your hat?" Virginia asked.

"Ripples," he curtly replied, utterly focused on landing his craft.

Sam flew a sharp, 180 degrees turn and set up for his final approach. He set the flaps to thirty degrees, reduced power, and brought the de-Havilland DHC-3 Otter into a glide. Using peripheral vision for cues, he observed the height of trees on shore, his eyes carefully observing the ripples on the water.

Just above the surface, he raised the nose. This made the aircraft flare, meaning to lose lift and stall, slowing its descent, causing its twin pontoons to softly hydroplane for a moment before it sank gently into the water.

"Nice," Virginia murmured. "I barely felt that."

"Sam knows planes," Tom observed, a note of pride in his voice.

Sam reduced the engine to an idle, before powering off. The engine coughed and the propeller stopped spinning. Unclipping his belt, he opened the door, and climbed down the ladder. Holding onto the wing support, he reached down and picked up his hat that was floating on the surface of the water.

Sam shook the excess water off his cap, jauntily placed it back on his head. Stunned, surprised, and a little awed, Virginia, standing at the door to the plane, laughed out loud. Tom muttered, "Show off," under his breath, but he chuckled, too.

"All right," Sam said, beaming a crooked, boyish grin. "Let's go find Holman's sunken aircraft."

CHAPTER FORTY-FIVE

S AM IDLED THE DHC-3 Otter to the edge of the silty, sandy
basin. Once there, he and Virginia used a set of ropes to
secure the aircraft, tying it between the base of two conifer trees.
Tom opened the luggage hatch at the back of the aircraft, and
nudged the container for the self-inflating twelve-foot Zodiac
out the door into the water.

On landing onto water, the sensors in the casing fired the
carbon-dioxide and nitrogen canisters. This inflated the boat in
a matter of seconds. The three climbed in, and Tom started the
two horsepower Suzuki outboard. He lowered the propeller,
and headed out into the deep water of the basin.

Once they were about fifty feet out, and the water was deep
enough that Sam could be confident that they wouldn't snag
anything on the shallow reeds, he dropped the sonar transducer
buoy and commenced towing it in a large grid formation.

Closing in on the third grid, less than twenty minutes into
their search, Sam spotted the outline of a metal object beneath
the water. The sonar started to ping, indicating something manmade had been located. Sam increased the frequency of the
sonar's soundwaves, which improved the quality of the image.
It was good, but nothing like the bathymetric equipment used
on board Sam's salvage vessel, the *Maria Helena*.

"Our luck is in." Sam grinned. "That's never happened
before!"

"What?" Virginia asked.

"Luck… we've never found something on the first run," Tom answered.

Sam shook his head. "He's right. That honestly never happens. After all these years of silence, who would have thought old Yago was telling the truth?"

CHAPTER FORTY-SIX

IT TOOK NEARLY forty minutes to set up their closed-circuit rebreathers and diving paraphernalia. They carried additional oxygen tanks and dropped spare oxygen tanks at multiple pre-arranged safety decompression stops from a dive line attached to a large orange buoy.

There was a reason Yago never tried to reach his father's plane, and it wasn't just the depth of the wreck. Altitude diving was dangerous — even for a trained diver. Diving a hundred feet at altitude was much different than being submerged to a hundred feet at sea level.

Few dive charts existed to correctly identify the rate in which compressed nitrogen dissipated from one's blood stream. The charts that did, such as those produced by the U.S. Navy, showed decompression sickness rates with a base line of sea level. None give depths at altitude.

Jack Holman's plane was buried under 350 feet of water, but also 1083 *above* sea level. Thus, the rate of decompression sickness would be in the realm of an educated guess.

Sam and Tom had no desire to push the limits, so they decided to make a bounce-dive. Racing to the bottom, searching the wreck and getting the hell out of there. It would then take nearly four hours to complete the decompression stops and reach the surface. Sam just hoped the batteries for his undergarment infrared heating system lasted that long.

He finished checking his equipment and turned to Tom. "Are you good to go?"

"Good to go," Tom confirmed.

Virginia said, "I'll have a fire going and some soup heated by the time you get back. Good luck."

"Thanks," Sam said, noticing her anxious expression. "We're going to find this thing and then we're going to get your father back."

"I know," she said. "Just don't get yourself killed in the process."

"We'll do our best."

Sam rolled backwards into the water, letting himself fall free from the Zodiac. He checked his gauges, searched for Tom, and confirmed that all was ready to go. A moment later, he deflated his buoyancy wing and began the long journey to the bottom of the lake.

It took nearly twenty-five minutes to reach the bottom of the lake. At a depth of 350 feet the pressure exerted on their bodies was the equivalent of a little more than ten atmospheres, which meant their time at this depth needed to be short. The dive line deposited them just about right on top of Jack Holman's wrecked aircraft.

Sam fixed his flashlight on the seaplane.

The visibility was excellent — surprisingly better at this depth than on the surface. The icy cold water made the perfect environment for preserving the aircraft. Sam recalled how the float plane had never crashed, but as Yago had told him, Stanford had intentionally sunk it after murdering Holman. Now, the sunken seaplane looked like a museum grade display of a 1920s aircraft lying in a bed of marine life to make the focus point of a manmade reef.

On the lakebed beside the open hatchway, a small pile of equipment, books, and personal belongings could be seen strewn across the ground. Despite their disordered clutter, as though a kid had simply thrown them out of the aircraft, they appeared amazingly well preserved.

He kicked his fins and headed toward the still open hatchway midway down the fuselage. Shining his beam across the aircraft, he noticed there was a fine layer of silt which had built up over the metal structure over the decades. It was to be expected, no matter how cold the environment. He stopped at the opening and spotted something that wasn't supposed to be there.

A single hand-print in the soft silt, indicated someone else had tried to open the door recently.

Sam's eyes raked the internal edge of the fuselage and the hatchway. There were another three handprints there. Tom's beam flicked across the hatch and then stopped.

Sam entered the aircraft. The inside of the entire fuselage, aft cargo bay, and cockpit were all stripped bare. Anything that wasn't bolted down had been removed. He swam up to the cockpit. Maps and maintenance books, which would have ordinarily been stored in the open console between the two pilot seats, were all missing. He flicked his flashlight around the cockpit. There was nothing else to see.

He turned around in the narrow compartment and headed back out through the opening.

Tom met him at the hatchway. "Let me guess... we weren't the first to reach the wreck?"

"It looks like it."

Tom turned his focus to the pile of junk that lay next to the languishing float plane. "It looks like someone else was looking for Holman's journal, too."

Sam sighed. "Yes, and it looks like someone else beat us to it."

CHAPTER FORTY-SEVEN

I T TOOK NEARLY four hours to reach the surface.

They weren't taking any chances with decompression stops, given their altitude. It was a long, slow, and cold process. Sam felt hypothermia start to encapsulate him by the time they reached the surface and Virginia met them with the Zodiac.

Tom climbed on board first and then helped pull his friend up.

Sam removed his facemask.

Virginia met his eye. "You didn't find it, did you?"

"No. Someone else beat us to it. Must have been recent. Maybe even in the last few days."

Her face became instantly etched in pain and fear. "It's all right. We'll work something out."

"Yeah. I'll have Elise track down the rest of my crew from the *Maria Helena.* They were owed some hard-earned vacation time and are currently scattered throughout the globe. They're an eclectic bunch, each professional to their core. Holiday or not, my crew will come running if I tell them I need help. Together, we'll come up with a plan to find your dad."

"Sure," she said, but even in his near-hypothermic state, Sam knew she was lying.

Virginia motored the small Zodiac to the shore where she'd left a small fire burning on the beach. Sam and Tom pulled the inflatable out of the water. Sam removed his dive equipment, dry suit, and then sat down next to the fire.

The effects of compressed nitrogen after a deep dive leading to severe fatigue were well documented. Right now, Sam felt as if he could have slept for days.

Virginia handed him a warm drink. "It's soup. You'll feel better."

"Thank you." Sam took it and slowly sipped a mouthful. The warm liquid stirred him alive as it moved down his throat.

Tom, tough as a full-grown oak, appeared undeterred by the cold or physical hardship. He took a couple sips from his own hot drink, put it down on a nearby rock, and then went in search of some more firewood.

Virginia smiled. "Does anything faze him?"

"Not much," Sam said taking another sip. "But when something does, you don't want to be on the wrong side of him. He's an unearthly force, a formidable warrior with the intellect and strength to win any battle."

Virginia smiled. It wasn't hard to imagine someone Tom's size as a lethal soldier. "How long have you two been friends?"

"Most of our lives. We grew up less than a block away from each other and went to the same schools. His dad taught us to dive and my dad taught us to sail. We joined the Marines out of school and learned to fly helicopters. After we left the military, I took over the search and recovery arm of my father's shipping company. I had the good fortune of convincing Tom to come along. We've worked together on some of the most unbelievable cases around the world."

"I've read about your exploits over the past few years. They're quite impressive."

Tom returned with a stack of firewood, sat down, and put another piece of flotsam on the fire. A few minutes later, Sam spotted a stranger approaching their camp. The man could have almost passed as Tom's twin, except for his height. He was roughly six foot-three inches, with a barrel chest and muscular physique.

"Afternoon," Sam said, without standing up.

"Afternoon." The stranger dipped his hat, smiled, and glanced down at the diving equipment. "I couldn't help noticing you were under the surface for a long time. Did you go all the way to the bottom?"

"Yeah," Sam said, without elaborating.

The stranger smiled. There was something familiar about him, some facial characteristic Sam couldn't quite place. "So you came to find Jack Holman's sunken float plane, did you?"

Sam gave him a firm nod. There was no point denying it. "Yeah. We had a look at his wreck. Didn't find anything though."

The stranger's voice suddenly turned icy. "Did my father send you here?"

"No."

"I know he sent you to find me and you got this far, so you must be good at your job... Mr.-?"

"Sam Reilly." Sam stood up to greet the man. "This is Tom and Virginia. Who are you?"

"David Perry."

Sam's heart started to hammer in his throat. "Senator Perry's son?"

"Yeah." David let his big shoulders slump forward. "You found me. Out here trying to track down Jack Holman's last whereabouts, searching for treasure. The question is, now that you've found me, what are we going to tell my father?"

"You haven't listened to the news lately?"

David shrugs. "Too busy, why?"

Sam sighed. "I'm really sorry to tell you this, Mr. Perry. Your father died a couple days ago."

"Really?" Hiding his reaction, David turned to stare at the

lake. Sam didn't feel the young man was surprised by the distressing news, but it was clear he was upset. "Where? How?"

"In New York. It might have been a heart attack. Or he might have been murdered."

Still turned toward the lake, David gave a long, unhappy sigh. "He loved me in his way. We were never close, but I didn't want him dead."

Sam asked, "Can you think of anyone who would have been interested in hurting your dad?"

"Yes," David answered without hesitation.

"Who?"

"Just about everyone he knows." David spun back to meet Sam's scrutinizing gaze. "Look, my father was a powerful man, but that power came at a price. He owed a lot of bad people."

"He owed them money?" Sam asked.

David shrugged. "Money, information, changes to the Senate, deals, you name it and my father owed it. That's why I came out here."

"To get away from it all?"

"No. Because I needed to find Jefferson Davis's Confederate Treasury. It was the only way to save my father's life, and now it's the only way to save mine."

"It looks like a lot of people are after this elusive Confederate gold, but I'm afraid someone beat us both to Jack Holman's wreck. The aircraft was stripped bare. There was nothing down there that could lead us to the ironclad he spotted back in 1930."

David grinned. "Of course, there wouldn't be. I removed Holman's journal yesterday."

A wry smile of incredulity formed on Sam's lips. "You did?"

"Yes. I've been reading the journal since yesterday and so far, I haven't found anything. It was stored in a watertight container, but with time some of the ink has faded. It makes it difficult to read. Besides, Holman's notes regarding the strange pyramid—

which we're all assuming must be an old Confederate ironclad — are so vague that it would be impossible to locate."

Sam nodded. "So, what do you want from us?"

"If my father hired you to find me based on an old legend regarding the Meskwaki Gold Spring, you must be one of the best. Now I have the journal and I need your help to save my life."

"My help to do what?" Sam asked.

David's mouth twisted into a cynical smile. "Why, to find Jefferson Davis's fabled Confederate Treasury, of course."

CHAPTER FORTY-EIGHT

T HEY ALL SAT around the fire together, Sam beside David, then Tom and Virginia. Virginia rustled through one of the duffel bags and brought out snack food, mixed nuts, potato chips, and a variety of cookies. With a glad cry, Tom went straight for the chocolate chip.

Sam tipped his bowl, finishing the last of his soup. "You'd better tell me what you know about this stolen Confederate Treasury, why your life depends on finding it, and how you think I can help you do so."

Exhausted, disturbed, or perhaps just on emotional overload, David rubbed his hands over his face. Tom offered him a cookie, which he turned down. "This is going to sound crazy," David said, "but would you believe me if I told you that the greatest treasure in America's history has been buried somewhere in the upper Missouri River since the Civil War?"

Sam's eyes lit with interest. "You mean could I believe it's remained a secret all this time?"

"Could you?"

"Sure." Sam nodded. "I've known treasure to stay hidden for centuries due to bad luck, or the earth's simple desire not to release the truth about the past. Tell me what you know about this secret."

"In 1863 as the city of Vicksburg was hunkering down," David began, "Union General Ulysses S. Grant prepared what would soon become a prolonged and arduous siege of Vicksburg. At the same time, Jefferson Davis, having received word from Lt. Gen. John C. Pemberton that it would be impossible to hold Vicksburg indefinitely, ordered a covert mission to retrieve the Confederates' treasury."

"Go on."

David took a sip, nodded his approval. "An ironclad, the CSS Mississippi, was inbound to Vicksburg with a bunch of Confederate prisoners. These were mostly deserters who were set to hang to discourage others from getting the same idea during the siege. One of Davis's most trusted men took the opportunity to load the treasury onto the ironclad. During the process, the river battleship was fired upon. The prisoners broke free and took control of the Mississippi."

Virginia poured hot chicken soup from a Stainless-Steel Thermos into a cup, and offered it to David. "You want something to warm you while you speak?" she asked. "It's a ration pack mixture, but it's not bad."

David took it. "Thanks."

Tom asked, "Where did the ironclad go?"

"It headed north. At the time there was a blockade of nine Union vessels to the south, making it impossible to retreat into Confederate waters. They turned the ship north and kept going. It is my belief that the prisoners, having realized they were now running from the Confederacy and the Union, attempted to flee to Canada."

"How?"

David took a sip and smiled. "Not bad. Anyway, they'd have headed north along the Mississippi River, changing to the Missouri at St. Louis, and taking it as far north as possible."

"How far do you think that would have been back in 1863?"

"I've done my research. The CSS Mississippi was state of the art at the time with a draft of only nine feet, she was surprisingly light and nimble. She could have outpaced any other ironclad on the rivers and my guess is she did just that, running from anyone who attempted to attack or approach her. With such a shallow draft, it would be difficult, but not impossible for her to reach modern day South Dakota, possibly even North Dakota and on to Montana given enough time. That far north, it would have been unlikely they were still being pursued."

Sam thought about that for a moment. The fire was burning down to embers. Tom pushed to his feet, picked up a driftwood log and laid it down gently on the fire. He dropped down cross-legged before the fire, and started picking on the mixed nuts.

"So you're saying Holman thinks he spotted the pyramid-shaped pilothouse of a Confederate ironclad in North Dakota?" Tom asked, voicing the question Sam was about to ask.

"Yes."

Sam raised an eyebrow. "But in the nearly nine decades since he was murdered, no one has spotted any sign of the CSS *Mississippi* along the Missouri River or any other tributary throughout North Dakota?"

"That's right."

"How do you explain that, given we're obviously not the only two people to know about those vast sums of gold?"

David finished his soup, put the bowl down. "I don't know."

Sam mentally pictured the upper Missouri River. "For that matter, if an ironclad did indeed reach the Dakotas back in 1863, why isn't there any record of it?"

"What do you mean? They were escaping. They weren't trying to publicize their travel destination."

"No, but think about it. Heading north along the Mississippi River, from Vicksburg, they would have turned into the Missouri River."

"So?"

"So," Sam said. "Even back in 1863 the river would have taken them past Jefferson City, Kansas City, Sioux City, and Fort Randal. All of which, would have had permanent lookouts, not to mention lots of surprised citizens, even then. It would be impossible for the sight of a Confederate ironclad to go unnoticed. Any ideas how to explain that?"

David smiled. "None."

"Yet you're still certain?"

"Why?"

David swallowed heavily. "All I can say is I'm a hundred percent certain the ironclad existed, and it carried the bulk of the Confederate treasury north along the Missouri River. That gold is now buried nearby the *CSS Mississippi*, which became stuck somewhere in the Dakotas. Based on what I've read in Jack Holman's journal. He spotted the pyramid shaped casement or pilothouse of that ironclad to the east of North Dakota."

"You know an awful lot about this ship's secret past." Sam smiled. "What the hell aren't you telling me?"

David crossed his arms, his eyes focusing on the still water of Dog Lake. "I don't want to say."

"Okay."

"Okay, what?"

Sam stood up, dusted off his pants, and offered his hand in a friendly gesture. "Okay, we'll be off, then. Good luck with your treasure hunt. It appears you'll be all right on your own."

Tom pushed to his feet once more. "Yeah, probably best we take off before the wind shifts."

David jumped to his feet, ostensibly to stop Sam and his friends from leaving. "Hey, I need your help, I can pay well. I'm willing to split the gold."

Sam shook his head. "I'm not interested in the money. I have a rule: never search for treasure with people you can't trust. I don't have many rules, but that one I tend to follow. It comes from the old days of pirates and their bounties. Everyone knows you can't trust a pirate. I don't trust liars. Period. And I don't trust you."

"All right, all right!" David opened his backpack and

removed the firm, leather bound, locked journal. He unlocked it, laying it upon a dry log well-lit from the fire. He flicked through more than a dozen old pages. Some of the dates spanned the 1870s through to 1920s. He found what he was after, removed a folded piece of paper, and handed it to Sam. "I know the gold made it this far north along the Missouri River because of this."

Sam took it. His eyes had barely glanced at the page, before he inhaled in surprise. Lips pursed, he shook his head.

"What is it?" Virginia asked.

There in front of him was an exact photocopy of the map Virginia had shown him back in New York.

CHAPTER FORTY-NINE

A LL FOUR OF them settled down around the fire again, prepared to hear the whole story.

Over the course of the next hour Sam listened as David explained that the surviving prisoners of the *CSS Mississippi* had indeed tried to flee to the north in a bold attempt to reach Canada.

Lies and secrets poured like water from a breaking dam. It might take a while for the first one to spill, but once the dam bursts, they flow like a river.

David said, "There were a number of problems they hadn't taken into account. The first of which was food and supplies. There were nearly twenty people to feed on board and very few supplies. This meant they would need to make regular stops to hunt for food. Up until Kansas City, this could be successfully achieved by raiding livestock from farms which ran alongside the Missouri River, but from Sioux City onward, the region was still predominantly occupied by Sioux Native American tribes, including the Dakotas, Lakotas, and Nakotas."

Sam said, "They were attacked as soon as they left the safety of the river?"

"Exactly. Even on the river the Sioux Indians could have easily overrun them, but they had no reason to attack. The ironclad appeared formidable, with little to gain from attacking it. The escaping prisoners from the *CSS Mississippi* were lucky, in the sense that they were simply allowed to pass through their tribal lands."

"So why didn't they make it all the way through to Montana?" Sam asked. "I thought the Upper Missouri River from the Dakotas through to Montana was easily navigable by early paddle steamers?"

"They were, but you have to remember, no one on board the ironclad had ever been that far north. These were Confederate men—mostly prisoners through desertion—and they had no understanding of the topography of the Missouri River or the lands throughout the Dakotas and Montana."

"So where do you think they got to?" Sam asked.

"Based on Jack Holman's journal, I believe what remains of the CSS Mississippi is laying somewhere along one of the tributaries of the Missouri River in North Dakota."

Realizing that the Perry family must have an intricate history with the ironclad and its treasure, Sam asked, "Why did they stop there?"

"They had been on the waterway for nearly two months since surviving Vicksburg and they needed to get the ship out of the water to make repairs. They had no idea where they were, or how close they were to reaching Montana, otherwise they would have probably just tried to keep going. As it was, they didn't. They agreed to enter a small tributary to do the repairs, eventually finding one with a natural oxbow lake, in which they could partially beach the ironclad."

Sam imagined the scene. "And they never got out again?"

David nodded. "They didn't, but not for the reason you'd think. You have to understand, the oxbow lake they'd found had recently flooded, sending a shallow course of water over miles of land. It served its purpose and they completed their repairs, but then tragedy struck."

Virginia, always interested in the classics, piped up. "It sounds to me like this story has all the elements of a Greek

Tragedy. The downfall of someone due to fatal error or misjudgment, suffering and catastrophe, all arousing pity, mystery, and fear on the part of the audience."

"Oh, yeah, I see it," Sam said. "A domino effect of accidents waiting to happen: A bunch of deserters who are supposed to hang, escape with a country's fortune in gold. Add inherent human greed to the mix. What could possibly go wrong after they beach the iron battleship they're using to flee?"

"Like I said, this was the end of June—somewhere within the Dakotas—the very height of tornado season."

Laughing, Sam cocked an incredulous eyebrow. "Seriously? A tornado struck them, sending them to... to Oz?"

"It's not as far-fetched as you would imagine. You see, the entire area was covered in shallow water. *The CSS Mississippi's* bow was out of the water..."

Sam nodded. "And she acted like a giant sail. The tornado ripping her free of where she'd been beached, and sending her skipping across the water?"

"Exactly. When the storm had passed, the men on the ironclad quickly realized that no amount of trench digging would permit them to return the ship to the main tributary and back into the Missouri River."

Sam studied the photocopied map. "They buried the gold nearby?"

"Yes. Realizing it would be impossible to move that much gold on foot, they buried it, creating the makeshift map that you see here."

Sam looked at the map in a new light. Suddenly everything made more sense. The unnamed ship marked on the map was the *CSS Mississippi* and all the topographical locations were noted in relation to the ship. "Find the ship and we find the gold."

"Right."

"But no one's been able to find the ship. Maybe they burned

it?"

"No. After they buried the gold, they headed north into Saskatchewan. But the environment was lethal to the unprepared men of the ironclad—almost all of whom were Southerners, used to the warm weather of the Southern States. It was the end of summer.

"As winter approached, the temperature dropped quickly. The bulk were killed off quickly from an attack by a local Sioux tribe. Those few who escaped, later died from a mixture of starvation, hypothermia, bear attacks, and rattle snakes."

"But someone survived as you know this story?" Sam said.

"Yes. Two people. An Irishman named Robert Murphy and a Southern landowner named William Chestnut. They agreed to split the gold between them. The Great Sioux War finally ended in 1877."

"But neither could find the gold?" Sam asked.

"No. They had the map, but never saw the *CSS Mississippi* again."

Sam smiled, staring at the map. "Are you going to tell us how you know all this?"

David grinned. "Because, for more than a century my family has searched for the wealth of the Confederate treasury. The gold that my great, great, grandfather, William Chestnut, helped bury."

CHAPTER FIFTY

S AM WATCHED WHAT had to be a ten-pound walleye jump out of the lake, silver flashing, making a splash in the still water. He turned back to the fire and asked, "If this treasure has been buried since 1863 and Jack Holman spotted it back in the 1930s, what's everyone been doing for the past nine decades?"

"Why didn't my grandfather find it?"

"Yeah."

David said, "Because he didn't have Holman's journal."

"Sure, but neither did you until yesterday. So, what changed three weeks ago, that sent everything into catastrophic motion?"

David's thick brow narrowed in a way similar to his father's. "You've already dived the *J.F. Johnson,* so I'm assuming you know about the Meskwaki Gold Spring and my family's dark past?"

"Yeah. Your grandfather, Stanford stole the tunnel from the previous group of rumrunners after Al Capone was indicted."

"Yeah, my father became a lawyer and went on to become the legal arm of the family business. Bright and motivated, he was appointed District Attorney in Minnesota by the time he was thirty-five. He then ruthlessly targeted any other organized crime enterprises throughout the region, getting a name for himself as an honest man, making the State safe for families, business, and the lives of its citizens."

"Taking off from the perfect runway into politics, he became a senator."

"Right."

"Did you enter the family business?"

"No. Don't get me wrong. I'm no angel. It was simply a case that by the time I came along, the Perry family were already wealthy and powerful in their own right. There was no need for me to enter the illegitimate part of the business."

"So you got to… what? Enjoy your life?"

"Something like that." David smiled. "That much you know. William Chestnut's son, Stanford, moved to Minnesota and entered the bootlegging business, later turning to full-blown organized crime, shipping various forms of contraband. Robert Murphy's family remained in Saskatchewan. There, the Murphy's started a small crime empire. By the time Prohibition came into effect in the US, Murphy's son, Rory, had set up a distillery and was mass producing rum.

"By the time Stanford entered the game, Rory was already the head of a dangerous and powerful family. Through their mutual fatherly connections, the two men became business partners. Stanford grew jealous, as the Murphy family always seemed to be more successful."

Sam tilted his head. "A bitter feud erupted between the families?"

"Yes, but not only that, Stanford became obsessed with the buried Confederate gold and determined to beat Rory to it."

Sam took that in. "Stanford died years ago, and Rory must have, too. So who is your family still quarrelling with?"

"The head of the Murphy's family is now a woman named Rachel. Three weeks ago, she came to my father, certain that he knew where the gold was. The Murphy scion threatened to reveal everything about our family's dark past unless he handed over the location of Jack Holman's wreck."

"Why would she think your father would know that?"

"Because my grandfather, Stanford, murdered Jack Holman. Stanford knew that Holman worked for the Murphy's, and if he wanted to steal the operation running out of the Meskwaki Gold Spring, he would need to remove Holman from the equation. After sinking the aircraft into Dog Lake to hide the evidence, he realized that in doing so, he buried the only link to the Confederate treasury. To protect my father and myself—not to mention to end this century old feud—I set about trying to locate the damned treasure before Rachel Murphy reveals everything."

"How did your father attempt to deal with her?"

"By blackmailing her, of course. She has deep ties with a New York crime syndicate. My dad was a powerful, cunning man. Years earlier, he had assisted with the appointment of the New York District Attorney. The man owed him big time. My dad had him keep tabs on her illegal connection to organized crime, without ever arresting her for it."

"Your dad wanted full control."

"Right. So when he saw the note you brought up about Stanford stealing the Meskwaki Gold Spring, my father saw it as a threat that she was going to try and take over his business. He headed to New York to set things in motion, but she must have had him killed first."

Sam recalled the young, vivacious Senator who had replaced Senator Arthur Perry. She looked stunning. It was hard to imagine her being a brutal killer. "You know that Rachel Murphy was the Gubnatorial appointee to replace your father at the Minnesotan Senate?"

David took a deep breath. His face hardened, his eyes filled with defiance. "She's won everything—but won't stop there. As Senator, she now has the power to destroy me. I have to find that gold, before more lives are ruined."

CHAPTER FIFTY-ONE

CROSBY MUNICIPAL AIRPORT—NORTH DAKOTA

T HE SIX-SEAT, high-performance, single-engine, Cessna Centurion 210, took off on runway 30.

At the controls, Sam angled the aircraft for its maximum rate of climb, leveling out at five thousand feet, and setting a course due east. Despite being summer, the air was cold and dense, making the controls sharp and responsive. Next to him, Tom made notes and inserted coordinates into the search grid. In the rear two seats, Virginia and David stared out the windows, maintaining a visual vigil in case they happened to pass directly over the top of the remains of the Confederate ironclad.

The familiar hum of the aircraft's Continental engine and the low level sibilant whine of the breeze on the fuselage of the small plane filled Sam with the feeling of happiness and home that only three things could give him. Flying, sailing, and diving. He thought of David Perry and considered how perhaps they weren't so different in their tastes.

He looked over his shoulder, back at Tom and Virginia and felt grateful for his time in the military, and for all he had learned before he left the marines. He could see their toughness, mental calm, and physical agility and was glad to have them as his friends. He knew that the experiences and challenges they had faced together had shaped him as a person and was sure it was the same for them.

He could just as easily have lived in his father's shadow in the business world and had an easy life. David Perry did, and Sam considered how David seemed to hate his father for it, never having a good relationship. Sam Reilly was always his own man. For that, his father had admired and respected him.

"Where did you get this plane again?" Tom asked, leaning over.

"A friend of mine owns it," Sam answered as casually as he would if someone lent him their car to go to the local store.

"Really?" David asked, betraying a hint of incredulity. "And I thought my dad had rich connections. You just borrowed a friend's plane?"

"Ira runs an aerial survey business up here in North Dakota now," Sam said, as though that answered everything.

Virginia said, "You really don't have to play by the same rules as the rest of us, do you?" Her eyes turned toward David. "You don't count either, your family ran an organized crime syndicate for close to nine decades and everyone owes your father something."

David shrugged. It was a reasonable point, and there was no need to argue against it.

Sam set the trim, so that the aircraft naturally remained straight and level. It was the same way you set the sails on a yacht. His eyes glanced at Virginia over his shoulder. She had a mischievous grin on her face and shook her head at him.

"I met Ira down South after Katrina. He was flying sorties mapping hurricane damage for the Federal Emergency Management Agency, and I was running logistics for Homeland. We had a few beers together, found stuff in common. He said if I was ever up North to look him up."

"And this is his Cessna?" she asked.

"It's a Cessna Centurion, modified for survey. From here, I can scroll through the monitor to view digital video, LIDAR, infrared and gamma electromagnetic remote sensing and readouts for electromagnetic and gravity."

"It's already all systems go." Tom said, having already switched the machine on, recording both digital video and LIDAR.

"What's LIDAR?" Virginia asked Tom.

Tom leaned over his shoulder to talk to her. "It's like radar only it uses pulses of light instead. Radar uses radio waves, sonar uses sound waves, LIDAR uses light. It's used in cars with assisted braking and lane keeping tech, and for surveys. It's good for us because the structure of a boat in this environment will stand out on the light spectrum compared to the wilderness."

"Holman had to divert south around here for a squall for two hours, which was when he noted seeing the wreck of the ironclad," Sam said. "Elise has done the numbers, isolating an area of 500 square miles of uninhabited National Park, and there's not much there for anyone to visit. There are little estuaries that run off the river all over the place throughout, so there's plenty of places the ship could have ended up high and dry. Those river boats hardly drew anything, so it could be anywhere depending on the rainfall that year."

"Wouldn't someone have noticed it from the air since then?" Virginia asked. "Surely planes have been over here since the 1920s."

"I'm guessing it must not be visible from the air anymore, but the LIDAR will penetrate the foliage of trees and give us a better chance of finding anything," Sam answered.

"I'm setting a standard north-south grid trawl plan for us on the GPS," Tom said.

"Got it," said Sam, finding and switching on the display unit. He dialed up the brightness.

Tom said, "Its gyro mounted to adjust for speed, pitch, and yaw so just stick on the yellow line."

"Understood," said Sam.

Tom scrolled through the specifications screen on the monitor in front of him. "It's got an inertial measurement unit built in, which will talk to the data recorder and give us exact latitude and longitude of anything we find. Your friend's old Cessna has a few tricks up its sleeve!"

"Like I said, Ira's a good guy. And I figure if Homeland Security contracts this little plane, I'm sure it will be good enough to find a lost boat in the woods."

After three hours, they had covered the designated search area. The LIDAR had produced a couple of log cabins, and a disused ranger's station that looked to have been mostly burned down in a forest fire at some point, but no boat.

"We've got about an hour's fuel left Tom, what do you think?" Sam asked

"I think Elise had to be wrong about something eventually, who knew?" Tom answered with a broad smile, unperturbed as always.

"I think we can short-cut back from here if we take a north-east heading around that knot of hills down there."

"Copy that," Tom nodded. "I'll look back over the footage and make sure I didn't miss anything."

Sam rolled the Cessna in a wide turn and set a new course on a bearing just outside of the designated search zone. The four rode in silence, wondering what they would do next.

It was at that exact moment the LIDAR sensor blipped.

"Oh man!" Tom shouted. "Have a look at this!"

Sam's eyes darted toward the LIDAR display monitor. An unmistakable shape of a pyramid stood atop the hull of a large ship. The image could have been of anything, but Sam was as certain he'd found the CSS Mississippi than as he would be if the LIDAR screen had located its nameplate.

A grin reached his lips. "Well done, everyone. We're about to get to the bottom of a hundred and sixty-year-old mystery."

Tom dropped an electronic pin on the map readout from the scanner, and checked the GPS reading on his watch to verify the coordinates—writing them down. The four occupants of the plane eagerly craned out the port side window of the tiny aircraft. Each tried to visualize what the wing-mounted sensor had picked up, but all they could see was the verdant green foliage of the thick woods below.

"Got it marked?" Sam asked, his face beaming with delight at his friend.

Tom matched his grin. "You bet."

Sam searched the map, locating a level meadow about three miles to the west. "I'm going to try to put us down in a relatively flat field to the west of here. Who's ready to go for a hike?"

CHAPTER FIFTY-TWO

THE ONLY AVAILABLE landing site turned out to be closer to a five-mile trek from the suspected shipwreck. Sam studied his hand-held GPS and plotted a course. There was no vehicle access anywhere nearby, and it turned out to be roughly a two-hour hike to reach.

Sam, Tom, Virginia and David made the trip on foot, slogging down thickly wooded, low hills, which they followed to a large flatland with densely forested marshes. The trio's desert boots sunk into the swampy ground, and the foliage became nearly impenetrable the closer they got to the final resting place of the ship. They were pushing through virgin scrub with no sign of mankind anywhere to be seen.

Insects bit them and buzzed in their ears. It was midsummer, and they were feeling every degree of the hot and humid wetlands. Their progress was reduced by trying to slog over the soft, uneven terrain. The stilled air was thick with birdcalls of ducks and water-fowl.

Sam wished they'd come closer and eat all the bugs that were attacking him.

"I still can't believe Elise was finally wrong about something!" Tom said as he held up a branch for the rest of them to clamber under.

"Well, she wasn't off by much" Sam replied. "She probably couldn't find any accurate estimates of what the prairie potholes did that year."

"Prairie potholes?" Tom asked.

"What we're in. They're the areas of low lying land across the northern states cut by glaciers ten thousand years ago. The glaciers scarred the land and left potholes known as kettles that hold water in the springtime each year. They support most of the agriculture up here—-in some places farmers rely entirely on them. The thing is though, between winter snowmelts, river estuaries and annual rainfall differences, who can say where water collected from year to year?"

It took nearly two hours before they reached the base of a small ravine. The climb up the canyon was a hundred feet of loose rocks and soft, earth-sliding hell.

Reaching the crest first, Virginia turned around and shouted, "Didn't you say the CSS *Mississippi* was an ironclad?"

Sam felt doubt rise like bile in his throat. "Yeah, why?"

"I hate to say this, but I think we've found the wrong shipwreck."

"What are you talking about?" Sam asked.

He immediately picked up his pace to the peak, until he could clearly see down into the gorge below. Sam kicked an innocent bush, cursing in a low, muffled voice. Right there below him, was a dilapidating paddle steamer from 150 years ago...

CHAPTER FIFTY-THREE

S AM RAN HIS eyes across the old paddle steamer. To the right of him, Tom shook his head with a combination of amusement, disappointment, and astonishment. "Well, would you look at that?" Tom's booming laughter filled the air.

"Yeah, I'm looking." Sam growled.

A paddle steamer? Really?

The damned thing looked like it belonged popped right out of an old western movie. Sam half expected the sound of an antique player piano to start playing honkytonk, envisioning a few cowboys sitting around a table with a deck of cards, reeking of tobacco and strong whiskey. The ship had three decks layered like a birthday cake. In ascending order from water level: he noted what constituted the main deck, the boiler deck, and the hurricane.

A series of old boxes lined the main deck where freight had once been stored. The boiler deck looked like it contained the cabins. The pilothouse jutted from the hurricane deck, in what Sam recalled the old-timers refer to as the Texas.

Twin smoke stacks rose amidships; once they carried sparks away from the ship's powerful boilers. Like other steamboats of its era, it had been painted white, with a red stern paddle wheel. The paint had faded, and in most places, had been stripped by the sun. Otherwise, it looked like it belonged in a museum of a bygone period of the far west Missouri River.

A small forest of Hybrid Polar, American Elm, and Flowering Dogwood trees surrounded the vessel as though by purpose, creating a canopy through which the paddle steamer had been hidden for probably some 150 or more years. A few Eastern Redbud's, still in full blossom, were growing from within the ship.

David stumbled to the top, bent over to catch his breath. "What's the problem?" he asked.

"We found the wrong shipwreck."

"Shit."

"That's what I said." Virginia turned toward Sam. "Now what?"

Just down in this gorge lay the unexplored remains of a ship. Good humor abruptly restored, Sam and Tom glanced at each other, excitement in their eyes. Together, they both replied, "Let's go check it out!"

"Have you two forgotten that we're on the clock here? If we don't find that gold, a lot of good people are going to die." David turned to Virginia. "You told me that we've got four days to find the Confederate treasury if you want your dad back alive."

"I know," Sam said. "But it won't take long to reach the paddle steamer and find out how it got here. Maybe the captain's left his pilot logbook."

"What difference is that going to make?" David asked.

"Look around you. The Missouri River is miles and miles away. There are no tributaries anywhere near here."

"So?"

"If the steamboat managed to be blown here, where it's remained all this time, there's a good chance the ironclad might be nearby, too."

David nodded, as though he were mentally considering the logic of that. Then, reluctantly, he replied, "All right. But let's make it quick. If we're not in the right place, I want to get back to the aircraft. There might be still time to refuel and make another run before nightfall."

"Agreed."

Sam led the group down the shallow ravine into the flat field. The sky darkened beneath the canopy of thick vegetation. The ground was soft, a silty mixture of sand and gravel. He made his way through the forest toward the portside of the ship. Surrounding the hull was a six-foot skirt of dilapidated iron, slanted outward at thirty degrees.

He grasped the side of it to see if he could climb up, but the rusty metal broke free, crumbling away in his hand. With a bit of time they could probably hammer through a chunk to climb up, but the thicker main section was unrelenting.

"What is this stuff?" Virginia asked.

"No idea," Sam replied, breaking another section off in an attempt to climb. "Maybe they used it as a defensive barrier to protect the ship from various rocky shoals along the sections of rapids spread throughout the unmapped river?"

"That's not its purpose," David said, with defiant certainty.

Tom smiled. "Go on. Enlighten us, what was it used for?"

"It's obvious," David said, matter-of-factly. "They were used for defense. You have to remember this paddle steamer sailed in a time when only the bravest adventurers would travel the Upper Missouri River. Fur traders, trappers, and gold prospectors. It probably dates back before the Great Sioux War of 1876."

Sam grinned. "Of course. Attack from Sioux Indians would have been a real threat. One of the few means of defense to a riverboat captain at the time would have been to stay in the deep water of the middle of the river, and make sure none of the attackers could climb up on board." To David, he said, "Good thinking. Come on, we'll head to the stern-wheel and see if we can climb up from there."

He followed the starboard side of the hull, walking all the way around, to the stern-wheel.

Once there, he turned to face the rest of the group, a broad grin plastered across his face. "Can you believe it? We've been wrong about *everything* all this time."

David stared, his eyes wide and his mouth open. "I don't believe it!"

Breathing fast with excitement, Sam felt his heart hammering in his throat.

For just behind the paddle-wheel, he saw two eight-foot bronze propeller screws.

CHAPTER FIFTY-FOUR

S AM CLIMBED THE false stern-wheel up to the main deck. Virginia, Tom, and David followed immediately afterward.

"So now we know the truth," Sam said, his eyes raking the ship with a new light.

David touched the side wall. It was made of cheap wood and crumbled in his hand. "This is why there were never any local reports of having seen an ironclad once steam up past this section of the river. They must have stopped somewhere earlier on one of the rivers, even as far back as the Mississippi. There they erected a cheap, wooden façade."

"It wasn't all that uncommon during the Civil War," Sam said, shaking his head. "We should have considered that."

"Really?" Virginia asked.

"Sure. There were a number of carpenters and shipbuilders along the Mississippi in the early 1860s who could apparently construct a disguise like this. That was the point, to change the shape and appearance of anything from a barge to a battleship."

Virginia stroked an old railing, her full lips curled with curiosity. "Whatever for?"

"Mostly for defense to scare away invading ships."

"With cardboard-like cutouts?"

"Yes." Sam took pleasure in seeing her astonishment. "There

are even reports of farmers transforming barges into ironclad battleships to chase away attacking Union warships."

Virginia studied what she could see of the ship. "And these men transformed an ironclad into a paddle steamer."

"Come on," Sam said. "Let's see if we can find the logbook."

It took them five minutes to walk a full circuit around the perimeter of the mighty warship come paddle-wheeler.

Once inside her outer façade, it became easy to see the ship's original purpose.

Even though the hull was rusted through in several sections, she was still a grotesque and powerful monument to the brutality of the era that spawned her. The whole design reeked of death. Every surface was engineered to withstand attack, and issue destruction.

The main turret stood proudly on the deck with the rusted remains of the smoothbore cannon still jutting from its fore-most side. They could see where the hull had been smashed by cannon shot in several places, and the thick armor that had survived the rust still bore the deep dents from solid shot strikes sustained during battle.

The outer holds below deck had been compromised by decay, but the main structure of the ghastly ship was intact due to the sheer thickness of the armor plating. It took several smashing blows from Tom's lump hammer to break the rusted seal on the main hatchway before the trio could gain access to the internal ship.

Climbing below decks the atmosphere was stifling. Eerily quiet, it felt entirely undisturbed. They all knew immediately that nobody had set foot in this ship since its original occupants left all those years ago. A tingle of excitement ran through Sam. He glanced at Tom, wide-eyed and eager. He looked like a child in a candy store who found a fifty-dollar bill, and now needed to decide what to spend it on.

Sam knew exactly how he felt.

They worked their way forward, through the boiler room and upstairs to the wheelhouse. The ship was littered with the remnants from the sailors. It was a time capsule to the civil war. A treasure-trove for a collector. Sam and Tom however, were of one mind. They sought the contents of the keep-safe on the bridge.

The bridge was badly damaged from a canon-strike, which had rent the iron skin from the frame in one corner. This had opened that part of the ship to the elements, and as a result most of the wheelhouse was rusted and rotted away. On his hands and knees, Sam instinctively dug down into the silt, which now lay where the bridge floor would have sat. He scooped up handfuls of thick, heavy dirt and methodically tossed each handful aside.

It must be here.

Without a word Tom shoved down beside his friend in the cramped space, and shoulder-to-shoulder they dug. After about five minutes they were rewarded when Sam dusted the dirt off the waterproof-wrapped parcel. He smiled broadly as the oilskin literally fell away in his hands, revealing the embossed leather cover: *C.S.S MISSISSIPPI CAPTAINS LOG – REGISTRY OF PRISONERS.*

CHAPTER FIFTY-FIVE

S AM RAN HIS eyes across the nearly 160-year-old document.
The first few sections included detailed ship movement
reports, including weather and any maintenance issues. He
skimmed through the document quickly, until the date May 17,
1863. There the captain had made a note about a series of
prisoners, mostly deserters, who had been picked up at Natchez,
Mississippi, and were being transferred to Vicksburg to hang.

This was nothing unusual at the time, Sam mused. Deserters
would hang at cities soon to be under siege, as a means of
deterring other would-be deserters.

What he did find interesting was the note regarding the last
prisoner, a Mr. William Chestnut. It noted that Chestnut was
previously ranked simply as a Major. There was no information
regarding his Service Branch, which ordinarily would have been
one of five areas: infantry, cavalry, artillery, engineers, or
ordinance. Instead, there was a single, handwritten scrawl,
underlined by the captain: This man is extremely dangerous. He
is highly intelligent. Deceptive. Manipulative. Not to be allowed
speech with anyone.

Sam felt his heart race and his chest tighten as he flicked
through to the prisoner register. The apple rarely falls far from
the tree. Were all members of Perry's family line cunning,
duplicitous, and dangerous?

He placed his finger along the list of names, running down

each until he reached the arrest document beneath the name of William Chestnut. While Virginia, Tom, and David continued searching the rest of the ship for any sign of the treasure, Sam read the full report.

Regarding prisoner William Chestnut–

Prior to the war, Major William Chestnut was a wealthy tobacco landowner and a well-respected shipping engineer with contracts from New York through to New Orleans. He was approached, personally, by President Jefferson Davis in 1861 for his assistance as a spy, due to his unique, wide-spanning network of engineering connections spread throughout the Union. For twelve months, it is believed he served his duty in this admirably, feeding the Confederacy useful information.

Something happened in 62 and William Chestnut changed his allegiance, becoming a double agent, working tirelessly to produce a secret list of wealthy Southern landowners and senior soldiers who could be enticed to consolidate into the Union on assurances that no financial or physical repudiation would occur.

By the time he was captured it is believed that he had secured enough powerful signatures to end the Confederacy. This Covenant has not yet been located, but as of this moment, it is considered the most dangerous document ever written. If it's allowed to reach Washington, it will spell the end of the Confederate States of America.

William Chestnut is intelligent, dangerous, and manipulative. I hereby sentence him to hang at Vicksburg, without delay.

It was then signed by the Senator of Texas, *William Simpson Oldham.*

Sam secured the leather binder and quickly tucked it in his backpack.

I wonder why David Perry never mentioned anything about a Covenant?

CHAPTER FIFTY-SIX

S AM SAT DOWN and ran his fingers across his forehead and through his hair. Fascinating as the ship was, there was nothing else of value discovered on board the *CSS Mississippi*. That she held historical interest was not in doubt. Yet for assisting his group to locate the treasure? Not so much.

Temporarily stumped, he unfolded the map David photocopied of the Confederate Treasury. On a digital tablet he opened up a Geographic Information System, which utilized both satellite images and detailed topographical maps, to view geological, forestry, and topographical information of their surrounding area.

He placed the photocopied map beside the digital topographical map. Then, he studied the two images.

The hand drawn map gave no reference to distance or direction. Whether it was designed like that because its maker was far from a cartographer, or because William Chestnut intended it that way so only he could make sense of it, Sam didn't know.

At its center was an unnamed boat—presumably the *CSS Mississippi*. From there, the path led across two small creeks to a large river that split into two. At the fork, a large anvil had been drawn and next to that, a pickaxe and a shovel. His guess was that the anvil indicated some sort of topographical or geological structure that could be used as a point of reference. As for the pickaxe and shovel, perhaps they signified a mine shaft, at the end of which, he hoped to find Confederate gold buried.

Sam glanced at the digital topographical map. There were no creeks nearby and only one large river nearly four miles away. He switched the digital version to geological formations. It depicted depth of the ground in different colors. Similar to a three-dimensional bathymetric map of the ocean floor, this portrayed the deeper depths in a color spectrum, ranging from blues to red, with blue the deepest and red the highest points.

Sam brightened, as suddenly the map looked very much like the one William Chestnut had drawn.

Two otherwise barely noticeable indents on the maps in light blue, indicated the shallow creeks from Chestnut's 1863 journey. Closer to the mine shaft, in which the Confederate treasure was supposed to have been buried, he spotted two deep ravines, indicating there had once been a conflux of two decent sized rivers.

"That's definitely our place," Sam said.

"Well done," David said. "I knew there would be a reason my father hired you. You're damned good. Thank you."

Sam smiled, modestly. "I haven't found the gold yet."

"You will though, you will!"

Standing on the ironclad's deck, Sam set a marker on his hand-held GPS. The last thing he wanted was to lose a ship that could prove to be responsible for some of the major historical events within the Civil War.

Tom turned up, dirty and ruffled. "Look what I found," he said with a grin. In his hands he was carrying an old revolver. "It's a Walch Navy 12 Shot Revolver. Walch only ever released 200 of the revolvers, and its design never really took off, but it was a remarkable bit of engineering for its age."

Sam made a thin-lipped smile. "Was it really?"

"Yes! It was a cap and ball revolver, with six-cylinder chambers, two hammers, two triggers and fires twelve shots!"

Tom's hazel eyes were wide with excitement. "Can I keep it?"

"It's yours," Sam said. "You'd better pack it up, we're leaving."

Afterward, he, Tom, Virginia, and David started their long trek east. The trail on the map headed due east from the ship, and continued until it reached the western shore of the main river. They were following the lay of the land as it descended gently down what would have been a watercourse. In the past, it may have been the kettle which had trapped the ironclad.

Half a mile out, Sam could hear the river — not the flow, but the chatter of birds by the thousand. The hikers broke through a thicket of dense trees. The moment they did, a cloud of waterfowl burst into the air from the bank nearest them.

From there, the crew followed the river north for about half a mile until the river forked in two, splitting along the base of two valleys. On the map, the image of an anvil was marked on the tip of the spur that separated the watercourses.

Standing on the western shore of the river, they stood staring at the landscape, waiting to make sense of the image on the map.

It was Virginia who saw it first, pointing north. "There!"

Sam followed her indication to a black igneous rock that sat just above the waterline and appeared oddly out of place. The sedimentary rocks around it had been eroded by the river over thousands of years, but the jet-black lump of hard stone had stood almost impervious — only ever being polished by the river's passing flow. The rock was shaped like a giant anvil, tall and proud, extending below the surface of the water.

"So according to Chestnut's map, the entrance to the mineshaft should be exactly where we are. I don't get it, everything lines up perfectly, the rock, the rivers," Virginia said. "The map shows the tunnel entrance right here, but there's nothing. Anyone got any ideas?"

Sam pulled out his tablet and started to zoom in on an image using the touch-screen. He looked at a topographical map of the region that Elise had found him after they checked in the exact location of the wreck.

Sam examined the map for a minute, glanced up at the rock formations, and then pointed to the side of the valley. "Assuming William Chestnut and Robert Murphy had some idea about how to draw a map, I'd say right there."

Virginia shrugged. "Okay mister treasure hunter, you got me, I can't see a mineshaft entrance. There is nothing there."

"Well, you wouldn't," Sam replied.

"Why not?" Virginia's eyes focused on the valley's wall. Sandstone and quartz lined the edge of the river and there were only a few trees nearby. "Where? I don't see anything."

Sam grinned. "That's because the entrance is about thirty feet below us."

David met Sam's wild declaration with incredulity. "Below us?"

Sam nodded. "Yes. I assumed you knew. This river was dammed in the early 1930s as part of Franklin D. Roosevelt's Public Works Administration Deal. Created by the National Industrial Recovery Act in June 1933 in response to the Great Depression, most of North Dakota started to dam its major rivers for irrigation and, in this case, raising the river's height by thirty-five feet."

"You said it was only thirty feet below us?" Virginia pointed out.

"Sure, but I checked. After a series of unusual weather events, the dam's reported water level is five feet lower than average for this time of year."

"All right. So that's great, really great. It's thirty feet down. Now how are we going to retrieve the treasure?"

"Simple. We simply need to dive for it."

CHAPTER FIFTY-SEVEN

I T WASN'T UNTIL the following morning that the four of them managed to fly into Minot in North Dakota and hire all the diving equipment required to retrieve the Confederate gold. The Cessna Centurion was replaced with David's de Havilland DHC Sea Otter. In doing so, they were able to now land on the dammed river, where the Confederate treasure was supposed to have been hidden.

All told, it was nearly midday by the time the DHC Otter had gracefully skimmed the slow-moving water, taxied to the beach, and was anchored along the dark bank of the river.

Sam surveyed the area. The sky was a pale, washed out blue, with a few puffy white clouds. A cold, northerly breeze was enough to make the river ripple. Once this entire area had run with cooling molten magma, creating the common extrusive igneous rock — basalt. Over time, silt and clay were compacted into sedimentary rock. Today the riverbank was comprised of hard granite, basalt, and lose black shale.

On shore, Sam, Tom and David donned their dry suits and dive gear, while Virginia began laying out the ropes, pulleys, and inflatable lift bags that would most likely be required to bring up the treasure chest. They were using a set of standard air tanks fitted to SCUBA equipment and a single pony bottle containing a small amount of oxygen for emergencies. There would be no need for the larger, and more complicated rebreather systems, because the depth was shallow. Submersion times would be kept comfortably short.

Frowning with concern, Virginia gave Sam a thin-lipped smile. "You're going to do this, aren't you?"

He squeezed her hand affectionately. "I told you we'd find it and we'd get your father back. We still have three days to retrieve the gold and to make a deal."

She squeezed his hand back. "Thank you."

"You're welcome," Sam said with a carefree boyish grin. Nodding to Tom and David, he put his dive regulator into his mouth, shuffled off the ledge of the rocky shore to the river, and into the icy waters below.

Sam gently released air from his buoyancy control device until he started to sink. He followed the natural slope of the bank, with Tom and David following right behind. Bright crepuscular rays penetrated the crystal-clear waters all the way to the bottom of the river nearly seventy feet below. He swallowed, allowing his ears to equalize as he descended.

Sam checked his depth gauge.

It read: 35 feet. A couple feet above one atmosphere.

He turned to face the river bank. With the visibility excellent, he had a good 270-degree view of the surrounding submerged slopes, but no sign of any entrance to a mine. For a moment he worried that the entire mine had been flooded with silt. It was a possibility, but he hoped the dark shale and quartz which lined the slope would have prevented that.

Sam turned to Tom, his palms raised in a confused gesture.

Tom shrugged. It wouldn't be the first time something wasn't where they'd expected it to be.

On his dive slate, Sam wrote: LET'S SPLIT UP. SEARCH NORTH AND SOUTH.

David shook his head. Wiped the slate clean and wrote: NO. WE STICK TOGETHER!

Sam nodded. He gathered that David had been crossed by his family so many times before that he would never truly trust anyone. That suited Sam fine. They could stick together. Three pairs of eyes instead of one, would have a good chance of finding the opening if it was still down there.

He swam north along the sloping bank of the river at a depth of thirty feet. After swimming nearly two hundred feet, Sam turned around. They three divers returned to the starting point and then headed south until they reached the fork where the river split into two. Keeping the bank to their left, Sam continued round the point, heading up the second river.

Thirty feet past this point, he spotted what they were after.

An eddy swirled in front of them—marking the entrance to the abandoned mineshaft. As expected, it was partially buried in silt, rock, and river debris. A series of jet-black shale lined the entrance, blocking two thirds of the tunnel. Rotten railway sleepers that had once formed the framework for the mine's adit had collapsed.

Sam switched on his flashlight and shined it inside.

The beam shot through the still water, to the shelf of a dark basalt boulder. A pair of wooden slats ran along the ground in the shape of a narrow-gauge mine rail. In its original form, gold is found in igneous volcanic hydrothermal veins where it is deposited along with quartz, amethyst, and other metal ores.

Several feet within, an old wooden mine wagon leaned on its left side, where a pile of quartz fell from its bucket. Sam guessed the original prospector who mined the shaft had used the cart, because it had been too difficult to bring metal rails to the rugged, Sioux occupied land.

Tom studied the adit's rotten framework.

Sam pointed to his dive slate, which read: WHAT DO YOU THINK?

Tom wiped the slate and replied: IT'S LOOSE, BUT I'M GAME.

Sam handed the slate to David, who simply nodded that he was keen to keep going. It would be dangerous, but it wasn't like any of them had much of a choice.

They needed to retrieve the Confederate treasury.

Lives depended on their success.

Tom and David switched on their headlights and hand flashlights. The remaining portion of the opening still clear was roughly three feet wide by two and a half high. It was going to be tight—especially for Tom—but the dimensions made the opening navigable.

To make it easier, Sam unclipped and removed his single air tank and fed it through first, before effortlessly swimming through the gap.

About ten feet inside, the tunnel opened up to a horizontal antechamber. Here the shaft was closer to four feet wide and five feet high. Small, but large enough to dive without fear of being unable to turn around if needed. Sam reattached his dive tank and waited for Tom and David to swim through.

When they were ready, he continued deeper into the shaft.

It ran approximately a hundred feet in a horizontal line. At the end of which, it took a ninety degree turn—straight down. Above them, a huge hardwood beam was still dug deeply into the sides of the tunnel to form a gantry from which objects were once craned down in the past.

Sam flashed his light down the vertical shaft.

It reached the bottom some twenty feet below. The width was fine to swim through, but it didn't leave sufficient space. Anyone swimming forward couldn't abruptly change direction. They would be forced to swim backwards.

Sam didn't need to explain that to Tom or David, who both realized the problem the second they glanced into the narrow, confining space.

Sam removed his dive cable, running it over the old wooden beam and attaching the end to his dive belt with a carabiner. It ran off a spool that was thick enough to be used both as a guidewire and for lifting purposes. It wasn't ideal, but it was the only back up possible, given their space and time constraints.

Lips pressed tightly together, Tom gripped the opposite end of the guidewire and said nothing. Sam knew his friend would move hell and high water to ensure he could be dragged back out if he got stuck.

Without any further discussion, Sam started his descent headfirst down the vertical shaft into the darkness below.

The bottom of the narrow shaft opened into a small chamber. It was big enough for a single diver to turn around, but not much larger. Sam swept his flashlight in a gentle arc. The walls were scarred with multiple two to three feet gashes, where prospectors must have once tested various quartz seams for gold. To the north, a new tunnel headed in a downward slope, before breaking off into two more tunnels.

Sam swallowed hard. If the shaft went much deeper, they were going to need a lot more equipment. He was about to turn around to tell Tom and David just that, when he spotted a large pile of black shale lining a hole in the ground below. The jet-black shale was out of place, at geologic odds with the pink or white of quartz.

He emptied the last of the air from his buoyancy control device until he was significantly negatively buoyant, with his knees firm on the ground. Sam set his flashlight down on the side of the tunnel. Once light was shining on the pile of shale, he removed the first flat, stratified rock with his hands, followed by the second. They were loose, light and easy to remove. Within ten minutes, he'd cleared away most of the stones.

Beneath the remaining pieces of dark shale, a rich blue emanated, glistening like jewels under the beam of the flashlight. It encouraged him to work faster, clearing away the last of the stones.

Mouth dry with anticipation and excitement, Sam worked to keep his breathing slow and even. There, laying in a bed of sedimentary rock, was an honest to God, treasure chest.

A treasure chest! This was it. This was what they had come

all this way to find!

Heart pounding, Sam picked up the flashlight, focusing its beam on his discovery.

The strongbox was metal-bound, likely made of oak. Painted in a decorative blue, it had the Confederate seal stamped into a raised badge on top. A hinged clasp hung on the front with a finely crafted thick brass padlock through its eye and thick, ornate handle rails ran along each end.

Sam thought he had rarely seen anything as beautiful in his life.

CHAPTER FIFTY-EIGHT

D ISCOVERING THE STRONGBOX was just the beginning. The harder part of their task was now to retrieve the heavy object from within the narrow confines of the mine shaft. Returning to his friends with the good news, they surfaced together. There, they created an intricate series of dead man anchors, pulleys systems, and buoyancy devices. The largest pulley was connected to the structural joist above the first vertical shaft.

Sam made the last dive to the Confederate chest. He secured it using a cradle of nylon mesh, connecting each of the four ends with a single carabiner. To this, he attached the first of four lifting devices—shaped like miniature hot-air balloons—the bags were then filled with air from his secondary regulator octopus, the small plastic mouthpiece the diver uses to breath out of.

He depressed the release valve and a burst of air dispersed out of the regulator octopus, filling the first of his lifting balloons. He followed with a second balloon, and on the third, the treasure chest started to lift. It didn't race toward the ceiling of the mineshaft, but it broke free of its bed of rock where it had been housed for nearly 160 years.

Sam tugged on the lifting rope, and a moment later, the line started to move.

Once the strongbox was level with the horizontal tunnel, Sam unhooked the rope from the ceiling. His job was to manage the buoyancy of the lifting bags so that the Confederate chest could be maneuvered easily.

There was one tricky little problem. As the box began to ascend, the volume of air within the lifting bags would expand, eventually causing the entire thing to rocket to the surface.

To counteract this, the lift bags had an inbuilt bleeder system in place, which Sam could control to blow off excess air volume. Throughout this slow process, the lateral movement of the chest was controlled by the pulley system, into which Tom and David exerted their strength.

Each of them worked quickly, in a controlled and coordinated discipline that would have made Sam's drill Sergeant proud.

Within ten minutes the treasure reached the main horizontal tunnel. Sam could see the fine light from the opening of the old mine shaft. On Tom and David's faces, he could see the unique mixture of manifest relief, excitement, and exhilaration.

Sam adjusted the buoyancy, until the chest became neutral once more. Tom then returned to the surface, where Virginia had set up a heavy block and tackle on a truss between trees on the water's edge in readiness for the final lift. David, true to his original word, was determined to stay with the chest the entire time, in case someone tried to steal its contents.

The cradle for the treasure chest was then attached to the end of a final rope by a carabiner, which reached all the way to the surface.

Sam waited, and within a few minutes, the rope started to move.

He and David followed the chest slowly along the tunnel until they reached the narrow entrance. There, they gradually helped ease it downward to fit beneath the partially collapsed opening to the mine shaft.

It slipped through seamlessly.

Sam and David followed afterward, then, each holding it with both hands for stability—they ascended. The last thing they wanted now was for the old Confederate chest to slip out of the harness, sending the entire contents to spread throughout the bottom of the river.

To make matters more difficult, the current flowed in a constant southerly direction. Sam carefully further inflated one of the lifting bags until the load slowly surfaced.

Once there, he filled each of the bags to their full amount, making certain that the chest wouldn't accidentally sink. Sam and David held the side of the chest, while Tom and Virginia quickly hauled the heavy barge downstream to the western side of the river and up onto the bank.

Sam and David slowly climbed out of the river, each one removing their dive tanks and equipment. All four of them then dragged the heavy chest another seven or so feet up the bank, letting it come to rest in a bed of black shale. Water drained from the heavy box through a series of small rust fractures. They all stood around the treasure, staring in an exhausted sort of awe and triumph.

David started to laugh.

Sam looked up, gave him a wry smile. "What is it?"

"Nearly a hundred and sixty years ago my great ancestor buried this here. Since then, so many generations of Chestnuts and Murphy's have searched for this place with no luck! I can't believe we really did it."

Virginia grinned. "Yeah, we did."

Tom said, "Well, let's open this thing up and see what all the hype was about!"

Sam contemplated the heavy box in silence.

Though corroded in places, it was still a beautiful work of sturdy, practical craftsmanship. The blue paint was worn through, but the workmanship was clearly of a high standard for its day. It looked exactly like what Sam had imagined for a Civil War era treasure chest

The sides were cut together seamlessly and the only sign of

the copper lugs that were hidden on the joints was the paint corrosion that had resulted from the electrolysis in the water. The seal of the Confederate Army sat proudly raised on a mini dais on the lid of the chest, while decorative handrails ran along the sides.

A hook and clasp on the front were locked with a heavy brass padlock, which was green and black from its years submerged underwater.

The water finally ceased draining from inside.

A tingle of adrenaline in the base of Sam's spine and gooseflesh on his forearms reminded him of how excited he was at this moment. He watched as Tom moved to the pile of gear and ceremoniously handed him a brick chisel and his lump hammer. Sam lined up the chisel on the inside edge of the non-hinged side of the lock and raised his right hand with the lump hammer held tightly.

For effect at such a moment, he paused, and smiled widely at the team gathered around. Then he brought the hammer down a mighty blow, which instantly shattered the weathered lock into pieces.

Sam opened the heavy lid. All eyes fixed on the contents inside.

It was empty.

Not entirely empty, but not full of treasure — it had perhaps five large rocks in it. That was all.

"What the hell?" Tom growled.

Virginia made a high, feminine gasp — a cross between a scream and a sigh.

David kicked the box and began to swear volubly under his breath.

Sam felt his heart hammer in his throat with disappointment. Crouching down, he pulled out each rock. Under them was one item, a single octagonal glass mason jar with a locking latch and a cork seal inverted on the bottom — its heavy glass lid overcoming its natural buoyancy, and a single gold coin. The coin weighed down a hand-written note.

He picked it up, and ran his eyes across it.

Sorry, Chestnut. I beat you to it. Nothing personal, but gold talks and I never cared about the Covenant — R.M.

CHAPTER FIFTY-NINE

T HE HEAVINESS OF exhaustion sank Sam into the rocky bank by
the river as he sat down with Tom, Virginia, and David. He
laid back and looked up at the sky, exhaling deeply, searching
for inspiration.

Eventually, he stood up and strolled to the edge of the river.
There, he rinsed the single gold coin—the sole reward for their
efforts.

Wandering back to the others, he sat down to examine the
coin. Despite its age, the precious metal had lost none of its
luster. He didn't have latex gloves to protect the old coin from
the natural oils and salts on his hands. At this stage, he didn't
care. They'd lost everything anyway. It was never about the
gold or the money.

It was about finding the Senator's son and saving Virginia's
dad.

The head of the coin, also known as the obverse side, was that
of Jefferson Davis. Superimposed were the number 20, followed
by the word, dollars. A fine indent marred the top edge of the
coin with another name, one he hadn't heard of before, C.
Bechtker. At the base of the coin was the date it was minted,
1863. On the reverse side of the coin was an image of an ironclad
warship, followed by the Latin words, *Deo Vindice*—With God
as our Protector.

Sam turned the gold coin around in his hand, like a gambler

might play with a $5,000 high roller casino chip. A slight grin formed on his lips. "There's something I don't get about any of this."

Sitting cross legged, David said sullenly, "Like who stole our damned treasure?"

"No. We know it was R.M. That's Robert Murphy, right?" Sam turned to Virginia. "Or, Rachel Murphy, but I can't see her apologizing to William Chestnut."

"No. It has to be Robert Murphy," David agreed. His curiosity abruptly triggered, he asked, "So what don't you get?"

Sam said, "If Jack Holman retrieved this gold in 1930 or 31 with Robert Murphy, that would have made Murphy..."

"Nearly ninety years old!"

Sam smiled. "I don't suppose he lived that long?"

David shook his head. "No. He died in 1928."

Sam cocked an eyebrow. "So, who came here in 1931 and took the gold?"

"Couldn't Murphy have returned for the gold years earlier?" Tom suggested. "Anywhere since 1863, he could have conceivably made it back here with a small army of laborers and dug up the treasure."

Sam shook his head. "Not possible."

"Why not?" Tom asked.

"For starters, Robert Murphy didn't become rich until later in life, when his son, Rory, started to make it big in the bootlegging business producing rum in Saskatchewan and selling it to Al Capone in the 1920s," Sam said. "Secondly, there's still the matter of where Jack Holman found the gold."

"What gold?" David asked.

"A few days ago, we ran into a man named Yago. He told us he was the son of Jack Holman. He said his father had come to the Ontario wilderness to find gold. Turned out, somewhere out there, in the process of it, he started to work for Murphy. In doing odd jobs, he located the remains of the CSS *Mississippi* and later returned with a number of gold Confederate coins."

David interrupted. "How did you know Holman found gold coins, let alone the Confederate ones?"

Sam flicked the coin in between his fingers and smiled. "Because his son, Yago, described it exactly like this one."

"But that doesn't make any sense," David argued. "I mean, no pilot or anyone else who found the ironclad would have deduced that there was buried treasure a few miles away, hidden beneath an old prospectors mine."

"That means, Holman must have come here with Robert Murphy."

David shook his head. "Can't have. Murphy was long dead by the 1930s."

"Agreed," Sam admitted. "But what if Holman came here to fulfill Robert Murphy's life-long ambition, perhaps a pact he'd made with himself or someone else, to find the treasure."

"Sure." Tom, who had been stacking piles of slate to make his version of a castle with a moat, looked menacingly at the empty Confederate chest. "But that still doesn't answer where the gold coins got to. I mean, if Holman took it, or even Murphy, the coins would've turned up somewhere by now, but there's been no record of them surfacing anywhere."

"What are you suggesting?" David asked.

Tom sat up straight. "How do we know there was ever any gold in here?"

Sam handed him the gold coin. "This looks real to me."

Taking the precious metal, Tom ran his eyes across it, then burst into sudden, unexpected laughter. "No, it isn't. It's a forgery and a very good one."

"Whoa. What are you saying?" David asked, his nostrils flaring. "This entire thing our two families have been searching for has been some giant hoax dating back to the Civil War?"

"No. But how much do you know about Confederate coins?

Everyone knows the Confederacy printed paper money, but have you ever seen a Confederate gold coin?"

"Hey, you're right," Sam said. "I hadn't even thought of that."

"No. The gold coin's real." David was adamant. "I grew up hearing of the unimaginable wealth of gold Confederate coins from the *CSS Mississippi*. Why would my father make up such a story? More to the point, why would people be willing to kill for it?"

"Who knows?" Tom said. "All I know is that the Confederacy didn't mint any of their own coins."

Virginia looked up from Holman's journal which she was still industriously reading from start to finish. "I can answer that."

"Really?" Sam asked, surprised. "How?"

She shrugged. "I collected coins when I was a kid. Some of the most valuable coins were those few which were minted by the Confederacy."

"Such as?" Tom asked.

"In January of 1861, the Federal government produced about 330,000 silver coins." She sighed and then paused. "Technically, they were only 90 percent silver and 10 percent copper. Either way, they were termed silver half dollars at New Orleans. Of course, when Louisiana seceded, the state took over the mint and continued production, turning out about 124,000 of the coins."

"If they made 124,000 coins, wouldn't eBay and other online auction houses be full of the old Confederate minted coins?" Sam asked.

"No, because it's impossible to tell the difference." She put Holman's book down. "You see they used the original die — the metal block used to cast the blank coin — so their coins still read, *United States of America*. The Confederate Treasury Department then took over and minted another 963,000 United States half dollars. Coins of this period contained approximately the amount of metal equal to the face value of the coin and these Louisiana and Confederate-produced coins had the same amount of silver as the U.S. produced coins and were thus just as valuable. There is no way to determine if an individual coin was minted by the U.S., Louisiana, or the Confederacy as the same workers used the same die and machines and the coins had the same amount of silver."

Tom smiled. "Okay, so I was right, the Confederacy never minted any gold coins."

"Technically, you're still wrong," she said. "Louisiana and the Confederacy also minted United States $20 double eagle gold coins in New Orleans. The product runs for these coins was about 5,000 by the U.S., 9,750 by Louisiana, and 2991 by the Confederacy. The South also minted approximately 10,000 United States gold $1 and $5 coins at Charlotte and Dahlonega before running out of stock and closing down these two operations."

"Sure, but those were still, fundamentally U.S. coins." Tom turned the gold coin over in his hand. "This has a clear depiction of Jefferson Davis's face, and an ironclad with a Confederate motto. How do you explain that?"

"The Confederate States, as an independent nation, wanted to produce their own coins, not just copy U.S. coins. My guess is these gold coins were privately minted for the Confederate States of America."

Sam asked, "Any way we could find out who that was?"

Virginia made a thin-lipped smile. "Who minted this batch of coins, you mean?"

"Yeah."

"Normally during that period, the name of the goldsmith would be imprinted on the coin, as a means of confirming its authenticity. A good craftsman earned his reputation by ensuring the specified amount of gold or silver to any other metal was found in the coin. What's the name on the coin?"

Sam said, "C. Bechtker."

"I've heard of Bechtker. He was a German-born industrialist from Carolina named Christopher Bechtker and produced gold coins from the first private mint in 1830. But he couldn't have minted this."

"Really? Why not?"

Virginia said, "Because Christopher Bechtker died in 1843. Some of his coins have fetched hundreds of thousands of dollars in today's markets."

Tom said, "So that proves it. This is a fake."

Virginia nodded. "I guess so. Albeit a very good one."

"No, it doesn't," Sam said, putting away his satellite smartphone after making a quick internet search. "The C doesn't refer to Christopher. It refers to his son, Charles, who had learned the family trade. As such, he'd been commissioned in secret to mint a particular batch of gold coins for the Confederacy."

"That makes more sense," Virginia said, returning to leafing through Jack Holman's journal. "But it still doesn't answer my question. If the Confederate treasure was real, where did it all go?"

CHAPTER SIXTY

Virginia continued to study Jack Holman's journal, while Sam contacted Elise to get her to do a search of Murphy and Holman's finances at their death, in the off chance they could pick up the otherwise cold trail to the treasure. Tom and David got a nice fire crackling. As it burned to lower embers, they began heating up ration packs for lunch.

There was something hidden in the journal. Like a sixth sense, Virginia felt certain of it, but so far, she just couldn't find anything to back up her gut feeling.

She turned another page. Sam had spoken about Holman's son telling stories about his dad getting drunk and showing off gold Confederate coins, but that could have simply been the imaginings of a young child. Still, there was more to it. She felt certain that Holman hadn't just spotted the pyramid-shaped casement of the *CSS Mississippi*.

He'd been inside and found the treasure.

His journal would prove it, she was certain.

"What do you expect to find in there?" David asked, bitterly. "Jack Holman didn't know anything about the gold. His relationship to this entire thing was that he spotted what he thought to be a pyramid in the middle of nowhere out from North Dakota."

"I've no idea, but it's the only lead I have right now, so I'm going to keep searching for it."

David shrugged. "Suit yourself."

Virginia flicked another page, looked at the date, and stopped. She went back a couple pages, and then skimmed forward. There was something wrong with the dating sequence. At first, she thought she'd made a mistake, turning the pages out of sequence, but now realized it wasn't her fault. Dates were all over the place. Events that happen on one day would be repeated several years later and vice versa. Three or four dates would follow a natural sequence of events, before fluctuating to a period sometimes years earlier.

How can that possibly be?

No one makes that sort of blunder. It was almost like a form of dyslexia, where the author of the journal had ended up writing the dates in a jumbled, disordered mess. It was hard to believe. Much more likely, Holman had intentionally made the anomalies.

But why?

The answer hit her like a heavy rock to the chest.

To protect the Confederate treasure if his journal should be discovered.

It was a simple code. Dates appeared as though they had been randomly placed, but there was a purpose hidden within. Regarding the year, the first two digits always remained unchanged—19—whereas the second two would fluctuate between 10–31.

Looking at just the year column in regards to dates in the journal, it appeared Holman had given each entry a year date entirely at random. Likewise, pairing the day and month appeared entirely random. It was only when the two were compared with each other, that Virginia started to see a sequence.

Her heart hammered as her eyes scanned the next page to confirm her theory. She had an analytical mind that naturally computed complex algorithms quickly. In this case, something simply didn't look right, until she'd stared at it long enough, for the code to reach the surface.

She was right.

Most of the journal was filled with trivial information, in which to bury the code. For example, on two pages, the month on the first page would be subtracted by the month on the second page, to achieve the actual month the event took place on the third page.

The same algorithm was applied to the day and year.

She tried it on an event that she already knew about and after applying the formula the date came to 12/5/1925 – the year Jack Holman won the Schneider Cup with his experimental Seaplane.

Her heart raced.

She flicked back to the page she'd marked earlier with dogears, where Holman discussed seeing a pyramid through the trees near North Dakota. The corrected year for 1931 became 1922. Six years before Robert Murphy died.

David shifted. "I'm going to get some more firewood."

"You want us to come?" Tom asked.

"Nah. You're all right. I don't need to collect much," David said as he pushed to his feet. "I just thought we might as well be comfortable while we have lunch."

Virginia continued to read. Some entries referred to routine flights, abnormal weather, important events coming up. Nothing that referred to the ironclad.

Virginia skimmed the barely legible writing that she recognized as Holman's scrawl. She turned to the previous page. The handwriting was similar, but not the same. She flicked over another four to five pages. There was no doubt about it.

Someone else regularly joined him on his flights.

Virginia quickly turned the pages back to the section describing the sighting of the ironclad. The notes were written as though by Holman, but it wasn't his handwriting. The revelation was startling as it was irrefutable.

Holman wasn't alone when he spotted the ironclad!

She folded a couple dogears into the paper, feeling a familiar twinge of guilt. Mrs. Brand, her fourth grade English teacher would have put her in the corner during recess for the abuse of the book, much less an old document like this one.

Frowning with concentration, she continued to scan more of the pages. If Holman wasn't alone when he spotted the ironclad, the real question remained, who was?

Sam interrupted her thoughts. "Food's ready, Virginia."

"Thanks. I'll just be a minute."

She continued to skim, confident she was onto something, but unwilling to mention it to anyone else until she was certain. It took several pages before she found what she was looking for.

There was a story regarding a car, an old rumrunner from the 1920s. She read the notes, and turned the page, where a black and white drawing of the car was still visible. There notes referring to the car's make and model appeared blotched and unreadable, but next to them were some other information that might help her identify the car. Color: burgundy. Year of manufacture: 1927. And a lot of technical gibberish that would only interest car lovers.

Virginia beamed a wide grin.

Sam took a seat next to her, still holding his pony-bottle of oxygen. The regulator seemed to have seized on the bottle and he was having trouble separating the two for the flight out. "What's so interesting?"

"This," she handed him the drawing of the car. "Any idea what sort of car that is?"

"That's a Model A Ford Tudor." Sam matched her smile, his lips setting deep creases in his cheeks. "What about it?"

She whispered, still afraid to jump to the wrong conclusion. "There's a chance this car still holds the Confederate gold."

"Really? That's what you think?"

"No. That's what Holman thought."

Sam asked, "And how did Holman work out the gold was hidden inside Murphy's car?"

Virginia answered, "He'd searched and ruled out every other location, but then he'd recalled that Robert Murphy loved his car more than any other possession. Murphy had even joked on multiple occasions, and I quote: 'within my car, is all that my heart has ever desired.'"

"But surely someone would have found the gold by now? It's not like the driver wouldn't notice the additional weight, is it?" Tom asked.

Virginia scanned the specific lines referring to the design of the Ford Tudor. "It was originally specifically built with double leafed springs, to take the additional weight of the contraband rum. There was a secret compartment built beneath the false floorpan, filled with lead weights to reduce the vehicles center of gravity. This improved maneuverability in the event of a police chase."

Sam's eyes widened, and his intense blue eyes lit up like sapphires in the sun. "Robert Murphy switched the lead for the gold. Anyone who knew the car would have instantly assumed the heavy weight was from the lead, never guessing it had anything to do with the gold of a nation."

Tom whistled. "Find the car and you find the gold."

"Find what car?" David asked, dropping the wood by the fire, suddenly interested in their conversation.

Virginia said, "A Burgundy 1927 Ford Tudor, heavily modified to make it fast and agile, as a rumrunner during the bootlegging era."

"Hey, my dad owns one of those. My grandfather bought it back in the 1930s."

"You're kidding. What color was it?"

"Burgandy. A 1927 Model A Ford Tudor," David said without hesitation.

"Certain about the year?" she questioned him.

"Yes. Of course, I'm certain about the year. It was a new model. Ford changed from the last run of the Model T in 1926 to the brand-new Model A in 1927."

"Where did your granddad buy it?"

"What's with the twenty questions?" David asked, curtly.

"It's important. It has to do with the Confederate gold."

David raised a cynical eyebrow. "Okay. Apparently, the car was Robert Murphy's pride and joy. Stanford liked the concept of owning it when it went to auction after Murphy died. Even though his father, William Chestnut had long been dead, he somehow felt it was a fitting end to a family feud that had lasted a lifetime."

"No joke? Where does your father keep it now?"

"At private residence in Minnestra Minnesota, where he lives when he's in office as a sitting senator. He's kept it meticulously maintained and has even shown it at various car events throughout the years." David smiled. "Why do you want to know?"

Virginia expelled a deep breath of air. "Because, according to Holman, there's a hidden compartment within that car, where the entire contents of that chest have been hidden all this time."

"Get out of here." David's face flushed red. "Are you certain? It's been in my family's possession all this time?"

Virginia handed him the book with the markings. "See for yourself."

David read the note enthusiastically.

"Okay, so Robert Murphy and Jack Holman went back in 1920 to find the treasure. Jack Holman helped the man return it to his home in Saskatchewan. Jack looked up to Murphy. Then, when Murphy died, and there was no mention about the gold, he started to search for it himself. He was certain that Murphy had simply decided to hoard it away somewhere like a miser."

"What do you think?" Virginia asked, her heart pounding.

David grinned. There was something reptilian in his wide eyes. "So, the gold has been hidden in my father's Ford Tudor all these years?"

"It appears so," Virginia said.

"That's amazing." David reached inside his backpack and retrieved a handgun. A Beretta 92. He leveled it at her. "I guess I don't need your help anymore."

CHAPTER SIXTY-ONE

S TARTLED, VIRGINIA OPENED her mouth to say something cutting. Thinking better of it, she quickly shut it again. Sam and Tom stayed stock-still in stunned silence.

"I'll have that journal now," David commanded, holding out his open palm.

Virginia, still frozen with shock, didn't move.

An instant later he flicked the side mounted safety of his Beretta 92 forward with his thumb to emphasize the point.

"Okay, okay," Virginia said, as she slowly reached over to place the book in his hand. "We don't want the treasure — that's not what we came for. The journal is all yours. You'll need it to unlock the hidden compartment."

David aimed his Beretta at her face. He remained silent, but his jaw set firm. The way his eyes intensely fixed on Virginia, suggested he didn't believe a word she'd said.

Slowly, David's trigger finger gently squeezed the trigger.

Sam kicked his diving pony bottle — containing compressed oxygen — into the fire. The plastic regulator nozzle broke on impact with one of the larger pieces of shale they'd used to surround the fire. This sent a burst of compressed oxygen into the fire.

Excited by the sudden burst of pure oxygen, the flame flared upward, like in a mini-explosion.

Virginia dived to her side.

The blast knocked David off his feet. He discharged multiple rounds as he fell, but the shots went high. It took an instant to recover, but his vision had been blurred by the explosion.

Holding his breath—a reaction to fear, Sam's eyes swept the scene, darting between Virginia, Tom, and David.

Sam exhaled, relieved. The bullets missed them all by a long shot. David was disoriented and his vision impaired, but he still held the handgun—he and it were out of reach.

Sam didn't have seconds to react and neither did Tom nor Virginia. Veterans of combat, their eyes met. Silent meaning passed between them.

They needed to move fast.

They needed to move *now!*

Without looking back, Sam, Tom and Virginia sprinted together into the thick forest to the west. It took time for David to gain control and regain normal vision.

Bang! Bang! Bang!

The lethal automatic made a thunderous, audible roar as David emptied the remaining rounds from his Beretta. The weapon hissed, bullets whizzed, slapping into the trees around them, but by the luck of the heavens, none of them reached their intended targets.

Sam felt his heart thumping in the back of his throat as he sprinted through the thin cover of trees. The large muscles of his legs burned. The trio ran for about a half-mile. Then, panting, they walked briskly to catch their breath.

They regrouped at a natural clearing near the edge of the wooded area, still breathing heavily. Leaning forward, Sam struggled to fill his lungs fast enough to keep up with his metabolic demand.

He looked up at Tom, who was grinning widely.

Surprised by his friend's incongruous grin, Sam laughed out loud. "You okay? What is it?"

"We're out in the middle of nowhere now, right?" Tom asked, as he bent down and unzipped his ankle pocket.

"We sure are," Sam said, waiting to see what could possibly make Tom so happy despite their current predicament.

"A hundred miles from civilization, you'd say?" Tom asked.

"Yeah. Why? What is it?" Sam asked, intrigued by his friend's levity.

"David's going to climb onto his plane, use it to return to his father's house, and claim his fortune in stolen Confederate gold, right?" Tom held his gut with both hands, just about curled over laughing.

Maybe it was elevated hormones as a result of a near death experience, but just watching Tom laugh so uninhibitedly, made Virginia join in. Sam, helpless to the situation, couldn't stop laughing either. It was like a stupid joke that wasn't really funny, yet in the mass hysteria of a sublimely ridiculous set of circumstances, became the funniest thing one could ever imagine.

Like trying to put out a fire, but the odd flame keeps jumping up unexpectedly, their irrepressible snickers and chuckles eventually died.

"Right. So, what's so funny?" Sam said, still waiting for the punch line. "We're about to be left here in the middle of nowhere, while that bastard gets to fly back to civilization, where he'll return to dear old dad's place, and retrieve his fortune in Confederate gold. What is so damned funny?"

Sam wasn't laughing now.

Tom met Sam's hardened stare. With one last chuckle, he replied. "I wouldn't worry, he won't get far."

"Why not?"

"Do you think he'll need these?" Tom answered, holding the keys to the airplane aloft.

"Nice!" Sam said. "You never trusted him?"

"Not for a moment." Tom answered, still smiling.

CHAPTER SIXTY-TWO

THEY WALKED THROUGH a more densely wooded forest, until the woodlands thinned out and became grassland. There, crickets chirped loudly in the afternoon sun. The three hiked across the prairie, spotted with kettles where water used to stand. Many were now filled with full grown trees.

The air was filled with the trilling sound of the blue-winged teal, the quack of a wood duck, an occasional Canadian Goose honking, as well as other waterfowl. Oddly the canopy of the tree line in these holes sat level with the surface of the prairie, creating a strange and ancient landscape, unlike anything they had ever seen before.

Sam pictured huge gangs of bison nosing in the grass in times gone by. Here and there deeper kettles stood ringed with fewer trees and mostly filled with water. The trio stopped for a rest on the edge of one of these waterholes.

Ten minutes later, Sam climbed a small hill and spotted a small gray snake in the distance, winding its way across the valley. Cars and trucks, no bigger than ants, wound across the horizon, too, much like a snake.

Sam took a deep, fortifying breath, and made a "this way, come along" gesture to his friends.

It took them only an hour to reach the four-lane highway of Interstate 94.

Walking gratefully into a large roadhouse, Sam smiled. The

place held the common, familiar noise of civilization—couples laughing, others talking, the sound of the TV. To speed things up, Sam moved to the counter to order a hot meal for each, while Tom and Virginia took a booth seat round the back. Sam sat down next to Tom. A waitress, smiling, chatting and cheerful, placed three glasses of cold water in front of them.

Virginia looked down. No one said a thing.

Still smiling, the waitress left.

Sam's eyes darted between Tom and Virginia. Both had turned a little gray. Small beads of sweat were forming on their foreheads.

"What is it?" Sam asked.

Virginia said, "We might have a problem."

"Really?"

Tom smiled. "They think Virginia killed Senator Perry."

Sam swallowed hard.

Virginia sighed. "And that I killed Malcom Bennet's son in New York and stole nearly a million dollars of his cash."

"How did anyone come up with that idea?" Sam asked, concentrating on working the problem.

"My face was on the news," Virginia said, looking at the TV that now was discussing celebrities playing golf in the snow with orange golf balls. "The coroner ruled that Senator Arthur Perry didn't die of a heart attack. It appears someone inserted an intravenous cannula into the large vein in his neck and injected a massive bolus dose of calcium gluconate."

Sam waited for her to explain what any of that meant. When she remained silent, he asked, "What would that do?"

"It would stop the heart, mimicking the signs and symptoms of a heart attack."

"So someone's suggesting Senator Perry was assassinated using a drug that paramedics carry?" Sam asked. "It seems possible, but obviously circumstantial. Surely your tracking log would show that you were at work all day. I can't think of a better alibi."

"Except Senator Perry was a very first case for the day. I'd only been at work for half an hour. Leaving a massive window of opportunity to murder him."

"All right. But even so, I don't think it will be hard to disprove."

"There's more," Virginia said, through a thinned-lip smile.

"Go on."

"The New York Police Department has revealed footage from inside an apartment in New York. It depicts a paramedic who resembles me awfully well, removing large bundles of hundred dollar notes next to a dead kid—Malcom Bennet's son, who'd never used drugs previously—and loading the cash into my medical kits."

Sam said, "Okay, so the New York Police Department thinks you're responsible for both their deaths."

Virginia says, "You know what this means?"

Tom said, "You're a hunted woman… If they think you killed a senator, they'll go after you with everything they've got. Biggest man—ah, woman hunt in a long time."

"It's worse than that," Sam said.

"What?"

"It means David Perry's out of the woods and he's painted a target on our backs."

Tom sighed. "If only we knew where Senator Perry lived in Minnestra, Minnesota, we might just beat David Perry to it."

Virginia smiled.

"What?"

She pulled out her smartphone and brought up a picture of the late Senator Perry's driver's license. Along the front was his Minnestra address. "Look what I just found."

Sam laughed. "Now all we have to do is reach that address

before David does."

On the TV opposite them, a news article flashed. It was a special announcement by the FBI. It showed Sam, Tom, and Virginia's faces getting into a seaplane at Minot. It described each of them and warned the general public to immediately contact the police if anyone of the party were spotted, anywhere.

Sam smiled.

"What are you smiling about?" Virginia asked.

Sam shook his head. "It's nothing. Just an intrinsic truth, that's all."

"Go on. What?"

"There is no problem sufficiently bad that it can't get worse."

CHAPTER SIXTY-THREE

S AM WATCHED THE big man filling up his eighteen-wheeler semitrailer with diesel. The guy had tattoos down both arms, his beard was long enough to reach his chest, and he wore a gregarious smile.

Sam greeted the driver. "Where are you headed?"

"Chicago," the man replied, without looking at him.

"You'll be taking I-94 through the Great Lakes?"

"Sure will. Why, you looking for a ride?"

"Yeah. Three of us are heading to Minnesota."

The driver turned to greet him, his blue eyes taking him in with a glance. "What are you, backpackers?"

Sam had learned long ago that the truth often worked better than the best fiction. "No. Honest people, in a world of trouble, looking for a favor."

The driver's eyes swept past him, across to Tom, and Virginia. His gaze rested with male interest on Virginia, then flicked back to remain on Tom. Sam guessed what he was thinking: a big guy like Tom could be trouble to deal with. Then again, Virginia was stunning, and it was hard to imagine a girl like her would be hanging out with a couple of troublemakers.

"Okay, why not. Come along. I won't be making any more stops until the morning."

"Great, that suits us."

The stranger offered his hand. "My name's Eddie Freitas."

CHAPTER SIXTY-FOUR

THEY DROVE THROUGH the night and arrived at Minnestra, Minnesota in the early hours of the next morning. From there, they walked several blocks off the main road, to the house that Senator Arthur Perry had once called home.

Sam stared at the mansion in the moonlight.

The place made the Senator's lakeside log cottage appear small. The house formed a large U-shape, towering three stories. According to Elise, it was heavily protected by a state of the art, back to base security system. Fortunately, Elise had topped her class at cyber encryption and hacking when she worked for the CIA.

Not only was Sam now equipped with the digital diagrams for the residence, but also the code to the keypad that unlocked its doors and neutralized the alarm. Behind the house was what appeared to be an oversized barn. Of course, looks can easily be deceptive, and in this case, the barn was made of specialized materials utilized for their high strength and density. Inside, the barn was home to a collection of twenty or more classic cars, with an approximate current value exceeding fifty million dollars.

With Elise's prep, it took just ten minutes to enter the main house and retrieve the digital key to the barn.

There were slate stairs up into a terraced garden area, complete with gazebo and water feature behind the house. At the top of the stairs a quartz pebble path wove through to the north toward a thick manicured hedge, which at ten feet high, provided a boundary at the rear of the yard area.

As they stepped through a gateway in the hedge, they could see two large khaki barns with a sprawling blacktop driveway giving access to both. The one on the left had sliding doors across the breadth of the front, like an aircraft hangar. The barn on the right had a double-width rolling door like a garage. There was a pedestrian door on the side, which was locked.

Sam inserted the security key into the slot beside the blast-resistant door, as though he were checking into a hotel room for the night. The heavy door was on automatic hydraulic arms.

The keypad light flashed green.

Surprisingly noiseless, the doors slid open.

The three of them all took a sharp intake of breath as they stepped inside the barn. Automatic lights blazed on with a buzz as the trio entered the spacious garage. Temperature and humidity controlled, the air was cool and dry, like a hospital.

Splayed in front of them sat two rows of vintage sports cars, astride a concourse of polished concrete which was painted yellow. Each car shone brilliantly and was a prime example of its pedigree. One side was all European sports cars. A 1979 Porsche 935, A red Ferrari 250 GT California Spider, An Aston Martin DB3S from 1956 in classic silver, and a 1955 D-Type Jaguar.

The opposing row was all American vintage muscle. At the front, a 1967 Mercury Cougar GT-S, a 1968 Shelby Mustang GT500-KR, a 454 cubic inch V8 1970 Chevy Chevelle SS, a black 1934 12-cylinder Packard coupe, a Pontiac GTO Tri-Power and in the back, opposite the Packard sat the Burgundy 1927 Ford Model A Tudor with a modified flathead V8.

"I think we found it," Sam whispered, approaching the old American beauty and running his finger down the smooth arch of the passenger-side wheel arch.

The Ford shone as though brand new. Color keyed red wheels with white-walled tires adorned her below the running boards, and the huge silver grille at the front gleamed in the barn's halogen lights overhead. Large bore exhaust pipes jutted rudely from the back of the running boards on both sides the only visual clue giving away the modifications made to the car.

The suspension in the Tudor had been up-rated in the tail end to stop her lying low on the road when loaded up with hooch, and the trunk and floor were modified to take extra cargo. The front seats sat up an extra six inches from the floor belying a secret compartment under the passenger cabin. Under the hood were modified truck carburetors, and extractor manifolds feeding into the large bore exhausts tailpipes. The tires were pristine. They looked as if they had been checked for air recently. Long-range fuel tanks were installed.

The tank meter read full.

Which was all very compelling, when you thought about it. Tom slanted a sly glance at Sam. Virginia grinned. They were all thinking about it.

In its day this Tudor could out-run any car she went up against. Sam opened the front door, turned the switch on the electric starter. Instantly, the proud and powerful elderly matriarch roared to life, blurting out a puff of blue smoke. She burbled away at a soft idle as though it was only yesterday she had been sprinting across the frozen lake in front of a convoy of rum runners. Nodding at the sound of a perfectly tuned engine, he let her warm up.

Sam climbed into the back seat. Rubber covered stainless steel where the rear passenger's feet would have gone. At a glance, everything appeared as Henry Ford would have initially manufactured it. It was only when Sam opened the door, and squeezed into the large saloon-style, leather rear seats, that he observed the ruse.

His knees bent all the way back to his chest. Unless the car was designed to sit children in the back, the floorpan was much too high, meaning there was next to no legroom. In fact, if Jack Holman's description was right, the false floorpan sat nearly six inches higher than the real one.

Sam felt his heart race as he examined the intricate metallic latches that held the floorpan together. There were no bolts or screws. Instead the entire thing had been manufactured to fit seamlessly. According to the original specs for the modified Ford Tudor, the spacing was filled with lead to keep the vehicle's center of gravity down low.

Sam unlatched the four locks.

The false floorpan slid effortlessly backward, revealing a series of metal sheets.

"I don't get it." Sam asked, "What did we miss?"

"Nothing," Virginia replied with a head shake that made one blonde lock drift in front of her face. "perhaps there's something buried beneath that."

Sam removed the first sheet of lead, followed by another one. Underneath the third layer was a shallow rectangular mahogany box. He tried to remove the chest, but it wouldn't budge. Either too heavy or fixed to the floorpan with bolts.

He unclipped a latch on its side and the entire top opened upward.

All three of them gasped—inside were the coins of the Confederate treasure.

CHAPTER SIXTY-FIVE

S AM'S HEART SKIPPED a beat. There were more gold coins than he had ever seen or even imagined. He felt like a kid who'd arrived at the Pirates of the Caribbean ride at Disneyland, and after falling through the rapids had been whisked away to a world filled with treasure. His eyes swept over more than a thousand gold coins. Lying at the center of the treasure, a single unsealed note was fixed to a bed of blue velvet, like a dragon guarding its hoard.

Sam opened the document.

The three of them read the Covenant together.

When they had finished, Virginia said, "Can you imagine how much of America's history would have changed if this had found its way to Washington in 1863?"

Sam grinned as he closed the lid, locked the latch, and began the tedious task of sealing the false floorpan again. "At least now, it will finally reach its intended destination."

Climbing out of the car, Virginia's back straightened with sudden alarm. "Did you hear that?" she whispered.

The three of them tip-toed toward the side of the barn. As they broached the hedge Sam heard boots crunch pebbles, and saw the flash of yellow lettering on the back of a blue bulletproof vest. He motioned with his hand.

All three of them stopped, and instantly dropped to the ground.

Taking cover in the hedge, they watched silently as multiple federal agents surrounded the house below them. From their vantage point above, Sam could count twelve agents on the northern side in standard covering formation, at the back door.

He watched as six prepared to insert themselves at the back of the house. They wore full black tactical gear with balaclavas, and were armed with M5 assault rifles. Two men on point, one held a door ram, the second man covering with a pump-action shotgun.

Sam indicated to Tom and Virginia to retreat to the barn staying low.

"Anyone up for a drive in the country?" Sam whispered to Tom and Virginia as they made it back to the relative safety of the barn.

"Better make it quick!" Tom answered, climbing in to the passenger seat of the Tudor.

Virginia pressed the automatic door button—the sliding doors opened at the back of the barn. She quickly climbed into the front passenger seat, while Tom took his position, reclining in the saloon style lounge at the back.

In the driver's seat, Sam switched on the ignition. Once more, the Flathead V-8 motor roared to life. He shifted into first gear, turned the wheel to full lock, and revved the motor hard, power-sliding the tail end of the giant car around in a neat 180 degree turn. He gunned it again, squealing the car across the polished concrete floor and out the back of the barn.

As they tore away, Sam watched in the rear-view mirror as two FBI agents in blue jackets burst through the side door and turned to see the Ford as the three fugitives bounced away in a stream of torn up dirt, mud, and stones.

The driveway behind the barn opened on to a trail across the northern side of the property, which led into the woods. Despite the summer weather, the fire access trail was muddy and slippery, with rocks and jutting tree roots that made the going very rough.

Sam wrestled hard with the steering wheel as it thrashed away from him. The Ford's rock-hard suspension was in danger of giving all three passengers internal injuries as they raced northward away from the sprawling lake house.

Sam looked again in the tiny rear-view mirror and saw Tom stretched out sideways across the saloon-style leather seats, while next to him, Virginia was holding on for dear life as the Tudor skidded, jumped and swayed its way through the densely wooded pine forest.

"Where are we going to go?" she yelled to him over the roar of the motor.

"Minneapolis Airport."

CHAPTER SIXTY-SIX

MINNEAPOLIS AIRPORT, MINNESOTA

S AM PULLED INTO the service lane that ran alongside the airfield, where the juggernaut Boeing BC-17 Globemaster III dominated the landscape. It dwarfed the rest of the airport parking and taxi traffic. The next biggest was a Boeing 737 passenger jet being used by a budget carrier, which at 102 feet long, looked like a nervous school bus cowering beside a hulking freighter.

The airlifter jet was a civilian version of the 'Moose' used by the US Air Force for heavy hauling sorties. It was 174 feet long, with a wingspan of 169 feet. It could deliver a payload of 77 tons on a dirt runway 3500 feet in length thanks to the brute force generated by the two Pratt and Whitney jet engines on each wing. It could even make a K-turn with its reversing function.

Sam pulled up at the security gate designated specifically for cargo carriers. A portly uniformed attendant at the security gate glanced at them. "You must be Mr. Sam Reilly?"

"That's me," Sam replied.

"The captain of the Globemaster advised me you'd be turning up with a classic car." The attendant appraised the historic vehicle, admiration in his hazel eyes. "She's a beauty."

"Thanks."

"You must be in a hurry." He opened the gate and waved him through. "Have a good flight."

Behind them, Sam heard the wail of police sirens. He glanced at the rearview mirror. There were more than a dozen police cars and FBI vehicles racing toward them. The attendant's eyes darted to the small army of FBI vehicles, and back to Sam. Recognition suddenly penetrating his gaze.

"Hey, wait…" the attendant shouted.

Sam jammed his foot on the gas pedal and the car lurched forward.

He spun across the service lane and onto the taxiway. Sam raced past the control tower, along runway 12 L. Past a Boeing 737 that was stopped at the intersection with runway 22, waiting for a small private plane to land.

In his rearview mirror he spotted the flashing lights now making their pursuit on the runway, a quarter of a mile behind them.

"We've got company," Tom said, rather unnecessarily.

"I see them!"

Sam gunned the accelerator and the Ford Tudor lurched forward with surprising ferocity. He glanced up at the sky where a private single engine Cessna was coming in to land from the north-east. He swung the wheel hard left, turning into runway 22.

Along the final third of runway 22, the Globemaster III started to move northeast, toward the end of the airstrip. The Cessna's pilot had already spotted it. He or she was set to land well past the taxiing behemoth — right where Sam's Ford Tudor was now racing at nearly eighty miles an hour.

The coachwork on the old car started to rattle.

Wide-eyed, Virginia stared at the Cessna approaching for landing. "Sam!"

"I see it! I see it!" Sam shouted, keeping his eyes fixed straight ahead and his foot hard to the floor.

Its single propeller blade spun in a blur, as the Cessna raced head on toward them.

"For God's sake, Sam, move over!"

"Why?" Sam asked, with a sardonic grin on his face. "We're heavier than he is, that gives us the right of way."

Virginia looked at him, her otherwise soft face, suddenly distorted with fear.

An instant later, the Ford Tudor passed beneath the Cessna's landing strip gear, the little craft safely landing twenty feet behind their transport and their car.

Virginia screamed. "You knew!"

Sam shrugged. "I had a pretty good idea."

Behind them, sirens blaring, lights flashing, at least ten Federal Agent cars raced to meet them.

Ahead, the Globemaster III lowered its massive rear cargo door. Sparks flew from the steel boarding ramp, where metal struck the runway.

Sam lined up with the ramp, easily matching the jet's current speed of eighty-five miles per hour.

Virginia tense, her mouth open, and her eyes round with disbelief. "You can't be serious?"

"Sure, he is," Tom answered, comfortably lounging in the passenger seat. "Have you ever known Sam to be anything but serious?"

"Yeah, what could go wrong?" Sam asked. "It's not like this is a war zone. You and I did this before in Afghanistan, didn't we?"

"Right," Virginia admitted. "But the cargo aircraft was stationary at the time!"

Sam glanced at his speedometer. It read: 90 miles an hour. "Technically, we're only slightly traveling only slightly faster than the Globemaster, so we're basically stationary."

The Ford Tudor edged closer to the dragging tail ramp. The

wheels touched metal and the Tudor launched itself into the Globemaster. Sam jammed on the brakes, pulling up at the end of the empty cargo bay.

Sam yanked up the Tudor's handbrake, opened the door, and quickly hopped out. Crossing around the front of the car, he opened the passenger door, for Virginia and Tom to climb out.

The huge tailgate, which had been slowly moving, closed tight.

Tom slammed the door shut, then the three of them walked to the side of the monstrous cargo bay, and dropped onto the bench seats there.

The loadmaster strode in. Nodding to the others, he raised a hand to Sam in a friendly greeting of relaxed familiarity. He immediately began securing the car with a set of fixed chains. Sam felt the aircraft brake hard as its pilot reached the end of runway 22, in preparation of making a sharp turn, ready for takeoff.

Virginia turned to him. "Whose aircraft is this?"

Sam said, "It belongs to my father's shipping company. He lets me borrow a little freight space now and then when I need it. It was on its return from Alaska after dropping off some engine components for one of his freighters in dry dock at Dutch Harbor. When I spoke to Elise earlier, I asked her to arrange to have it meet us here. I told her to let them know we might have unwanted guests."

The four Pratt & Whitney F117-PW-100 turbofan engines increased pitch to a constant whine in preparation for takeoff. The entire aircraft began to shudder, as it dragged against its locked brakes.

Sam clicked his seatbelt and used part of the fuselage rigging for support.

Virginia shook her head. It was all a game to him. They were being chased by the FBI and dangerously entangled with a violent takeover by organized crime, and he was grinning.

With a lurch, he felt the pilot release the brakes. The monstrous cargo carrier launched forward at a rapid pace. Unburdened by anything other than the Ford Tudor, and three extra passengers, the Globemaster III moved with the spritely ease of a much smaller aircraft.

Sam felt the nose lift. Moments later the entire aircraft effortlessly soared up into the air.

One of the flight engineers approached the cargo hold. His eyes darted between, Sam, Tom, and Virginia — taking them all in at a glance, and fixing on Sam. "Sam Reilly?"

"Yeah."

"The captain wants a word with you."

"What about?" Sam asked.

The flight engineer sighed. "We have a problem."

CHAPTER SIXTY-SEVEN

S AM RACED UP into the cockpit of the massive cargo aircraft.

The captain greeted Sam with familiarity, but his open salvo was, "We have a serious problem."

"So I heard." Sam gripped the side of the third seat in the cockpit — the engineer's chair — to brace himself, while he ran his eyes across the important instruments. The aircraft looked stable in the air, for now at least. "What's going on?"

"The control tower has requested that we return immediately."

Sam said, "That was to be expected."

The pilot's brow narrowed. "Sam, how long have I known you now, fifteen years?"

Sam nodded. "Sixteen."

"In that time, I've learned that your word is like an ironclad contract, as solid as it is unbreakable." The pilot met his eye. "I just broke a number of laws just by taking off, not to mention nearly killing some FBI agents who tried to stop me. I did so based on your word that the FBI were currently working for organized crime and you've got with you, the only evidence to end their entire operation."

"That's right," Sam said.

"I believe you. Even so, when I land, I'm going to be arrested, lose my wings, and my freedom. So, what do you suggest I do about the control tower's request for us to return to Minneapolis?"

"Nothing." Sam shrugged, maintaining his characteristic stance of insouciance. "What are they going to do about it?"

The pilot bit his lower lip. "Well, apparently three F16s from have been scrambled from the 148th Fighter Wing out at the Minnesota Air National Guards. They should be here within a few minutes to escort us back down to the ground."

Sam expelled a deep breath of air. "That will be Good."

"Good, what?" The pilot looked confused. "How is that good?"

"While the F16s are on our tail, we're less likely to be attacked by the people we're *really* running from."

Sam pulled out his cell phone and began to casually scroll through it.

Jaw tight, the captain said between gritted teeth, "What do you want me to do about it?"

"Nothing. Keep going, continue on your flight plan."

The pilot's brows drew down. "And what do I say when our country's finest men and women with really expensive jets tell us to land?"

Sam continued to indifferently scroll through his cell, as though he was finding a number to arrange a coffee date. "I'll sort it out."

The pilot, red faced from fear, his raising blood pressure, or perhaps helpless fury, the pilot slowly, clearly enunciated, "Did you hear a word I said, Sam?"

Distracted, Sam looked up from his cell phone. "What?"

"I asked what the hell you suggest I tell the F16 fighter pilots when they ask me to land?"

Sam grinned. "Tell them to wait one minute while I finish speaking to their boss."

The captain's eyes darted toward the radar screen. Three

small green blips could be seen entering their airspace, moving ominously toward his vessel. "We've got company!"

Sam pressed the call button. It reached the message bank. He left a short message, asking the person to ring back as soon as they got the message.

The three F16s took their escort position around them.

The pilot shot Sam a concerned look. "They've requested we return to Minneapolis."

"Did you politely decline?" Sam asked.

"Did you notice their array of armaments?" the pilot replied.

"All right," Sam said, equably. "Tell them you'll need a minute to program your landing vectors."

"Okay." The pilot exhaled a breath of relief, and began inputting the return flight details.

Sam said, "Not yet."

"Why not?"

"I need you to drag this out as long as possible."

"Why?" the pilot asked.

Sam said, "I'm still waiting on a call."

At three minutes, the captain's face darkened further as a message came over his headphones. He turned to face Sam directly. "Sir, we've been officially given two minutes to turn around and make our descent into Minneapolis."

"All right. I want you to wait until 119 seconds have passed before beginning your turning circle. Then you'd better take us back to Minneapolis."

The captain nodded, visibly relieved.

At the two-minute mark, the pilot made a gentle bank to the left, to make a 180 degree turn back to the Minneapolis airport.

The captain mumbled under his breath as they made their final approach, "There's a hell of a lot of FBI agents back at the airport… we're about to be in a world of trouble."

Sam's cell phone started to ring.

He picked it up. His lips curled upward into a winning smile. "Yes, madam Secretary, I did call. You're right, the situation is urgent. You see, I might need your help…"

CHAPTER SIXTY-EIGHT

DULUTH INTERNATIONAL AIRPORT

S AM AND HIS friends sat inside the gracious Ford Tudor motorcar. The lovely lady had been the best of her time.

The Boeing BC-17 Globemaster III landed with surprising ease along Runway 27, Duluth's longest landing strip. The monstrous cargo carrier applied its reverse thrust and used up every inch of the 10,162 feet of concrete runway. The aircraft immediately taxied, following the three F16s that had been escorting them, into the 148th Fighter Wing—Minnesota Air National Guard's base, which shared the civilian international airport.

The Globemaster III came to a complete stop.

Over the intercom, Sam heard the pilot say, "All right, Mr. Reilly. We're now inside the 148th Fighter Wing's Airbase. I hope you know what you're doing. Good luck."

Sam turned around to see Virginia in the front passenger seat and Tom stretched out in the saloon style backseat. "You might want to buckle your seatbelts."

Tom said, "We don't have any seatbelts."

Sam raised his hands, palm upward, shooting him a devil-may-care shrug. "What are you going to do?"

The flight crew removed the vehicle tiedowns and opened the

massive hydraulic cargo tail door. Sam pushed his foot down firm on the heavy 1920s style clutch, pushed the gearstick into reverse, removed the handbrake and accelerated down the steel ramp onto the tarmac. He swung the wheel around, changed into first gear, and headed toward the gated guardhouse toward the end of the 178th Fighter Wing Airbase.

Two soldiers stepped out to greet him. Sam slowed the car to a stop, his eyes glancing over the two men. He recognized the blue beret of an Air Force Security Officer on one of the men. The other gentleman was wearing full Service Dress Uniform with the insignia of a silver eagle dominating the Great Seal of the United States across his left chest, indicating that he was an Air Force Colonel.

"Sir," Sam addressed the Colonel.

"You must be Sam Reilly," the Colonel replied coolly. Without waiting for a response, he said, "I don't know what your connection to the Secretary of Defense is, but all I can say is that you have friends in some very high places. I have questions — many extremely sensible questions. Despite the fact that the FBI made an official request to have my F16s locate your Globemaster and bring you back to the Minneapolis Airport — I've been ordered to let you through, no questions asked."

Sam remained silent. It was a tactical move. Years in the Marines had taught him when to keep his mouth shut.

"Do you have anything to say?" the Colonel asked.

"No, sir."

"Very well. On your way, son."

Sam grinned. "Thank you, sir."

The Air Force Security Officer opened the gate and Sam drove through. Once out of the Airbase, he accelerated hard. The car had been extensively upgraded from its original specifications back in the 1920s to make it a more formidable rum runner during Prohibition. Nearly a hundred years old, it still had plenty of power in its engine.

Virginia asked, "Where are we going?"

Sam turned south onto Route 53. "Fond-du-Luth Casino."

She cocked a skeptical eyebrow. "A casino?"

"Yeah, why?" Sam put his foot down and quickly took the Tudor up to 65 miles per hour. "Are you feeling lucky?"

"Sure, but I still don't know how we're going to get my dad back. In case you've forgotten, he's still being held prisoner by either David Perry or Rachel Murphy."

"Don't' worry about it." He shot her a glance, waggled his eyebrows up and down. "I've got a plan."

Fifteen minutes later, Sam pulled up to main entrance of the Fond-du-Luth Casino. A valet in a tuxedo opened the door for him. The three of them climbed out the doors. Sam handed the valet the keys and a hundred-dollar tip. "Be sure to take good care of this grand old lady. She's on loan from my father and he's going to kill me if I bring her back with any dents."

The valet handed him a ticket. "Yes, of course. We'll take very good care of her."

Sam and Tom entered the Casino.

Virginia stared at him, her mouth agape.

"What?" Sam asked without stopping.

"You're just going to leave the car with the valet. Did you forget there's the entire wealth of the Confederacy still inside the car?"

Sam shrugged. "Technically, the valet's going to park the Tudor in the commercial parking lot and then leave it on its own... but no, I didn't forget about the gold. How could I? It felt like I was driving a heavy boat the damned thing was so overladen."

"Are you nuts?"

"Don't worry about it. Besides, it's been seen around here for the past nine decades. No one's stolen the gold yet, so why would they start now? In fact, here's probably the safest place for it. If we'd left it under guard somewhere, someone would be bound to get suspicious."

Sam continued walking, moving with the determined stride of a professional soldier. Like a cargo ship, Tom sailed through in a similar manner, the big man leaving waitresses and customers alike, trailing in his wake.

Virginia asked, "So are you going to tell me what we're doing here?"

"Not here," Sam said, as he opened the back exit at the far end of the casino. "The marina across the road from here."

"Okay, what are we doing at the marina?"

"Getting on a boat of course. Keep up with me, will you?"

Virginia laughed. "A lot of people changed after Afghanistan. Not you. You haven't changed one bit since I first met you."

Sam crossed the road, and started heading along the jetty until he reached the marina. A security gate blocked them from going any farther. He rifled through his wallet and removed a digital key. He swiped it on the security door. The light flashed green and the gate opened.

Sam raised his palms upwards and grinned. "Hey, what do you know, it still works."

Sam walked to the last finger of the marina, where a sleek *Blohn and Voss* sports cruiser was tied up. On the transom of her carbon fiber hull were the words, *Annabelle May.*

He and Tom untied the mooring lines and stepped onto the splendid teak deck. Merely moments after Virginia boarded, the sports cruiser's powerful twin MTU Rolls Royce engines started up. Sam casually went about the business of putting away the side fenders and mooring lines.

When he was done, Sam headed toward the bridge.

At the helm was a slim woman in her mid-twenties with facial features that betrayed a Eurasian ancestry. Slightly shorter than the average American female of this generation, she wore cargo pants and a light blue polo shirt. Her arms were toned and muscular suggesting a lifestyle that required regular exercise. Captain of the vessel, she maneuvered the large pleasure cruiser out of the marina with the adept agility of a seasoned sailor.

Once outside the narrow channel of the marina, she turned to face them, her striking violet eyes on Sam. "Welcome back."

Sam smiled. "Virginia, meet my computer hacker, and probably just about the smartest person to ever live, Elise."

"Pleased to meet you," Virginia said.

Elise nodded. "Likewise."

Sam looked at Elise. "Well?"

"Hey Tom, takeover while I show Sam why he pays me the big bucks."

Tom took the helm. "Where am I headed?"

Elise grinned. "To Isle Royale, of course. We have a meeting. It would be rude to be late."

CHAPTER SIXTY-NINE

S AM AND VIRGINIA followed Elise to the navigation station, where her laptop was open. Virginia inhaled deeply. "Is that honest to God percolated coffee I smell?

Elise gestured to an alcove. Virginia poured herself a cup. "Anyone else?"

"Sure," Sam said, dropping into a comfortable chair.

"No thanks," Elise said.

Virginia wandered over, handed Sam his cup, sat down and hummed with pleasure at the first sip. On the computer monitor were two open audio files. One named Rachel Murphy and the other, David Perry.

Gulping hot, black coffee, Sam studied the screen. "You said you found it?"

Elise grinned. "Sure did. Child's play. I thought you said these people were smart?"

Virginia looked at him, a vacant expression on her face.

Sam said, "I asked Elise to hack into Rachel Murphy and David Perry's cell phones."

"She tapped their phones?" Virginia asked.

"It's surprisingly easy these days if the target uses a smartphone," Elise said. "With landlines we need to tap specific telephone cables, but even then, we're only really capable of eavesdropping. Whereas with smartphones it's more like hacking a website. Once you're in, you have control. I can issue my own texts from either of the cell phones, delete texts I don't want them to receive, and even send digitally enhanced audio files."

Virginia asked, "Digitally enhanced audio files?"

"Basically, we take a collection of the known audio files, or recordings of their conversations, and then use individual words to make them say certain things."

"Like a mashup?" Virginia grimaced. "Wouldn't they see through that in an instant?"

Elise shook her head. "Amateur versions, sure. But we can do something a little more professional here."

Sam asked, "So what did you find?"

Elise said, "They're retrieving it now for us."

"Retrieving what?" Virginia asked.

Sam turned to Virginia. "Do you remember when we were in Dog Lake, Ontario and we first met David Perry, he mentioned his father had a small army of private detectives dig up information on Rachel Murphy's involvement with organized crime?"

"Yeah, he said that his dad had a copy of every single connection she had with organized crime in New York."

"Right.

"Yeah." Sam looked at Virginia. "Well, it got me thinking, if David was telling the truth about that then it stands to reason that his father probably made some record of his own involvement in corruption and organized crime."

"Why would he do that?" Virginia asked, crossing her legs.

"Because his way of life was all about leverage. Arthur Perry needed to know who knew sensitive information about his family business. That way he could control any vulnerabilities. More important still, he needed to have leverage over anyone who had something on him."

Her intelligent blue eyes widened. "Senator Arthur Perry kept a database on every single person within his organization and any competing organizations — AKA Rachel Murphy's New York operation!"

"Right. Find those dossiers, directories, and documents. Then we'll shut down our adversaries, and get your father back at the same time."

"But how will you do that?"

"Elise took an in depth look at the lives of Rachel Murphy and David Perry. It turns out little of what we've seen is true. Senator Perry told us that his son was a nobody who, though born into riches, never achieved anything on his own."

"That's not true?" Virginia asked.

"No, far from it. Turns out David Perry was the smartest of the Chestnut descendants. He went to Stanford University like his father and grandfather before him, but he didn't fail or drop out as reported — -he was an A+ student. But he wasn't the only gifted student that year. He shared the University Medallion for highest achievement in the field of Law with a woman." Sam looked at Virginia. "Any guesses what her name was?"

Virginia frowned. "Rachel Murphy?"

"You betcha. It turns out that Rachel and David didn't just go to Stanford together, they were lovers."

"Seriously?" Virginia's mouth dropped open. "Two star-crossed lovers from feuding families? It's a modern day Romeo and Juliette, except David — the traitor — after what he did to us, is playing the role of Macbeth. Did David's father know?"

"Yes. From what we can tell Arthur Perry hated the idea, but unable to suppress the relationship outright, he tried to use his leverage to make Rachel break it off. Three weeks ago, he threatened to reveal incriminating evidence proving her criminal involvement."

Virginia nodded, it was all coming together.

"David found out and decided to do the same thing his

grandfather did—topple the head of the family and take his place as the boss of a newly organized crime family. A joining of Murphy and Perry. Kill two birds with one stone. Get rid of his father who had him on a tight leash by controlling his finances, then integrate the two businesses into one."

Elise sighed. "But to do that, they would need Senator Arthur Perry's um, *Leverage Records*."

Virginia bit her lip. "So Elise, what did you find?"

"I'll show you."

"This was a message I spotted about three hours ago, when the three of you escaped Minnestra." Elise pressed play on an icon of David's cell phone.

It read: What went wrong? Sam Reilly escaped. You were supposed to kill him. RM

David then wrote back: He got away. You've still got Virginia's father. Sam will negotiate. The Confederate treasury is still ours.

Elise said, "This is where it got interesting. You see, I looked into the Meskwaki Gold Spring. Previously, shipments would only pass through the secret tunnel every month or so. But three weeks ago—the same time David Perry attempted to make a bit extra from his father's company—someone started to make dives of the *J.F. Johnson* every night."

"I thought that was strange, too," Sam said. "Then Tom pointed out that inside the hull were potentially hundreds of barrels of Prohibition era rum that would fetch a small fortune. We wondered if that was what the divers were searching for."

Elise smiled. "Sure, but they might make a million or two if they're lucky, but nothing to warrant the risks they were taking. Particularly when you think about the fact that David Perry planned to usurp his father's throne and an illegal kingdom worth hundreds of millions of dollars."

A wry smile formed on Sam's lips. "So what were they looking for inside the Meskwaki Gold Spring?"

"I'll show you," Elise smiled and scrolled down to the next set of messages. "First, I set the hook with Rachel Murphy, by making her think that Sam Reilly had found the *Leverage Records.*"

Sam smiled. "How could you possibly achieve that?"

"Easy." Elise stood up and began to pace up and down the room. Sam and Virginia, entranced, followed her movements. "You see, I knew Murphy had deep financial ties with senior members of the New York Police Department. I had no idea how deep the network went, but what I did know was that the two detectives who were there when Virginia found the drug dealer's money — which turned out to be Malcolm Bennet's son. They were also the same people who kidnapped Virginia's father. So we know they were both involved, and highly trusted by Murphy."

"You hacked their phones?"

"Yeah. Then I sent Murphy a single message from Detective Eric Greentree's cell phone. It read: *Sam Reilly knows about the Leverage Records. He's retrieving it tomorrow.* Murphy of, course, replied immediately that she would make sure they were no longer there to be taken."

Awed, Sam and Virginia both stared at Elise.

Elise paused, gave them a wry grin. "I deleted both messages before Greentree had the chance to read them."

Sam laughed. "You set Murphy up to convince David to retrieve the documents?"

"Yeah." Elise dropped back into her chair. "Pretty simple. She called him and explained the situation. David sounded confused, telling her that it had taken him three weeks to find the Meskwaki Gold Spring. She asked why he didn't retrieve the document then, but he warned her that Sam Reilly and Tom Bower were inside the tunnel with him. It would have been too difficult to retrieve the underwater safe, while they were down there with him."

Sam turned to Virginia. "With the *Leverage Records* we'll know every single step of their operation, with enough information to arrest potentially hundreds of people, and close down the entire system. More importantly, we'll be able to locate where they're keeping your father."

The room went silent while they all contemplated the current fortune of Virginia's father.

To Elise, he then said, "When will they make the dive?"

"Ten p.m. tonight."

Sam grinned. "Tom and I will be there by 9:30."

CHAPTER SEVENTY

S UBMERGED UNDERWATER, WITH a strong sense of *déjà vu,* Sam and Tom waited inside the wreck of the *J.F. Johnson.* Sam reflected that it felt like they had come full circle.

Sam waited behind the first hatchway that led into the lower decks of the shipwreck, while Tom was stationed all the way inside the ship's bilge. They were well prepared this time. Having been through this game of cat and mouse enough times to know how to win it, they weren't taking any more chances. They each had a pair of military grade bolt-cutters, to prevent either of them from becoming trapped. They were both armed with a sharp knife and a pneumatic hand-held spear gun.

Watching the hatchway through infrared night vision goggles, Sam waited silently in total darkness. He was a predator, fully expecting and prepared for his prey to come to him.

Right on time, he spotted two dive lights — presumably Murphy and Perry's. They used sea scooters. Careful not to kick up the silt, they still moved quickly. They stopped, and locked the hatchway, as David Perry had done last time.

Sam followed the divers as they progressed through the wreck, descending down into the lower two decks, through the locked door, and down the hatchway into the bilge.

Inside the bilge the twin sea scooters whirred as the divers raced to the opposite end of the old secret cargo hold from the ship's Prohibition days. The two divers reached a barrel that had been turned on its side. There were small handprints in the silt over the top of the barrel.

Sam watched as one of the divers untwisted the fake lid, before retrieving a small sealed box. It appeared to be made of plastic, and small enough to fit into someone's hand. Sam was expecting something larger, but actually, this made sense. Everything Senator Arthur Perry knew about every aspect of his company, could now be kept on a single 1Terabyte Flash Drive.

Smiling much like a crocodile waiting by a waterhole, he watched the first diver place the storage device within his or her dive vest.

A moment later, the two divers squeezed the twin triggers of their sea scooters and raced out through the cracked hull of the *J.F. Johnson* and into the subterranean cavern of the Meskwaki Gold Spring.

"After them!" Sam yelled through his dive radio.

Tom came out of his hiding place. "I'm on it!"

Sam squeezed the twin throttles. His scooter whirred into life and he shot forward, and through the opening.

On the other side, his world opened up into the cavern. Through his night vision lens, he searched his new environment. He had a clear line of vision through the crystal-clear waters of the Meskwaki Gold Spring. But up ahead, there was no sign of the diver's lights.

Sam swallowed hard. Where did they go?

Sam's heart raced, his thoughts went blank. *Where did they go?*

An instant later, he heard the blast of a shark-stick being fired.

The propeller of Sam's sea scooter whined and tore itself to pieces, bringing him to a standstill.

CHAPTER SEVENTY-ONE

D AVID FELT A sharp burning pain in his left thigh.

Adrenaline surged throughout his body. His heart hammered in his throat and his chest tightened. He glanced at his leg. Sam Reilly had shot him with a spear gun! He squeezed the trigger throttles and his sea scooter shot through the Meskwaki Gold Spring.

Next to him a second sea scooter raced.

After fifteen minutes and nearly a mile, he reduced his speed, and they began their gradual decompression section of the dive.

He scanned the area behind them. His two pursuers had remained on board the *J.F. Johnson*. He switched on his flashlight and shined it at Rachel. He felt his heartrate ease as the light confirmed that she was unharmed.

Safely ascending, they slowly reached the surface of the Meskwaki Gold Spring. The subterranean cavern was alight with the green sparkle of glowworms.

David removed his facemask and dragged the dive gear to the water's edge. He was breathing hard with the pain and exertion.

Rachel wrapped her lithe arms around him in a fervent embrace, "We did it!"

"Yes, we did." He hugged her back. A moment later he tried to step on his injured leg and stumbled from the pain.

She swore. "You're injured."

"A little. That bastard, Sam Reilly, shot me with a spear gun."

"Are you going to be all right?" she asked, concern in her voice.

"I'll live. We just need to get the flash drive somewhere safe."

"We can help with that." A voice from the dark commanded. "Now hand the flash drive over."

David looked up. Surrounding them, weapons drawn, were more than thirty members of the Royal Canadian Mounted Police.

CHAPTER SEVENTY-TWO

DULUTH MARINA

S AM TOOK A seat on a leather chair inside the *Annabelle May's* main living space. Feet apart, arms behind his head, he relaxed back in the comfortable recliner.

"I've made some calls," Sam said. "Your father has been rescued from a safe house in New York. The FBI found where he was being held captive."

Virginia leaned down and wrapped her arms around Sam's neck. A formidable woman, she embraced him with all of her heart — and the superhuman strength of a python.

"Thank you," she said, giving him a kiss on his cheek. "Thank you for everything." She then turned to Tom, "You too, Tom. I'm so grateful for what you've both managed to do."

"You're welcome. Really, it was fun. Hey, I think this deserves a celebratory drink." Sam stood up, walked over and rummaged at the expensive, well stocked bar.

"What have you got?" Virginia asked.

Sam shrugged, looking through cupboards. "I'm pretty sure the good Senator has something nice lying around here."

He came back a few minutes later, carrying three drinks on ice-cold rocks — actual rocks — the traditional way to cool rum without diluting it as the ice melts.

Tom brought the first glass up to his lips so that he could smell it. "There's a first-rate aroma here."

Sam raised his glass with Virginia, Tom, and Elise. "Congratulations. That was really something. We did a good thing today."

Virginia gave a crooked grin. "Yeah, we sure did." Silent teardrops running down her cheeks were the only sign of the emotional pressure she'd been under throughout the last few weeks.

"Will your father make it through his cancer do you think?" Sam asked, his voice serious.

"Only time will tell, but the trial has been achieving great results, and his treating oncologist says she feels confident my father got in early enough."

Sam held his glass up high. "To Charles Beaumont's good health."

"To Charles Beaumont! Here, here!" they all cheered, as glasses clinked.

Tom took a gentle sip, savoring the fine tastes. He turned to Sam and said, "It tastes like nothing I've ever tried. There's a smooth oak taste and a full body woody flavor I can't quite pick. Whatever sort of rum did you find?"

Sam said, "I don't know. Just something I found lying around. I'll go get the bottle."

"Whatever it is, it's very, very good," Tom reiterated. "The best, actually."

Sam returned a few seconds later and handed Tom the bottle.

Tom carefully picked it up. His eyes were wide, his agape mouth speechless, as he stared at the old bottle. It bore the tenderness of a bygone skill of delicate craftmanship. The label was white with the words: *Philadelphia 1876* set at the top — most likely a reference to the year Bacardi rum had earned a gold medal at the Philadelphia Exposition of 1876.

Below that were the words *Ron Bacardi Superior* and at the

bottom of the label it read, *Graduacion 44–5.* The intact cork had been carelessly tucked back into the bottle. To its side were the remnants of a foil seal with the Bacardi Bat embossed. At the bottom of the label were the words, *Santiago de Cuba* and below that, *Habana – New York.*

Tom turned to Sam and said, "My God, Sam, where did you get this?"

Sam grinned. "I found it when we were coming out of the *J.F. Johnson.* Technically, it was outside the shipwreck and thus not breaking any shipwreck pilfering laws. I noticed it bore the same description and Bacardi Bat as the other broken bottle you found earlier." He gave them all a pirates grin. "I just thought I'd bring it up and see if it was as nice a drop as you suggested."

Virginia laughed. "Did you like it?"

Sam grimaced. "A fine rum is wasted on me. I don't like rum in general." He frowned. "To be honest, it has the distinct palate of sweet tasting tobacco, leather, and wood to me."

Tom shook his head. "Do you realize you just destroyed a 50,000-dollar, rare bottle of Prohibition era rum, produced in the Bacardi Habana-New York distiller in the final weeks before Prohibition came into effect?"

"Destroyed? No way! Whether I like it or not, I'm drinking it!" Sam took another sip, grimacing over the taste. "Anyway, you guys are going to help me drink it." Grinning, he added, "And tomorrow, we're going to return the entire treasury of the Confederate States of America to its rightful owners."

He finished his drink and went to bed. Sam slept well, catching up on some much-needed rest. In the morning they handed the keys for the *Annabelle May* to the marina manager.

After that, they strolled back to the Fond-du-Luth Casino, handed the ticket to the valet, who promptly returned the Ford Tudor.

Sam climbed into the front seat, tipped the valet, and headed down Route 53.

CHAPTER SEVENTY-THREE

PENTAGON—TWO WEEKS LATER

T HE OFFICE OF the Secretary of Defense was a large room with blue carpet, a massive oak desk, and two small tables for meetings—four seats each. It wasn't the kind of place for a big, open gathering. Just a few generals and maybe a head of state or two.

Secrets passed through the room day and night.

The Secretary of Defense picked up the morning's briefings.

Inside the first one was a two-page executive summary of more than a thousand-page dossier on the recent shut down of an organized crime family dating back to the 1920s. It had incredibly pervasive ties to politicians, judges, high ranking police officers, border patrol, and prosecutors.

The man who'd started the organization had stolen it from a Minnesotan offshoot of Al Capone's bootlegging enterprise. That person's grandson, David Perry, had recently murdered his father, a sitting senator from Minnesota, in an attempted coup of the business.

More than a hundred arrests had been made, including two high ranking city officials from New York, and a number of police detectives.

The Secretary of Defense studied the photo of an extremely good-looking detective—Eric Greentree. The guy wore a pressed New York Police Detective's uniform, and had a number of citations next to his name. His face was fixed in the oval shaped proud smile of a man who was born to serve, yet behind that face, was the corrupt ruthless greed of a man bought by organized crime. A professional enforcer, he was willing to murder, remove evidence, and arrest anyone who got in their way.

There was another note about a woman who was instrumental in the breakthrough. Her name was Virginia Beaumont. The Secretary of Defense examined the image of the woman in a paramedic's uniform. Her facial features were striking. She looked confident and intelligent in her uniform, but the Secretary guessed she would have been just as impressive as a model or an engineer.

The Secretary of Defense had a head for names and faces. Searching her memory for the name, she felt the face seemed familiar, but distant too. Lips pursed, she cast her mind back.

Ah! That's right, Virginia Beaumont worked with Sam Reilly in Afghanistan. There was an incident where Sam had been shot.

Virginia Beaumont had saved his life. The Secretary smiled. Funny how life's events can turn on the flip of a coin.

Next, she read the news about Beaumont's father having made a miraculous recovery from a rare type of lung cancer following a recent drug trial. They used a new treatment using genetic engineering to trigger his own immune system to fight the cancer.

The Secretary of Defense, a slim, muscular woman with stark red hair, wore her dark business suit and her permanent scowl with equal severity. Yet the note brought a thin-lipped smile to her otherwise permanent scowl.

Six degrees of separation. Oh, I think not.

The man's daughter had served with Sam Reilly in Afghanistan. She had been a long-term friend of his.

She moved to the next briefing note...

The page depicted a handwritten letter, laying back in a blue velvet box. At the top were the words Ironclad Covenant for the Reunification of the Union. It was dated May 14, 1863.

Her eyes ran across the document with intense interest.

It described an agreement signed by several wealthy landowners, senior military officers, and sitting Congressmen from the Confederate States of America to rejoin the Union, after being given specific assurances that no further financial consequences would take effect by doing so.

At the bottom of the lists was an agreement to be bound by the terms of the covenant, signed by two signatures.

She glanced at those signatures.

Jefferson Davis and Abraham Lincoln

This was merely a photo of the real document, of course. The real document was now being held on display at the Smithsonian Institute in Washington, D.C. alongside the remnants of the Confederate States of America's once great wealth.

Closing her eyes, she imagined how many American lives might have been saved if the Covenant had reached Washington back in 1863.

Her thoughts were interrupted by a sharp knock at her door. Her assistant advised her that the Joint Chiefs of Staff needed to see her.

"Send him in," she commanded.

The Chairman of the JCS entered her office, interrupting her thoughts.

"I'm sorry, ma'am. We have a problem."

She leaned forward on her leather chair. "What's happened?"

"Some hikers have discovered the wreckage of an old bomber plane from World War II within the outskirts of Washington, D.C."

Her eyes narrowed. "A World War II bomber plane in Washington? We never lost any of our bombers in the area as far as I can recall. Although our history department would have a better idea of that."

"I'm sorry, ma'am. You misunderstand me. It wasn't one of our bomber planes."

Pushing back her chair, she stood up, and shot him a curious, incredulous smile. "Not one of ours. Then whose was it?"

"Germany's, ma'am. And it gets worse. Preliminary reports from our team on site suggest the aircraft was carrying a primitive nuclear bomb."

"Good God!" she said, taking in the full ramifications of the statement. Forgetting historical relevance and significance, she turned her focus on the immediate problem. "Has a team been tasked to secure the nuclear waste?"

The General looked away, crestfallen. "It appears someone has beaten us to it in the past twenty-four hours since the hikers located the wreckage."

"What are you saying?" She met his eyes. "Did someone try and steal a nuclear weapon?"

The General swallowed, his prominent Adam's apple bobbing in his throat. "What I'm telling you, ma'am, is that we currently have a Broken Arrow, right here in Washington D.C."

THE END

WANT MORE?

Join my email list and get a FREE and EXCLUSIVE Sam Reilly story that's not available anywhere else!
Join here ~ www.bit.ly/ChristopherCartwright

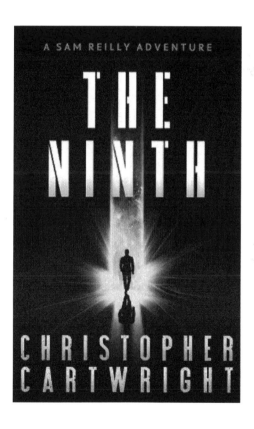

Printed in Great Britain
by Amazon